HER CONFESSION

The Black Door Trilogy, Book Two

By S. Valentine

HER CONFESSION

Limitless Publishing, LLC
Kailua, HI 96734
www.limitlesspublishing.com

Formatting: Limitless Publishing

ISBN-13: 978-1-68058-778-4
ISBN-10: 1-68058-778-1

Dedications

This book is for my family, friends and wonderful readers. Also those that were kind enough to spread the word on book 1. THANK YOU!

Author's Note

Please note that safe sex is practiced by all persons throughout this novel, unless otherwise stated.

Chapter One

Gabi

Present Day

As Gabi wrapped her fingers around Darion's, it brought little comfort. Her heart continued to pound at a frenetic pace, causing her stomach to knot. She drew in a deep breath, willing her muscles to relax. If there was ever a time her body needed to display confidence, it was now. Having crossed the rope, and being mere metres away from the black door, her gaze lowered to the familiar red glow that seeped from the bottom. Anticipation coursed through her veins, thick and heavy.

Although what lurked behind the door was one of the reasons Gabi was anxious, it wasn't the sole reason. She had been behind the door before, stepped into another world miles away from her own, and crossed boundaries she never thought she would. At that moment, pleasure may have been on Darion's mind, but Gabi knew that pain would inevitably follow. There was something she needed to do.

She observed the bar area for a final time, silently praying the very person she feared wouldn't appear.

As usual, Darion's confident demeanor displayed that he was eager, as always. His pupils held a wicked gleam, and the corners of his mouth were upturned ever so slightly. A seductive, dangerous aura emanated from him, in the way that he moved effortlessly, destroying women he passed with a sweeping, intense gaze, leaving them coy. Gabi knew the effect he had on them, for she felt it too. Darion Milano—a man of fantasies, who wanted it all and more.

Gabi tentatively took steps forward.

"Are you sure you wanna do this?" Darion leant closer, his voice soft, the warmth of his breath tickling her neck. He always sought reassurance that she was happy to participate in the playrooms.

Withdrawing her hand, she wanted nothing more than to turn on her heel and flee from the club. But there was no point. There was nowhere to run and nowhere to hide. She believed the truth always caught up with her in the end. As silence descended upon them, she noticed a flash of concern cross Darion's face.

"Gabi?"

"I'm sure," she answered quickly, hoping her smile appeared genuine. She tucked a blonde strand behind her ear before straightening her posture.

As they proceeded through the door, they were met with a corridor, which was bathed in the gentle illumination of red spotlights. Either side of it was playrooms. The club overall was glamorous, provocative. Anything anyone could ever want to be fully satisfied was on offer.

At a leisurely pace, Darion led her into a room which resembled an erotic dungeon. Gabi swallowed, linking her hands together. Although she had been in that room with Darion before, it had been alone. Now the door was wide open to the viewing members.

There was a large mirror on one wall, leather cuffs on straps hung on the wall opposite, and a table held handcuffs, paddles, and whips. A leather swing occupied one corner and a king-size leather bed the other.

"Darion…" Gabi hesitated for a second, gathering her courage. "Can we talk?"

Darion stilled, pinning her with a questioning look. Then his features softened as he cupped her face in his hands. His eyes, filled with love and longing, bored into hers. "I know you're nervous, Gabi, but I promise you, you'll enjoy it."

"It's not that. I—"

Darion shushed her. "Later."

His face broke into a slow smile, then he kissed her tenderly on the lips. Gabi reluctantly responded. As the kiss deepened—his tongue finding hers—her stomach tightened with desire. Burying her fingers in his hair, she closed her eyes and attempted to give in to temptation, to savour the moment. She couldn't.

"What's wrong?" Darion pulled back, obviously having sensed the distance between them.

3

Gabi wished she could keep the secret buried, hidden forever, but she couldn't do that to him. She at least owed him the truth. She knew that once the confession rolled off her tongue, she could lose him forever. She couldn't bear the thought. But maybe she didn't deserve him.

"Darion…" she whispered so quietly she could barely hear her own voice.

"What is it?"

"There's something I have to tell you." She fiddled with her cross necklace. It was too late for prayers.

As soon as he caught sight of her expression, which she knew would have displayed nothing other than terror, she noticed his face pale. She could see the lump that had lodged in his throat. Shoving a hand through his hair, he let out a low laugh. When Gabi failed to respond, he took a step closer, towering over her.

"What do you need to tell me, Gabi?" His tone now had a chilling bite to it.

Gabi wrapped her arms around herself protectively, feeling herself shrink in fear, her heart twisting inside her chest.

The atmosphere in the room changed dramatically, and now, all she could see around her were objects for torture, a red glow resembling hell, and a murderous glare that only the devil would possess.

Gabi was unable to stop the tears that rolled down her cheeks.

Chapter Two

Three Months Earlier

Gabi lay still, her gaze transfixed on the ceiling. Lost in a complete daze, she wouldn't have minded if the ceiling had some sort of patterns, swirls to follow, anything…yet it was smooth and white. Plain. She had been awake for fifteen minutes. The sound of her alarm had yet to pierce through her ears. She tried to recollect what had jolted her awake. A nightmare perhaps, a niggling worry…yet her mind failed to enlighten her. In all fairness, it could have been anything. Her emotions alone were filled with confusion and curiosity mixed with revulsion. She allowed her thoughts to bring forth the recent events at The Black Door. She had surrendered herself to the playrooms.

Before she could replay everything, she felt the jab of Darion's elbow as he rolled onto his back. Stretching her limbs, Gabi was unable to stop from smiling. She leant on one elbow and stared down at him. His dark tousled hair splayed across the pillow, his full lips slightly parted, his long-lashed eyes shut. He looked sweet when he was asleep. Innocent even.

As he returned to the fetal position, the covers left his body. Gabi got a glimpse of his tanned, firm ass, trim waist, and muscular arms. Warmth radiated through her body as she felt giddy with lust. She liked the fact he slept naked, the perfect antidote to an otherwise bleak Monday morning. He was irresistible in every sense of the word.

Gabi slid across the bed, hooking her arms around him, and burying her face in the crook of his neck. Darion turned over to face her. Slowly blinking his eyes open, he met her stare, and a lazy, mischievous smile surfaced on his face.

"Morning…" his tone was silky smooth.

"Morning," she responded brightly.

His fingers met her cheek, tracing across it slowly, tenderly. Then his focus settled on her lips for a moment. He leant over and pressed his mouth against hers. Gabi expected a quick morning peck, but his tongue slipped in, tantalising and teasing. Groaning into her mouth, he was soon on top of her, his hands roaming her body. Gabi smiled against his mouth, feeling herself melt under his touch. Darion Milano. Would she ever get enough of him?

Gabi had met Darion at the gentlemen's club he owned, The Black Door. Daring, intriguing, and unpredictable, he was unlike anyone she had ever met. Being engaged at the time hadn't deterred her from entering his world. The love, affection, and friendship she had lacked practically pushed her into his arms. Gabi had hated herself for having an affair with him, for betraying her ex-fiancé Lawrence. However, she had been unable to resist, regardless of Darion's warning that he may hurt her, and by being with him she would no longer recognise herself. He'd told her they were worlds apart—that much was true. The magnetic pull that drew them together was as strong as ever, and they were helpless to the undeniable chemistry and attraction they had toward one another.

"I have to get ready for work." Although she was aroused, Gabi reluctantly tore herself away just in time to stop the bleeping sound of the alarm clock.

Darion rolled onto his back, kicking the covers off. She opened her mouth to take a small breath as she took in his toned body. She felt a hot ball of fire in the pit of her stomach which spread through to her loins. Her fingers ached with the need to reach out and touch him.

"Not even time for a quickie?" His irises twinkled dangerously, his brows raised suggestively.

Gabi felt her heartbeat increase, and the burning of her presumably blushed cheeks. She swallowed, wondering how a man who was now her 'boyfriend' had a way of unnerving her with his fierce stare. She hated that at times he made her feel like a coy, inexperienced teenager, and yet loved the fact that other times, he made her feel like the most desirable woman in the world.

Breaking out of her daze, her shoulders drooped as disappointment swept over her. "I don't think there's time." She padded toward the bathroom. "This is another reason you should stay at my place more. It's nearer to my work."

And further away from his ex-wife, Eva, who was back in town. The woman that Gabi felt threatened by, who owned half of The Black Door, and who she feared was in Westhaven to reclaim both the club *and* Darion.

Gabi pushed the thoughts to the back of her mind before she got upset, or worse, angry. The rollercoaster of a relationship with Darion was testing at times, and she'd faced more obstacles in the months with him than she ever had in the seven years with Lawrence.

"What are your plans for today?" Gabi asked, climbing into the shower.

"I need to check on the club, finish off some paperwork," Darion replied, appearing in the doorway. "Gabi..." He stepped forward with a groan, staring at her longingly through the glass. "Let me join you."

Gabi was lathering soap in her hands when Darion slid the shower door open and climbed in. Pulling it shut, he turned around to face her, already hard and ready. Gabi hesitated. So she'd be a tad late for work. Ten minutes at most. Besides, it wasn't like she made a habit of tardiness. Darion made her break a lot of rules.

Her lips moved desperately over Darion's, their tongues crashing together, wrestling hungrily. With no time for foreplay, the tip of his cock nudged her already moist entrance. A moan escaped her lips as he gripped her ass, pulling her into him. As he pushed partway in, she noticed he was watching her closely, gauging her reaction like he always did.

Darion liked nothing more than to know what pleased her sexually.

Her breathing grew heavier, her pulse quickening. A wicked smile curled the corners of his mouth, and with a powerful thrust, he slammed her against the glass. Darion continued to pound into her fast, filling her, sending delightful spasms through her whole body.

"You feel so fuckin' good." He tightened his grip on her buttocks, pulling her as close to him as possible, his length sliding in deeper.

Their bodies, wet from the water, moved together in sync. Their lips and hands explored one another as they groaned and panted, unable to get enough. Gabi's heart slammed frantically against her chest. Her inner muscles tightened and quivered, the pleasure intensifying.

There was sheer lust in Darion's eyes as they travelled over every inch of her. Gabi buried her fingers in his hair, pulling his head down, and taking his tongue in her mouth. Their teeth clashed as they kissed savagely, greedily.

When Darion picked her up in a swift action, moving her up and down, supporting her in his strong arms, she cried out. Tension coiled in her stomach as the pressure began to build.

"Look at me," Darion demanded, grabbing her by the chin, and turning her to face him. He knew she was close.

As he bucked his hips upwards, Gabi felt an aching sensation in her abdomen, the desperate need for release. As Darion found her nipples, kneading them roughly, circling them into hard peaks with his thumbs, Gabi whimpered. She threw her head back, silently wishing he wouldn't stop, lost in sensations coursing through her body.

She tried her hardest not to surrender to the orgasm that was seconds away, but it was a battle she was losing fast.

"Darion…" she murmured, closing her eyes, gasping for air.

As Darion continued to slam into her endlessly, she took a deep breath, followed by another. Clinging onto his shoulders, she exploded around him, shuddering and crying out incoherently.

It took a moment for her to regain her composure. When her heavy breathing and hammering heart slowed, she opened her eyes. She caught sight of the triumphant grin on Darion's face. He was a good lay and he *knew* it. He let out a dirty sounding laugh, then picked up his pace, plunging in and out of her.

"So sexy…Gabi."

His lips met her breast, his skilled tongue circling her nipple greedily. Taking it in his mouth, he tugged on it with his teeth, making her gasp. Grinding into her, simultaneously sucking and feasting on her breasts, Darion's face strained with obvious pleasure. He gripped her even tighter, and she felt his cock twitching.

Biting his lip, unable to control it any longer, he let out a cry. She felt him throbbing inside her as he climaxed violently, falling apart. Clutching Gabi, he plunged into her until she felt the spasms begin to ebb. Obviously fully satisfied, he stilled and collapsed his weight against her. A tangled mass of limbs, they remained rooted to the spot. A comfortable silence loomed upon them.

"Do you love me?" Darion eventually spoke. His tone sounded desperate, needy, and his confident persona faded for a moment. Darion rarely ever showed his vulnerable side, and when he did, it surprised her. Looking at him, he didn't seem the sort of man who needed to seek clarification on whether he was loved. Who would be so crazy as to *not* love him?

"Of course I love you," she responded with utmost sincerity.

He ducked his head down with a small chuckle. "This is all new for me, Gabi. I've been out of the relationship game for a long time."

"I know," she soothed, knowing he was uncomfortable with verbalising his feelings. Gabi had learnt over time that Darion preferred to show that he cared through his actions. Sex, for him, was as close as he could possibly get to a partner, the way he proved his feelings.

Sucking in air, he gently lowered Gabi to her feet. He wrapped his big protective arms around her and kissed her forehead. When he finally pulled back and stood under the water, Gabi watched as he soaped his face and body. She bit her lip, and was then unable to stop the smug smile from straining her cheeks.

Darion caught her staring. He winked at her, a slow inscrutable smile appearing. When he'd finished washing himself, Gabi caught his mouth in a kiss. Darion reciprocated, his tongue brushing against hers, taking as much of it as possible. His stubble was sharp against her face, but it didn't deter her from deepening the kiss. Eventually, she extricated herself to catch her breath.

"Now, get out of here," she joked. "Some of us actually have work to do."

"Like ensuring the strippers are dancing sexily enough isn't a job?" he teased.

Gabi pushed him playfully. Careful not to get her blonde locks wet, she leant under the water, allowing it to pour down her skin. She breathed in the scent of vanilla soap, luxuriating in the warmth of the steamed room.

"Am I seeing you tonight?" Darion asked, exiting the shower and patting himself dry with a towel.

"Sure."

"You fancy having a drink at the club?"

Gabi stilled. Would Eva be there? She wasn't sure whether she could face her yet—face the person who had destroyed Darion's trust in women, the person who had introduced him to a dark world of sexual exploration—the very thing that would make or break their relationship.

"Maybe some other time."

Darion looked up, his eyes boring into hers. "Are you gonna avoid the club now?" He secured the towel around his waist.

"What do you mean?" She feigned ignorance.

"Just because Eva's back, it doesn't mean that anything needs to change between us, Gabi. You know that, right?"

She nodded.

When Darion left the bathroom, she rested her

head in her hands with an exasperated sigh. She didn't know anything of the sort. A small part of her suspected he still loved the bitch.

Chapter Three

It was 9:10 a.m. when Gabi discreetly slipped into the office. Luckily no one caught on that she was late. Her colleagues were either in the kitchen, fighting over the kettle, needing an instant caffeine fix for the long day ahead, or they were at their desks gossiping about their weekend antics.

Gabi had worked as an editor at Miller & Co. Publishers for a while. She liked to lose herself in a story, discovering journeys and lives that were different from her own. At one point, she'd experienced feelings of jealousy at some of the characters. They'd appeared to be having more fun than she was in her once miserable, lonely relationship with Lawrence. At least that was a thing of the past.

"Hey, sweetie." Her friend and colleague Mallory walked into her office, gently kicking the door shut behind her. "Bought you a coffee." She placed two cups on the table.

"Thanks, Mal." Gabi smiled. "How are you?"

"Great. How are you?" She dropped onto the

chair at the opposite side of her desk. "I haven't had a chance to properly catch up with you lately. My workload is crazy at the moment."

"I know the feeling." Gabi waved a hand to the pile of papers on her desk.

"So, what's new with you?"

Gabi blew out air. "I told you about Eva, right?"

"What? Who?"

"Darion's ex-wife." Gabi reached for the coffee and took a long swig. "She's back in town. For good."

"Seriously?" Mallory stared at her incredulously. "Why is she back?"

"Apparently she wants to ensure Darion sells the club." Gabi set her cup down. "Either that or she still wants in on the club, and to get Darion back."

"Shit. What are you going to do, Gab?"

Gabi shrugged, exhaustion suddenly overcoming her. "What can I do, Mal? I'm afraid to lose him."

Mallory's features softened with sympathy. "It's one test after the other with Darion." She pursed her lips. "You've both been through so much. How are things on the trust front?"

"I think Darion will probably always have trust issues with women." How could he move on from his past when it was back to haunt him?

"All you can do is be there for him, Gab."

"I wouldn't mind, but I've got my own issues to deal with." Gabi slouched in her chair. "Every time he goes to the club, I worry that he'll hook up with one of the dancers again." He did have quite a history with them. "Or worse, reconcile with Eva."

"I don't think he would," Mallory soothed.

15

"I hope he wouldn't."

Mallory rested her hand on Gabi's supportively. "How are things at The Black Door? Has he, erm…you know…asked you to do any freaky shit lately?"

"No." Gabi omitted their most recent experience in the playrooms.

That was another of her worries. Darion was extremely sexually adventurous, and more experienced than she was. He liked to push boundaries. She wasn't sure whether she could keep up with him, or whether she wanted to. She knew he liked to constantly seek sexual thrills. It wasn't as if by being in a relationship he could all of a sudden turn his back on his fantasies and settle for ordinary 'vanilla' sex. A man definitely couldn't change overnight. Gabi knew that much. Even being cheated on by his ex-wife in the playrooms didn't deter the enjoyment he got from participating in them. He wanted someone he could trust, who would enjoy the club as much as he did.

She prayed that once she eventually got closer to him, got him to open up, that he'd leave his dark desires and fantasies behind, and commit to a solid, ordinary relationship. Failing which, he'd strip Gabi's identity, and any innocence she had left. Did she want to go down that route?

"Darion sure leads a colourful life," Mallory said, pulling her back to reality.

"Too colourful."

"Yeah, but c'mon, Gab." Mallory grinned devilishly. "He's hot as hell, and it sure beats a predictable lifestyle."

16

"I'm not so sure anymore, Mal."

"Just relax, have fun. Surely Darion would never pressure you into anything you're not comfortable doing."

A comfortable silence descended upon them as they paused to sip their drinks.

Gabi cradled the warm cup in her hands. "Anyway, how's Steve?" she asked, eager for a change of subject.

"He's good." Mallory beamed.

"You get up to much over the weekend?' Gabi touched the spacebar on her keyboard, causing the computer screen to light up—thirty unread emails. She groaned inwardly. She was in for a busy day.

"We went to Sasha's for a couple of hours. It was fun."

"I miss that place."

Sasha's was a bar that she, Lawrence, Mallory, Steve, Suzie, Marcus, and some of her other friends used to go to on Friday or Saturday nights.

"You should come one night. Maybe even bring Darion."

"No way." Gabi shook her head. "I wouldn't want to run into Lawrence."

"I haven't seen him there in a long time." Mallory drained the last of her drink, and rose to her feet. "Anyway, I better get some work done." She made her way to the door, pausing to soothe Gabi's worries. "Darion loves you. Have faith that it will all work out."

Gabi smiled tightly. When the door closed after Mallory, she attempted to give a manuscript her full attention. She hoped that if she kept her mind busy, it would keep her niggling thoughts at bay. Twenty pages in, she was already feeling restless.

Pushing her chair back, she rose in her black Louboutin platforms and ventured toward the window. She took in the street below, the bustling crowds, and beyond that, trees and high-rise buildings underneath a sky which would have been perfect if not spoilt by the grey clouds.

She stared at the view in a trance-like state, suddenly wishing she was anywhere but cooped up in her stuffy office. She returned to her desk and kicked off her heels. Picking up the papers, she forced herself to concentrate on the words before her. She knew she needed to separate her personal life from her professional life. After a page, she tucked her legs underneath her and became engrossed in the story. It was gripping. Feeling optimistic, she smiled to herself, knowing that the passion she had for literature would never cease.

A few hours later, her iPhone vibrated in her handbag. Placing the manuscript on the desk, she fished it out and glanced at the clock on the screen. The afternoon had flown by. With a perfectly manicured finger, she clicked into her messages. Darion's name appeared. A hint of a smile played on her lips.

Darion: Hey, baby. I've got a surprise for you.

The giddy rush slipped away as Gabi's heart twisted in her chest. She stuffed the mobile back into her bag and sat back with a long, heartfelt sigh. She wondered what he had in store. Darion's surprises were *never* ordinary.

***

Darion

Darion switched off the laptop and reluctantly pulled himself off the sofa. Internet shopping. He always got carried away with it, teased with side-bar and pop-up advertisements that made him buy things he didn't need: electrical gadgets, iPhone accessories, stuff for his motorbike, and cars. Taking in his modern, lavish apartment which consisted of a humungous wall-mounted television, computer consoles, CDs, DVDs, top of the range kitchen appliances, expensive aftershaves, clothes, and watches, Darion knew he had a spending problem. He never liked to go without. Ever. However, now he was spending money faster than he earned it. He forced the thoughts out of his mind. He had bigger fish to fry.

Although he'd pretended to Gabi that Eva being back in town to stay wouldn't change things, he'd been lying. He feared Eva would destroy his world for the second time. Darion hadn't seen her in years—since she'd cheated on him, betrayed him. When she'd left town for good, although he'd been distraught, heartbroken, drinking whatever he could get his hands on, gambling away his hard-earned cash, and sleeping with almost every woman that came his way, a part of him had been a little relieved. He'd hoped it'd help him forget her.

How wrong he'd been.

How could he have forgotten someone that sexy, outrageous, adventurous? She was the female version of him. Together they'd been a dangerous match. Trouble. Their relationship had been intense, the sex filthy, and the games they played to test one other, exciting.

The only woman that had come close to what they had was Gina, one of the dancers at his club. Although it had only been a brief fling with Gina, she had fulfilled Darion sexually.

Then Gabi came along. He smiled just thinking about her. Gabi fulfilled him in other ways. Yeah, she was great in bed, and he was gradually getting her to open up, lose her inhibitions, and explore her kinky side. She also had a hold of his heart. He strongly believed he'd be a real mess without her. He'd met her just at the right time, when he'd been close to self-destruction. He hoped he didn't go down that road again.

What the hell was he meant to do with Eva back on the scene? He ran his hands over his face, feeling his spine stiffen. He'd spoken to Eva briefly a couple of nights ago, at the club. He'd been in a very awkward position with Gabi in the playrooms at The Black Door, to say the least, when she'd appeared out of nowhere. It was just like Eva to make an entrance. She'd screamed abuse at him, about why he was being uncooperative with her lawyers about the sale of the club. She wanted The Black Door sold, Darion didn't. All of his hard work, sweat, blood and tears had gone into that business.

One thing was for certain—Darion wasn't going

down without a fight.

He yanked on some black jeans, and teamed them with a matching shirt. He rolled up the sleeves, ensuring three buttons at the collar were loose. His semi-casual-smart look was complete when he slicked his hair back with gel and spritzed on some aftershave.

Grabbing his keys, he decided to take the Audi to work, to arrive in style. Besides, it drove like a dream. He hoped the smooth journey, the comfort of the leather heated seats, and the sound of the vocal rock CD in the stereo would calm his raging hormones.

It was time to face Eva.

Chapter Four

The car came to a halt, the tyres crunching against the pebbly tarmac. Darion switched off the engine and climbed out. Locking the door with his key, he inhaled a deep breath. He rubbed the tense muscles in his neck as he made his way toward the club. Rolling his shoulders back, he straightened his posture, feigning confidence. With any luck, Eva wouldn't be there.

The club was situated in the town centre of Westhaven, where he also lived. Ever since Darion had been a boy and his dad had taken him to several bars and gentlemen's clubs, he'd dreamt of owning one. He'd worked hard to make it what it was—glamorous, provocative, compelling—complete with lavish interior and stunning exotic dancers. That included the upstairs too. Behind the actual black door was another matter entirely…a dark world that either intensified your relationship or destroyed it. A lifestyle that he'd introduced to Gabi not so long ago. The impact it'd have on his relationship with Gabi was unknown. There was only one way to find out.

Sauntering toward his establishment, he stilled once he was near. He retrieved a box of cigarettes from his pocket. Popping one in his mouth and lighting it, he took in the building. There were only windows upstairs, which were blacked out, except for one. Even in the daylight, you could see the red glow that cast on the street below. The large overhead sign that read **'The Black Door'** was lit up, flickering on and off. As Darion blew out smoke, he took in the fluorescent sign of a woman dancing.

He'd put his all into the club's reputation, building an impressive membership list, marketing it online and in public, promoting it via leaflets and matches, complete with the club's logo. He was proud of his business. The parties that had taken place between those walls were enough to shame even the craziest of rock stars.

Taking a final pull on his cigarette, he tossed it to the ground and entered the premises. The main room, consisting of a bar, red velvet sofas overlooking a main stage, and private booths on either side, was empty. It was too early for customers. In an hour or so, the regulars that fancied a beer, a game of cards, or a private dance would be flooding in. Rock music vibrated from the speakers, although the volume was low enough to allow conversation. At night time, it was turned up a notch, and the party really started.

"Hey, boss," Lexi greeted him from behind the bar, flashing him a grin. "I didn't think you'd be in today."

"Why would you think that?" He slid onto a stool.

"Correct me if I'm wrong, but isn't the wicked witch back?"

"Word spreads fast."

"It's all anybody can talk about. Might there be a reconciliation in the cards?"

Darion stiffened. "You of all people know what she put me through, Lex." He shook his head. "Besides, I'm with Gabi now."

"Well." She leant over and squeezed his hand supportively. "You know I'm here for you."

"I'm sure I can handle Eva." Darion intended his voice to come out confident—instead it was shaky with emotion.

He rose to his feet and strolled behind the bar. Grabbing a glass, he dropped two ice cubes into it and reached for a bottle of whisky. Darion didn't care that it was a little early in the day. As far as he was concerned, there shouldn't be a time restriction on enjoyment, and a glass of liquor certainly made him feel good. Filling the glass halfway, he held it to his mouth, the rich scent filling his nostrils. He downed it in one, wincing as it tore through his throat and chest like hot flames. He remained rooted to the spot for a moment before setting the glass and bottle down.

"What's up with Gina?" he asked, noticing her sitting at the far end of the bar, staring into space.

Lexi pursed her lips. "She's not been herself lately, Daz. I don't know whether it's because she's still got feelings for you, or whether it's Eva being back, or what." She shrugged.

Although Gina had given Darion her blessing over Gabi, he knew she had always hoped that they would one day be an item. Darion groaned inwardly, wishing he wasn't the reason for her mood. "I better talk to her."

He casually sauntered toward Gina, shoving his hands in the pockets of his jeans. As he approached, he scanned the room. It was immaculate as always. The bar surface was gleaming; the glasses on the shelves glinting under the spotlights, and the vodka, spirits, and liquor on show were of a large variety. As always, everything seemed under control.

"Hey, G." He came to a standstill before her.

She blinked a couple of times, as if just coming back to reality. "Hey, Daz."

"You okay?"

"Yeah." She nodded with a smile, although he wasn't convinced.

He leant back slightly, evaluating her. Her eyes were glazed. He felt his chest tighten as he became riddled with guilt. He realised he hadn't been paying attention to the girls or the club for a while. He had been so wrapped up in his own life and problems that he had failed to ensure everyone else was fine.

Gina had been his rock for so long. He especially owed it to her to be there in return. He reached out and stroked a blonde strand away from her face. She looked up at him from beneath her long lashes. With his thumb, he slowly traced down her cheek. He noticed a flicker of gratitude cross her face.

"You know I'm here for you."

"Thanks, Daz."

"What's with the dress?" he teased, trying to lighten the mood. The black dress she wore, although short, was a far cry from the corsets and miniscule skirts she was usually seen in. "You look like you're about to go to a funeral, not twirl around a pole."

She pushed him gently on the shoulder. "If you hadn't been so wrapped up in Gabi you'd have noticed that I haven't danced in months."

He chuckled, pleased to see that she hadn't lost her fiery attitude.

"I've been behind the bar."

Really? He curled his hands together. "Any particular reason?"

"Unless he's with me, Johnny's possessive," she confessed.

"You want me to have a word with him?"

She shook her head with a soft laugh. "It's easier behind the bar. Besides, I kinda like him."

"As long as he treats you right." Darion was protective over the girls. He'd never let anything happen to them. The only reason he had never taken it beyond friendship with Gina was because he didn't trust himself not to unintentionally hurt her. She was fragile. They'd be dangerous together. Also, besides sex, they didn't have much else in common.

"I suppose I better get some work done."

Before he had chance to retire from the room, Gina surprised him by hooking her arms around his waist. Darion could feel the heat of her breath on his neck. He hated himself for becoming a little aroused. He'd yet to see the day when Gina failed to seduce a man with her beauty and bold personality. Gina, with her full lips, womanly body, and blonde waves cascading down her back was tempting.

Reluctantly, he embraced her back for a moment. His head fell into her hair as he breathed in the fruity scent of her shampoo. He screwed his lids shut. For a second he was unsure of whether he was comforting her or seeking comfort himself.

He tensed when he heard a creaking sound coming from upstairs.

"Oh, Eva's here," Gina informed him.

He swallowed, his mouth going dry. He had never felt uneasy at the club before. Regaining his composure, he disentangled himself from Gina. He told her that he'd be in his office should she need him.

When he was eventually inside, he locked the door. He didn't want any disturbances. Striding across the room, he collapsed in the leather chair in front of his desk. A whirling sound came from the computer's fan as he switched it on.

After an hour of sifting through new membership applications online, his mobile rang. He snatched it up. He glanced at the image on the screen before he answered. It was Gabi's naturally beautiful face smiling up at him, and for a moment, he forgot about everything but her.

"Hey, darlin'," he drawled coolly. "You okay?"

"Yeah. What are you doing?"

Was she asking out of mistrust, or because she was interested? "I'm in the office." He propped his legs on the desk.

"I'll be a bit late tonight," she began. "I just

remembered I've got dance class." She paused. "What's this surprise?"

Oh. He'd almost forgotten about that. "If I told you then it wouldn't be a surprise."

Gabi laughed, but it sounded more uncomfortable than happy.

"You'll have to wait and find out."

"You know I hate surprises."

"Get used to them. There will always be surprises as long as I'm around."

"I'll see you later then."

"See ya, Gabi."

"Bye."

Darion placed the mobile on the table and twisted his body around to face the computer. A loud knock at the door reverberated through the room. He froze, his heartbeat quickening. He felt a hot flush spread up his chest. Slowly rising to his feet, he caught sight of the bottle of rum on his desk. He quickly poured himself a glass and necked it back.

"Who is it?" he dared to ask, although he had an inkling of who it was.

"Darion…it's me…Eva."

Chapter Five

A wash of anticipation spread through Darion's gut as he made his way toward the door. His heart leapt in his chest as he unlocked it. Slowly pulling it open, he took a few tentative steps backwards. His focus remained on the desk as Eva walked in, her heels clacking against the floor. His nostrils were filled with the scent of her sweet perfume, the familiar smell that he used to inhale when he buried his head in the crook of her neck, kissing and biting her passionately. His knuckles turned white as he gripped the door handle. *Get a fucking grip, Darion.*

Without asking, Eva flopped down on a chair at his desk and began pouring herself a drink. By the time Darion sat opposite her, she had finished it. Going by her relaxed demeanor, one would never think that the woman before him was someone he despised. He watched her take in the surroundings, a small smile on her face. It felt as if he had been miraculously transported back to the past. His rubbed the tense muscles in his neck. He didn't like the hurricane of feelings revolving in his brain.

"Just what I needed," Eva's voice brought him back to the present. She wiped her mouth, studying him. "So, Darion." She leant back, smiling a slow, inscrutable smile. "It's been a long time."

"Yeah, it has." He reached for a cigarette.

"How's life?"

His jaw tightened as he clenched his teeth. His patience was wearing thin. "Cut the small talk, Eva. Let's get on with it."

"Sure, if you wanna play it that way." She flicked her hair back. "I'm sorry about our little run-in the other night," she said, although her eyes didn't appear to be in the least bit sincere. "I didn't mean to barge into the playrooms. I got your message from my lawyer, and what can I say." She shrugged. "I was fucked off, Daz."

Darion lit the cigarette and took a long puff. He blew the smoke out slowly. If he remembered correctly he had told Eva's lawyer to tell her to 'fuck herself,' and to see him if she wanted to discuss the club. He didn't actually think she'd show up.

He watched as Eva removed her black jacket. He got a full view of her impressive cleavage and petite arms, decorated with tattoos. That body. That body he knew so well, that he'd pleasured, worshipped, and brought to intensifying orgasms. The body that used to belong to him. Those piercing green eyes that had always stared at him full of addiction, lust. That long black glossy hair that he'd wrapped around his wrist more times than he could remember. He swallowed the lump that appeared in his throat and averted his stare.

"I've changed my mind about the club." Resting her hands on the table, she leant forward slightly, pushing out her chest and arching her back. "I don't want to sell it." Her penetrating eyes held his.

He didn't look away this time. If the bitch thought she could intimidate him, she was mistaken. He doused his cigarette in the ashtray. "I don't understand what you mean." He smiled widely, to appear outwardly unaffected. "For months, you've wanted the club sold."

She rose to her feet and sashayed toward him, standing at his side of the desk. Perching on the edge, a mischievous smile crawled across her face. "I've been thinking about the agreement we've had up until now."

Darion folded his arms across his chest, leaning back in his chair. "You mean splitting the club's profit fifty-fifty?"

She nodded. "I think I'm happy to stick to that arrangement."

What? "Why the sudden change of heart?"

Leaning toward him to create a bond of intimacy, Eva lowered her voice. "Oh, there's never been a change of heart, Darion…ever."

He knew she wasn't talking about the club. He begged to differ. "Well." He pushed to his feet abruptly. "The club has been fine without you here so the agreement can continue as it was—me running things, and your half going straight to your account."

She shook her head slowly. "I'm back in town now." She stood up. She was so close he could feel the heat radiating from her body. "And as partner,

I've decided I want to be more *hands on* this time around."

"I'd rather sell the club," he responded quickly.

"Now that's not very nice, is it?" She pouted, pretending to look offended.

Darion tapped his foot anxiously on the floor. "I'm not gonna put up a fight any more." He decided there and then that he would sell The Black Door. He didn't want to. It pained him, but he felt he had no other option. It was easier than having to face her every day. He needed her gone. There would be nothing but trouble with her in town, complications he didn't need. Besides, her being before him made him feel uneasy. She brought back emotions he'd tried to bury.

"Don't let personal issues affect business," she said sternly. "For starters, you aren't pulling in enough money."

"What would you know about my finances?" He cocked his head. "You're a fine one to talk."

"I've been speaking with Tiana. I wanna fix it, Daz."

Darion glared at her, although his confidence was diminishing rapidly. He couldn't deny that Eva was hard working and had a fine eye for detail. She seemed to know what the clients wanted, and a long time ago, the club had been bringing in money faster than he could spend it. He'd never admit he could probably use the help. His bank balance could use some extra zeros. The sooner he paid off his beloved vehicles, which he could never bring himself to sell, the better.

Fuck. Why did it have to be Eva, of all people, to

give the club a boost? As long as she stayed out of his way, he supposed he could just about live with it.

Clenching his fists, he stepped closer to her, so his nose was a small fraction away from hers. "Okay," he said through gritted teeth. "You can take on the upstairs, and I'll continue running the downstairs. But I'm warning you now, Eva, when I use the upstairs facilities, I don't want you around. Do you understand?"

She giggled. "Don't worry. I wouldn't wanna ruin your fun."

Darion sidestepped her and poured himself another drink. He tried his hardest to stop the shaking of his fingers. "Are we done?"

She grabbed her handbag and strolled leisurely toward the door, pausing to say, "We're far from done, Darion."

When she left, his fingers curled around the glass. Unable to stop the rage that engulfed him, he threw the glass to the wall with force, watching as it smashed into a million little pieces.

Chapter Six

Gabi

Gabi was sat in her Mercedes convertible, nodding her head along to "Undisclosed Desires" by Muse. Glancing in the rear-view mirror, her chest tightened, her breathing suspending. She was almost certain that a silver Toyota Yaris had been behind her for quite some time. She craned her neck, trying to get a better look, however there were two other cars separating them. Turning another corner, she sighed in relief as the car took a different direction. *Stop being paranoid, Gabi,* she told herself.

Now stationary at the traffic lights, her mobile rang. She snatched it from the passenger seat. With a perfectly manicured finger, she swiped to answer, pressing the speaker icon.

"Hi, Gabi."

"Suzie!" She beamed, turning the music down a notch. "How are you?"

"I'm good," she replied. "Better than good, in

fact. How are you, Gab?"

"I'm great. I've just come from dance class."

"How's that going?"

"It's great. I really like it. What are you up to?"

"Well...I literally just got off the phone to Mallory. I've got some news..."

Gabi felt excitement building, knowing what was coming next.

"I'm pregnant," she squealed in delight. "Me and Marcus are having a baby."

"Congratulations, Suze. I'm so happy for you. We have to celebrate soon."

"Absolutely...Marcus is calling me...I'll call you soon, sweetie."

"Bye, honey."

Gabi placed the mobile in her lap and pressed her foot on the accelerator as the lights turned green. As the car smoothly veered around the corner, she was unable to stop smiling. She couldn't have been more pleased for her friend.

She was about to turn the volume on the stereo higher when her mobile rang again. She predicted it would be Mallory to share her own excitement over their friend's news. Glancing down, she saw the screen displayed Darion's name.

"Hello," she breezed cheerily.

"Gabi."

"Everything okay?"

"Can we cancel tonight?" An exasperated puff of air filled the line. "I've had a long day at the club. I'm exhausted."

Gabi's shoulders sagged as she felt herself deflate. Darion rarely ever cancelled arrangements.

She instantly expected the worse. "Is something wrong?"

"Nothings wrong, darlin'," he responded, although the uncertainty to his tone made her think otherwise.

She was silent, expecting him to explain further. When he didn't, she said, "Are you sure?"

"Eva's changed her mind about wanting the club sold."

"Well, isn't that good news?"

"She wants back in on the business."

Gabi swallowed. Her suspicions being confirmed caused her stomach to somersault. She gripped the steering wheel.

"I'll call you tomorrow."

"Sure," she responded quickly, wanting the conversation terminated. "Bye."

A heavy ache rose in her chest as she ended the call. She wound down the window and sucked in a breath of cool air, willing herself not to get worked up. She knew she was being stupid and way too sensitive, but something wasn't right. Eva was up to something. She knew it. Darion had only been back at the club a day and the drama had already begun.

She swerved the car around, changing direction, and headed for her apartment. Once she was in the comfort of her living room, she kicked off her heels, and collapsed on the sofa. She lay there for a moment, staring at the television absentmindedly.

If only she could figure Darion out. If only she knew what he was thinking, then she could maybe help him. She had no idea what he wanted—now, or in the future. She knew for certain he had a passion for what he did though—he loved his club. As much as Gabi hated it, she hadn't wanted to give him an ultimatum and make him sell it, regardless of what he'd said when she'd almost left him previously.

Unable to take on all the obstacles that came with Darion, Gabi was close to leaving him less than a week ago. She couldn't handle it all: the club, his ex-wife, the dancers, his head-fuck issues, and damaged past. To win her back, he'd told her that he'd do *anything*. She wondered if he even remembered saying it, and whether it was said purely out of desperation to win her back.

She sighed heavily, deciding not to dwell on things. She climbed to her feet, heated up a ready-made meal in the microwave, and settled in front of the television to watch an episode of *Sons Of Anarchy*.

When it finished, she had a long hot soak in the bath, instantly feeling her muscles relax, and her worries begin to ebb. The sweet smell of the aromatherapy oils hung in the air, and she breathed it in, smiling in contentment. Closing her eyes, she lay there, enjoying the peace and quiet until the water turned lukewarm, and her hands went wrinkly.

As she dried and changed into a pink silk night dress, she contemplated reading a magazine in bed, or perhaps even start a new manuscript. She was literally under the bed covers for two seconds when the doorbell rang.

Who the hell would be calling so late? It wasn't like she knew any of her neighbours yet. She hadn't lived in the apartment for that long. It couldn't be

Mallory, she usually rang first. She climbed out of bed hastily. Trudging down the hallway barefoot, she peered through the peephole. It was black. Whoever was on the other side must have had their hand against it.

"Who is it?" she asked, knotting her hands together.

No answer.

Fuck. She hooked the chain across the door and gripped the handle. She pulled the door open, leaving a small gap, big enough to see out of. She sighed in relief, and smiled. It was Darion.

"I thought I wasn't seeing you tonight." She unhooked the chain and allowed him to enter.

"I changed my mind."

He booted the door shut behind him and picked her up. He caught her mouth in a kiss, his lips moving desperately over hers. Gabi responded to his firm kisses, feeling an excited shiver run up her spine. He pulled back to kiss her neck greedily, repeatedly, groaning as he did so. Gabi could feel the tension coiling in her stomach. She grabbed fistfuls of his hair, closing her lids, savoring every single second.

Backing her up against the wall for support, his hands buried under her nightie before he yanked it over her head. She felt exposed and vulnerable being naked, on display for him, a little shy. It was the way he looked at her—his eyes raw and glowing, the animalistic smirk that crept across his face.

His mouth met her breast, his hand cupping the other one simultaneously. Heat surged through

Gabi's body when he tongued her nipple, causing it to harden and tingle. She felt her internal muscles spasm, a needy ache persisting between her legs. It felt so good.

"Darion…" she moaned softly. "Shall we go to the bedroom?"

He shook his head, and lay her down on the soft carpet. "I can't wait any longer," he said huskily, his stare fierce on her. He unzipped his jeans.

Gabi seized his face, bringing it down to hers. Her tongue darted inside his mouth, roaming inside. She then freed his erection, her hand sliding up and down the shaft. Darion ran his tongue across his top lip seductively.

His hand buried between her legs as he rubbed her clit in circular movements. Gabi felt the pleasured vibrations shoot through her as her sensitive clit swelled, responding to his touch. When his index finger probed inside her, she threw her head back, arching her spine. Desire bloomed in her stomach.

"Gabi…" he murmured against her breast before sucking it into his mouth. "I can't get enough of you."

She found herself giggling softly. As she slid her hands up and down his length, Darion's features screwed up, his lips parting. She could see the rapid rising and falling of his chest, he was obviously as aroused as she was.

His wet tongue lapped at her breast, then he tugged on it with his teeth. Gabi gasped, gripping his cock firmer, pumping it faster in her hand. She rolled her thumb over the lubricated tip, eliciting a sharp growl from him. She desperately wanted to feel him inside her. She needed to be filled, to rid herself of the teasing ache in her body.

She rocked her hips onto his hand, feeling his finger slide deeper into her wetness, filling her satisfactorily. His thumb circled her engorged clit at the same time. She sucked in air. A hot flush spread through her body. Her heart raced wildly as her inner muscles ached and clenched around his finger.

"Darion..." she murmured breathlessly.

Darion pulled back for a moment whilst he slowly slid down her body. He left a trail of firm, rough kisses down her chest and over her smooth stomach before finally settling between her legs. He lifted them over his shoulders, giving him full and easy access.

Gabi squirmed when the tip of his tongue teasingly flicked her clit. His wickedly gleaming irises burned into hers, as he watched her. She felt her cheeks warm even more, however she was unable to look away. As he sucked with abandon, she gripped his muscular shoulders, greedily thrusting herself upwards onto his stubbled face.

Tension coiled in her stomach as he parted her with his fingers. His mouth stretched wider as his tongue dove into her, lapping up her juices hungrily. His soft mumbles sent vibrations between her legs as he devoured her, and she knew that he enjoyed every bit of it.

Gabi bit her lip to stifle her groans. Her nails clawed his shoulders, silently begging to feel more of him. Rocking her hips impatiently, she felt his smile on her skin as a dirty chuckle filled her ears.

"Come here…" she pleaded.

He jabbed her with his tongue, in and out repeatedly, pleasuring her with his mouth. His chin and cupid's bow glistened with her wetness.

Desire pulsed between her legs, a throbbing ache making his name spill from her mouth. She swiveled her hips, feeling his thick tongue fill her deeper. Grabbing his hair, spasms of pleasure rippled through her. Her abs tightened with every lick, her thighs trembling. She thrashed her head back, knowing she was close.

Darion looked up at her from beneath his dark lashes, his smoldering erotic stare almost sending her over the edge. She felt her legs stiffen, her sex fluttering and burning, close to release. With one last slow, torturous lick, Darion pulled back.

"Don't stop," Gabi spluttered. She pushed his head down, grinding onto his lips. He bit her clit playfully, but roughly, causing her to grimace.

"I want you, Gabi…" his voice was ferocious.

Dropping her legs to his waist, he shuffled up, catching her mouth in a kiss. Her tongue explored his with an overwhelming urgency, licking, tasting, sucking. She hooked her hands under his firm buttocks and pulled him into her. When he entered, hard and throbbing, she cried out involuntarily. It was painful at first, until her inner muscles relaxed and accepted his length. It was almost impossible for Darion to be any more blessed.

Her jaw ached as their lips smashed together. They kissed until they were breathless and both panting for air. Gabi looked at him. She could see beads of sweat forming on his brow. His eyes were dark and possessed as they always were in the throes of passion. His mouth curled back in a dangerous smile.

"Faster?"

He slammed into her forcefully, moving in and out of her endlessly. Gabi buried her face in the crook of his neck. She lost herself in the musky scent of his aftershave as she planted a trail of firm kisses across his skin. As she nipped gently with her teeth, she noticed Darion's jaw clench as he tipped his head back, giving her further access. The deep guttural groans that eased out of his throat turned her on. She liked nothing more than seeing him in pleasure.

She hooked her legs tightly around his waist, jerking her hips, meeting him thrust for thrust. As he plunged into her even faster, she squeezed her lids shut, her nails digging into his back. It was almost too much to bear. Each time he hit her sensitive spot, she felt ready to explode, to succumb to the orgasm that was threatening to tear into her.

"Fuuuck…" Darion ground his teeth.

Gabi clenched around him as she felt him twitch inside her. The thickness of his shaft filled her perfectly. Their stares locked, the raw passion between them visible. Gabi could feel an orgasm building. She sucked in air, her heart slamming against her chest.

Rocking her hips to meet his fast rhythm, she winced as Darion grabbed a fistful of her hair, bringing her mouth to his. His tongue dove in, invading greedily.

Gabi's core tightened, her muscles contracting

around him. She gripped hold of Darion, anchoring him to her, wanting to feel every bit of him if she could. As deep as possible.

"Gabi…" Her name came out a weak cry.

She felt him expand inside her. He grunted as he pushed in deeper, coming over and over, letting his climax overtake him. Gabi moaned out, shuddering, as her own orgasm rippled through her body. Her muscles throbbed as she surrendered to the divine release. Wave after wave of pleasure washed over her, making her legs tremble.

Eventually her body went limp. Gabi lay there, catching her breath, willing her heartbeat to slow. Darion's body weight crushed her, but she didn't want him to move. She could feel the beat from his chest on her own, could feel the warmth radiating from him.

She reached up and stroked his hair. She felt her heart swell. He was so sexy. He was easily the best lover she had ever had. She couldn't imagine this kind of pleasure with anyone else. It was addictive. She craved him. Darion Milano certainly knew what he was doing.

After a few minutes, he pushed himself into a seated position. His gaze lingered over her body, and he flashed her a satisfied smile.

"What am I going to do with you?" She giggled.

"Everything," he said, his expression serious.

"Let's go to bed," she said softly.

Her limbs were aching, her eyelids heavy, and she was shattered. She wanted nothing more than to sleep naked with him, skin on skin, cuddling, listening to the sound of the blowing wind outside her bedroom window. There was nowhere else she'd rather be that was so soothing, relaxing.

Darion rose to his feet and held out his hand for her to take. She did, allowing him to yank her up. As she headed toward her room, she felt his hand skim between her legs gently, making her sex flutter. She groaned inwardly. Darion was such a tease. She doubted she'd get any sleep.

Chapter Seven

The next morning, Gabi was pulling on her nude heels when Darion strolled down the hallway, a cigarette hanging from his mouth. He ran both hands through his hair, smoothing it back, and took the cigarette between his fingers, blowing out smoke. Gabi glanced up at him and felt the fluttering of nerves in her stomach. She was insanely attracted to him—the forever naughty glint in his eyes, and the slow smirk on his face that held some sort of secret. He was as mysterious as he was intriguing.

He stubbed the cigarette in the bin and took his coffee from the side, taking a long swig. Gabi found herself studying his full lips, the stubble that surrounded his mouth, and his strong, defined jaw. She felt the urge to kiss it. Catching her staring at him, Darion placed the cup on the side, and slowly approached her.

He hooked his arms around her waist, his gaze on hers. She could look at him all day, every day, and never get bored. And that was *with* clothes on!

As he brushed his lips against hers, she felt her heart drumming inside her chest. Tightening his grip, he pulled her against his firm body. Gabi melted into his embrace, her tongue searching for his desperately. They worked their lips together in sync, soft moans escaping, their hands burying in one another's hair. A wave of longing washed over her, and she felt that familiar needy ache for his touch.

"How long do you think this honeymoon stage will last?" she asked with a giggle, curiosity sweeping over her.

His brow furrowed in confusion.

"You know, not being able to keep our hands off each other."

"Forever, I hope." His tone was serious.

He sat down and pulled her onto his lap. They stared at one another in silence. When together they forgot about the world and its problems. The only thing that mattered was each other. They felt happy and safe in their little bubble, if they didn't overanalyse everything. It was nice not thinking about things now and then, just enjoying the moment, the relationship for what it was.

In an ideal world, Eva wasn't in the picture; neither were the dancers, and neither was the club. But then Darion wouldn't be the person he was. A small part of Gabi was actually drawn to some of his flaws and insecurities. He was like a puzzle she wanted to solve. How could she ever get bored if she was constantly trying to figure him out? One day, she'd get to know the real him. She hoped.

Noticing the way he was intently watching her,

she felt a sudden attack of insecurity. What was it he desired about her so much? She felt attractive with her naturally long blonde hair, pretty face, and slim body, complete with curves in all of the right places. She took care of her appearance and dressed well.

However, she'd seen the type of women Darion had attracted in the past: wild looking, with tattoos, collagen-injected lips, and silicone boobs. They were the sort of women that wouldn't be out of place on the pages of men's magazines. Gabi glanced down at her navy knee-length skirt, matching blouse, and high heels. She anxiously fiddled with her nails, wondering if she looked plain in comparison. Was she enough for Darion, or would he leave her when he needed a new sexual thrill?

"Do you think I should get a tattoo somewhere?" she asked him outright. "Just a small one?"

"No," he responded without a moment's hesitation. "I don't."

"Why not?"

"You're different to every girl I've ever been with." He traced his thumb along her bottom lip gently. "Let's keep it that way."

"What about a piercing somewhere, or something?"

"Gabi, you're naturally beautiful. You don't need to accentuate anything. Believe me, you stand out already."

Gabi felt herself swell with confidence. As he returned to his coffee, she faced the mirror, pulling her hair into a high ponytail. She then added mascara to the lashes that framed her brown eyes, and wiped a slick of pearly gloss over her full lips.

"Fancy breakfast?" he asked. "We have plenty of time."

"If you're making it." She smiled.

"Gabi, you know I like the simple pleasures in life, and food is one of them." He made his way toward the cupboards and began searching through them.

"Do you like cooking?" She plopped herself onto a chair at the table.

"I suppose. I don't get time to do it often. Everything is always so hectic in my life."

"I can see that," she muttered under her breath.

"I can rustle up some pretty fancy dishes, but there's nothing better than going to a restaurant." He turned to face her. "What are you in the mood for? Omelette, pancakes, waffles, quiche, scrambled egg muffins?"

"I'm impressed you can cook all of that from scratch. You're a man of many talents, Mr. Milano."

"I learnt how to cook growing up. I had no choice." He paused for a second, and a flash of what appeared to be sadness and disappointment crossed his face. "Anyway, what will it be?"

"Um…" Gabi bit her lip, wondering why he cooked his own meals growing up. Gabi knew that cooking wasn't one of her specialties. Her mom had never let her lift a finger when she lived with her. From laundry, to cooked dinners, to cleaning, she did it all. Now that Gabi thought about it, she supposed she'd been a tad spoilt. Gathering her wits, she said, "An omelette sounds good…thanks."

As Darion began making breakfast, Gabi smiled and took out a gossip magazine from her handbag. Setting it on the table, she began flipping through the pages. *I could certainly get used to this.* She was engrossed in a story, when ten minutes later, Darion placed an omelette before her. She inhaled the divine smell.

"This looks delicious."

"Enjoy." Darion winked, sitting down.

"What do you have planned for tonight?" Gabi asked, digging her fork into the omelette, and popping some in her mouth.

"Not much."

"You not going to the club?" she found herself prying.

"Yeah, I'm gonna pop in."

She stilled for a moment, holding her fork in mid-air. She couldn't help but wonder why he hadn't invited her along, like he usually did. Shrugging it off, she continued to devour her breakfast. When her plate was empty, she glanced at the wall clock.

"I guess I better get to work."

"Me too."

When Gabi had gathered her handbag, mobile and car keys, she followed Darion out of her apartment. She gave him one final kiss before climbing into her car. As she started the engine, she stole a quick glance at him. He was talking on his mobile. She felt a pang of jealousy. She prayed to God they both could overcome their trust issues before they tore them apart.

Chapter Eight

Darion

It was early afternoon when Darion arrived at the club. He immediately sensed something was wrong. Gina, Lexi, and Marnie were stood in a circle, their features twisted like they'd been sucking on lemons. Silence filled the air as he approached them.

"Don't stop talking on my account," he said, pulling out a stool. He looked at each of them questioningly. "What's going on?"

"We're not happy, Darion." Marnie folded her arms across her chest, causing her breasts to rise up.

He remained silent waiting for her to explain.

"It's Eva," Lexi informed him. "We can't work with her, Daz. She's driving us nuts."

Darion retrieved a silver tin from his pocket. Snapping it open, he took a cigar, popped it in his mouth, and lit it. "What do you mean?" He took a long drag, prior to blowing smoke from the corner of his mouth.

"She thinks she's in charge of this damn place.

She's laying down too many rules," Marnie said.

Darion clenched his teeth. "I told Eva to stay upstairs." He slowly rose to his feet. "She knows I'm in charge here."

"Well, I suggest you speak to her," Gina said firmly. "She's obviously not on the same page as you."

"Another problem I don't need." Darion sighed heavily. "I'll sort it."

He exited the room, making his way toward his office. He loosened several buttons on his top, feeling a hot flush sweep up his neck. He massaged the back of it in an attempt to soothe his aching muscles. He couldn't keep letting Eva get under his skin. The atmosphere in the club was usually relaxed, with the girls drinking and enjoying themselves. He didn't like seeing them worked up and stressed.

Taking a final puff on his cigar, he stubbed it out and poured a glass of rum and Coke. He finished it in several gulps. Slamming the glass on his desk, he sank in his chair, closing his eyes. Women. They seemed to be every problem he had at the moment. He needed to sweeten the girls up, that was for sure. They hadn't had a lock-in for a while; perhaps he'd party hardcore with them soon, like the good old days. One thing he couldn't let Eva affect was his relationship with the girls. He couldn't afford to lose them.

He spent the rest of the day responding to client query emails and calls. The club's membership list was ever-growing, and a few private parties had been booked over the next few months. He tore open a parcel on his desk and took out shiny leaflets. He ran his finger along one, taking in the photographs of the lavish club upstairs, and the crowd of beautiful people—voyeurs, fetishists, exhibitionists, sadists, masochists—fun, free-minded couples and singles of all sexual preferences.

He felt his cock strain against his jeans as memories of the playrooms invaded his mind. When they were married, Darion had been introduced to the world of swinging by Eva. She was after a new sexual high, and there wasn't much they hadn't done. They'd drunk booze and flirted with other couples online. There were thousands of members on the swinger's forums and chat-rooms. They'd met a couple and engaged in soft swinging before attending parties and swingers clubs. When they eventually participated in partner swapping, Darion had feared he'd be jealous and unable to go through with it. However, watching the woman he loved, the woman that was going home with only him, being pleasured by another man right before his very eyes was arousing. It was like a live porno. And so he and Eva had been hooked. The rest, as they say, is history.

Darion had a taste of that world and couldn't give it up. It was like an addiction. When he and Eva had split, he'd enjoyed sexual freedom. Every girl in the club was available, and Darion sure took advantage. He was living every man's fantasy.

He knew Gabi was nervous about the whole swinging lark, but he believed she'd come around to it. She hadn't once asked him to give the lifestyle up, nor given him any ultimatums. They'd played in the swinging rooms in the past, although they'd only stuck to one another. Gabi had shared a few kisses with other people, but that was as far as it had gone. Gabi was definitely heteroflexible. She was curious about women—he was sure of it. He couldn't wait until the day when Gabi could fully let go of her inhibitions, and they could enjoy swinging to its full potential. They would move on from soft-swinging, purely to satisfy one another.

As long as the rules were adhered to, Darion didn't believe swinging was classed as cheating. How could it be cheating if all involved knew about it and agreed to it? As long as both parties regularly communicated, agreed what level to take swinging, and what rules to abide by, then nobody could get hurt. Darion was open to everything. He only had three rules: no sex unless both agreed, safe sex always, and no separating. All sexual activity *had* to take place whilst they were in the same room. Unlike Eva, he was pretty confident Gabi wouldn't break that rule and tear his heart into a million little pieces.

Darion separated his sexual life and his emotional life. In the real world, he wanted a loving relationship with one woman, and one woman only, with *no* secrets. Never would he betray a girlfriend, especially outside of swinging, and he expected the same in return. He found it difficult to trust women, but hoped that in time, Gabi would *fully* restore his faith.

Chapter Nine

Gabi

Gabi slung her bag over her shoulder and waved at the tutor with a smile. As she exited The Royal Dance Academy, she was hit with a busy street of people rushing past. The sound of traffic filled her ears. The smell of damp air met her nostrils. It must have rained whilst she was indoors. Usually the dull weather would have her high spirits plummeting. Not anymore. She was always on cloud nine when she'd had a lesson. The exercise released feel-good endorphins, made her skin glow, and made her muscles become firmer. If there was one thing Gabi was passionate about, it was dancing.

Heading for the car park, she hummed the hip-hop song she'd just danced to. In the past, whilst Lawrence had told her dance classes were ridiculous for a woman of her age, Mallory had spurred her on. She'd pleaded with her to do something she was passionate about. She'd seen Gabi become a shadow of her former self, her self-esteem at an all-time low. Lawrence's constant criticising, controlling, and neglectful behavior had turned her into a pathetic, needy woman, desperate to be adored, to be wanted. Gabi hadn't wanted to join assertive classes to feel like her old self, and so she'd joined the Academy she used to attend when she was younger. As for confidence boosting, it was sure doing the trick. She'd even met a handful of friends there.

Whilst she was unlocking the car door, she felt the hairs lifting on the back of her neck, as cold chills washed over her. Like that time in traffic, she had a feeling she was being followed. She spun around and checked her surroundings apprehensively. She couldn't see anyone acting suspiciously, nor paying attention to her. Deciding she was being stupid, she climbed into the car.

Her heart almost exploded in her chest when her mobile rang. With a soft giggle when her breathing had resumed to normal, Gabi dived into her bag, and retrieved her iPhone. Swiping the screen with her finger, she held it to her ear.

"Hello?"

"Hey, Gab." It was Mallory. "Are you free tonight?"

"Yeah, I am." With her free hand, she strapped her seatbelt across her body.

"Great. Suze called me. She wondered if you fancied going to Sasha's later. It doesn't have to be a late one."

"I don't know." Gabi weighed up the options in her mind. Go to Sasha's bar, have a little dance, and down a few cocktails. Or go home, dress in her warm pyjamas, pour a nice glass of wine, and watch an episode of *Gossip Girl*.

"Come on, Gab. Suzie's feeling shitty about being cooped up all the time. Besides, it's been ages since we all went out."

A girls' night out was long overdue. "Okay," she agreed. "What time?"

"Suzie won't be drinking, so said she'll pick us both up after eight."

"Great. I'll see you later."

Gabi placed her mobile back in her bag. She was actually looking forward to it. Driving home with a grin on her face, it didn't take long until she was in her bedroom. Thumbing through the clothes in her wardrobe, she bit her lip, unsure on what to wear. Eventually she settled on a white dress, which she knew would compliment her golden skin. She had her dad's genes to thank for that.

She stripped her clothes off and placed them into the laundry basket in the bathroom. Not wanting to get her hair wet, she scooped it into a ponytail, and climbed into the shower. The water was warm and soothing. She closed her lids for a moment, and savoured her time in the now steamy, silent room.

Cautious of the time, she stepped out of the shower, and began drying. It didn't take her long to dress and perfect her make-up and hair. Finally confronting her reflection in the mirror, she decided she looked reasonably attractive. Gabi could look like a million dollars and she'd still downplay her appearance, which in effect only made her appear more beautiful—an attractive woman without the arrogance to go with it.

You look good, she told herself sternly. Twisting and turning, she scrutinised her image. Her blonde hair hung in loose waves. The dress she was wearing clung to all the right curves, the plunging neckline skimming just over her nipples. She'd accessorised with diamond earrings, which sparkled under the lights. She towered in red six inch heels, the type of heels Darion would tell her to keep on during sex. He had a thing for heels. Scratch that, he had a thing for everything. She half smiled, shaking her head.

Forty minutes later, she, Suzie and Mallory were sat in Sasha's bar. The place was lively, with music and laughter all around. Suzie was on non-alcoholic cocktails, whereas Gabi and Mallory ensured they took advantage of the night out, and so their table was laden with cocktails and shots. Gabi was on her third drink already, and starting to feel a little light-headed.

"I mean, I won't mind the getting bigger part." Suzie fiddled with the straw in her glass. "It's the morning sickness that will drive me crazy. Oh, and Marcus treating me like I'm fragile. He already won't let me lift a finger." She groaned.

Mallory squeezed her arm. "Soon you'll have that little bundle of joy in your arms, and all that will be a distant memory."

"Yeah. You're right." Suzie beamed. "Anyway, enough about me droning on." She giggled. "I want to know what you've both been doing lately. And we *must* get together more."

"Agreed." Mallory nodded. "And I'm afraid I haven't got much gossip. Same old for me. Steve is still a darling, our relationship is well, and work's going fine."

"Any children on the horizon?"

Mallory shrugged. "Maybe. We're not being careful, if that's what you mean."

Gabi turned to look at Mallory, knowing the shock wouldn't be missed from her face. "You didn't tell me you were trying?"

"I'm not trying, but I'm not not-trying, either. If it happens, it happens."

Although she was extremely pleased for her friends, Gabi felt envy twist her heart. Suzie and Mallory were both on the right track to a future they wanted—a happy family, whilst she was in the dark about her future with Darion. But surely the relationship was much more than fun and games; after all, they did love one another. Was love ever enough, though? The question always seemed to linger in Gabi's mind. Sometimes it wasn't enough. Sometimes it didn't conquer all. Sometimes, a person's love for themselves, or some things, overrode the love they had for another. She shook her head as if to erase her thoughts, and not dwell on the 'things' that Darion loved, and whether they were more important to him than she was.

"So, what's new with you, Gab?" Suzie broke her concentration, looking at her questioningly.

Gabi was just about to sigh in exasperation when her mobile bleeped. Darion. He'd stated that he was busy with club stuff, missed her, and that he hadn't forgotten about her surprise.

"I'm seeing someone," Gabi responded with as nonchalant a tone as she could muster. She tapped her finger on her mobile to respond to his text message.

"Yeah, and he's hot as hell." Mallory laughed. "Show her your screensaver image, Gab."

Gabi held her mobile before Suzie's line of sight. Her mouth fell open slightly. "Gabi, he is gorgeous," she swooned. "He's so different to Lawrence."

"He's different all right." She felt her cheeks straining with the grin that surfaced.

"Yeah, and he's a kinky bastard," Mallory informed Suzie.

"Mal." Gabi shook her head.

"Well, do share." Suzie swigged her drink.

Gabi threw Mallory a look. She didn't want Suzie knowing that Darion enjoyed the life of a swinger. She was only just coming to terms with it herself. She couldn't bear to hear any judgmental or negative opinions, should they come. She'd only shared with Mallory as she told her everything, and as they worked together, it was impossible to hide anything from her. Mallory had the ability to read her like a book.

"He's...um...into the usual." Gabi sipped her drink in a bid to end the conversation, but Suzie never let her off the hook that easy.

"The usual? Come on, Gabi, we're amongst friends."

Threesomes, orgies, hardcore bondage, toys, being watched, watching others, sex in public, role play...

"You know..." She shrugged. "Outdoor sex, role play, a bit of light bondage." She wasn't about to disclose the rest.

"He *is* different from Lawrence." Suzie laughed uproariously. "Well, he sure looks like he's making you happy. You're glowing."

"Really?" Gabi's high-pitched tone surprised her.

"Gabi, you were miserable when you were with Lawrence. No matter what issues you have with Darion, no relationship is perfect," Mallory told her. "Apart from feelings of doubt here and there, you *are* much happier."

Gabi felt her heart swell, and found it difficult to hide her joyous expression. Regardless of the obstacles she and Darion faced, she *was* happy the majority of the time. The girls were absolutely right.

After they'd finished the drinks on their table, they decided to hit another bar nearby. Mallory, knowing the bouncer, managed to get them into the VIP section. Past the rope, they ordered another round of drinks, and let loose on the dance floor. Swaying bodies surrounded them, excitedly moving to the pounding beats. Gabi wiped a strand of hair out of her face, and waved her arms in the air.

"I'm going to the bathroom," she shouted to the girls above the music, a moment later.

Gabi wobbled slightly in her heels, the alcohol having taken effect. She clamped a hand over her mouth, feeling as if she'd vomit. Her stomach was churning. Joining the queue for the bathroom, she felt vibrations from her bag, which was pressed against her waist. She fumbled for her mobile.

"Hello…" she slurred, when she'd finally retrieved it.

"Gabi," his sexy, husky voice came down the line. Gabi heard a blowing sound and realised he was smoking.

She grinned. "What are you up to?"

"I'm in the office. I've literally just finished everything that needed taking care of."

"Sounds like you've been a busy boy."

"Where are you?"

"I'm…um…" She paused, trying to remember the name of the bar. Shit, what was it called? "Oh…Havana Bar."

"Are you drunk?" She detected humour in his tone.

"Maybe," she admitted sheepishly.

He groaned. "I wish I was there."

"Come and meet me, then."

"Perhaps. I need to speak with the girls first. They're bitching and whining."

"Why?"

"I'll tell you when I see you."

Gabi entered a cubicle and locked the door behind her.

"What are you wearing?" His voice was now low and seductive sounding.

"Um…" She dropped onto the toilet lid, hiccupping. "A white dress."

"Wanna video chat?"

"No…" She groaned. "I'm drunk, Darion…I look a mess."

"Gabi, you never look a mess."

She wouldn't have minded seeing him. "Okay." She caved in.

A second later Darion called back, and she could

see him on the screen. Her stomach flipped with excitement. The grey polo shirt he was wearing was unbuttoned, revealing the top of his smooth chest. Gabi desperately wanted to brush her lips across it. She became wildly aroused, heat surging through every cell in her body.

"Let me see you." His full lips blew out smoke from the cigar he was smoking.

She positioned her mobile on the toilet tank, which was waist-level. Crouching a little, Darion must have gotten a glimpse of her cleavage. A strangled cry of satisfaction escaped his lips.

"Now I *really* wish I was there."

Gabi giggled.

"I'll be there soon."

Gabi put her mobile away and touched up her make-up. She then found Mallory and Suzie being chatted up by a few men on the dance floor. The girls enjoyed a little harmless flirtation, although they'd never act upon it and cross the line. Gabi was introduced to them all, prior to being asked for a dance. She declined. Darion didn't like sharing her when he wasn't present.

A sultry voice came from the speakers. "Bang Bang Bang Bang" by Soho Dolls was playing. Gabi swayed her arms and hips, as did the girls. She gasped when she felt one of the drunken men squeeze her behind. Ignoring him, she continued to dance.

After a couple of songs went by, the girls retired to their table, and sat talking and giggling for a while. Gabi's limbs were aching, her head spinning, and she knew if she so much as touched another drop of alcohol that she'd probably be flat on her back. However, she didn't want the night to end. She was having way too much fun. She reached for her glass of water and drained half of it.

"Let's go dance again." She turned her attention to Mallory and Suzie, unable to sit still.

"You pair go ahead. I need a moment's rest." Suzie leant back in her seat and rubbed her belly.

Gabi smiled ruefully. "Aw, Suze. Why did you suggest a bar? We should have gone to a restaurant, or for a coffee somewhere."

"Nonsense." She waved a hand in the air as if to dismiss Gabi's words. "I've been bored stiff lately and tonight has been fabulous. I wanted it to be like the old times." She beamed.

"I can wait until Darion comes," Gabi said decisively.

She had butterflies in her stomach, wondering what Suzie would think of him.

Chapter Ten

Darion

Darion switched his computer off, stuffed documents in his drawer, locked it, and scanned the room. Everything was neat and in its place. He was pleased he'd had a productive day. The dancers, barmaids, security guards, and other members of staff all seemed to be content. Well, for the moment, anyway. The club was making a profit each night, although not as much as he'd have liked, but he knew he'd get there. Although the clientele was built by Internet marketing, flyers and word of mouth, Darion still had a niggling feeling to renovate the place. He wanted to change the colour scheme so that it was all black. He knew that the chandeliers would really stand out then. He supposed he had time to achieve his goals.

The bar area had been swarming with customers, as usual. The atmosphere was lively as ever. However the best thing about the day was that he hadn't bumped into Eva. If he could leave the club with no drama for one day, his prayers would be answered.

He walked toward the leather sofa, which held a pile of his clothes. He thumbed through them, wondering what to wear. A black shirt was his best bet, as he was meeting Gabi in a bar. He yanked his t-shirt over his head and dressed in the shirt. He buttoned it up as he made his way toward the wall mirror. His brown hair, skimming his collar, hung loose. He scooped some gel out of the pot on the shelf, and rubbed it in his hands. Sweeping his wet palms through his hair, he ensured it was styled perfectly neat.

Car keys, he thought, as he examined the room. He spotted them near the mini bar in the corner. He was about to collect them when a tap at the door echoed through the room.

"Yeah?"

"Daz, it's me, Gina."

He felt his muscles instantly relax. "Come in."

Gina entered, closing the door gently after her. He perched on the edge of his desk. He had to look twice, and as he took in her appearance, he wondered what the hell had taken possession of Gina. Usually caked in make-up and a cigarette hanging nonchalantly from her fingertips, in front of him was a woman he barely recognised. Her usually immaculate blonde hair was tied back, her make-up the bare minimum. Instead of her confident strides, she stepped into the room unable to meet his stare. She looked exhausted, like she had the weight of the world on her shoulders. Was Johnny wearing her down, intimidated by her sexiness? He hoped not.

Never would he sit back and allow someone to control, manipulate, and change Gina's fiery personality.

"Is Johnny bothering you?" He narrowed his eyes, surveying her.

"It's worse than that, Daz." She bowed her head for a second before looking back up. "My mom's sick." He was certain he could see the glistening of tears teetering on her lower lids.

"Gina." He strode toward her, cupping her face in his hands. When she began sobbing, he pressed his lips against her forehead, and closed his eyes.

"She's got stomach ulcers. She needs surgery."

"It will be okay," he soothed.

"She's so sick, Daz. She's lost so much weight, and she's passing blood." Gina pulled back, her face etched with worry. "What if the surgery goes wrong? What if she doesn't heal? She's all I have."

"I promise you it will be okay." He had no idea if it would, but Gina needed all of the hope she could get.

"I need to go to her."

"Take as much time off as you need." He took a step back. "You want me to take you home?"

She shrugged, which he took as a yes.

"Come on." He grabbed his keys and jacket and led her out of the office. "Is your mom still based in London?"

"Yeah." She swiped a loose strand out of her face.

Darion realised that Gina actually looked prettier without a face full of cosmetics. She looked younger. He hated seeing her vulnerable side though. When she clasped her fingers around his, he didn't have it in him to edge away. She tightened her hold. Their gazes met. Admiration and longing was apparent on her face. What used to come next was her smashing her lips against his, burying her hands in his hair, scratching, and biting. *Fuck.* He turned his back on her and ensured he strode a couple of steps in front, their fingers still intertwined.

"Where's Johnny when you need him?" He'd meant to mutter it but it came out louder than he'd expected.

"Our relationship is always on and off." She twisted her mouth in distaste. "Nothing is ever straight forward in my life, Daz."

"Do you think you'll sort it out? I don't want you going to London alone, G."

She shrugged a shoulder. "We'll see."

Darion gripped the steering wheel as he drove to her apartment. He maintained his hard stare on the road ahead of him. Would Gina be safe going to London to see her mom? If he was single, he'd accompany her on the trip at the drop of a hat. He could trust himself around her now. The only thing was, could he trust Gina? He didn't want to land more rejection on her, distress her anymore than she already was. Leaning back in his seat, he decided it was probably best if he left her to it.

When the car eventually came to a halt outside her apartment, he turned to face her. Eyes shut, her mouth was slightly ajar, and she was snoring gently. Usually when he'd carried Gina to her door, it had been hurried and impatient, and for one thing only.

He was pleased to find that he didn't miss those days one bit. Gabi definitely did have a hold over him.

"G." He shook her gently. "We're here."

"What?" she murmured, opening her eyes.

"We're here."

"Oh." She sat up and unclasped her seatbelt. As she looked for her handbag, Darion climbed out of the car. He sprinted around it to hold the door open for her. Silence descended upon them as they made their way toward her door. He felt a stabbing pain in his chest. He hated goodbyes, even if they were only for a short period of time. He'd been so used to having Gina around that he knew he'd feel a little lost without her.

"Thanks for the ride, Daz." She rummaged in her bag and retrieved her keys. "I guess I'll see you when I see you."

He nodded. "Send your mom my wishes."

"I will."

"Make sure Johnny meets you in London."

"I will." She understood he was worried about her and chuckled. "Make sure you keep that bitch in check," she added, and he knew that she was referring to Eva. Gina had never been a fan. She'd always sensed there was something odd, perhaps even sly about Eva, and she had been right. "And look after Gabi."

He nodded. He would try his hardest to.

Chapter Eleven

Gabi

From the corner of her eye, Gabi noticed Darion weaving through the dancing crowd. He hadn't noticed her yet. He garnered looks of admiration from several giggly women he passed. He strode tall and confident, towering over most of the men with his 6'2" frame. As he scanned the bar, Gabi caught his attention by giving him a wave. His stern features softened, and a smile tilted his lips.

"What do you know..." Suzie chuckled. "He's even better looking in person."

Even Mallory was transfixed. She'd always been fond of Darion since he'd rescued Gabi from 'soul-destroying-Lawrence,' the nickname she had given Gabi's ex. Although Darion had his issues, Mallory knew he had a good heart, and his intentions were good.

Darion nodded to the girls in acknowledgement when he was before them.

"You know Mallory. This is my friend, Suzie."

"Hi, Suzie." He flashed her a slow, devilish smile that must have unnerved Suzie, as her cheeks flushed slightly red.

"Hi." She waved.

Darion then leant down and brought his mouth down hard on Gabi's. She expected a quick peck, but his tongue massaged hers with a possessive urgency. His hands cupped her face, and he kissed her more powerfully. Gabi felt herself sliding slightly back in her seat from the pressure of him against her. Public displays of affection didn't bother Darion. He didn't care who was around. If he wanted a kiss, then he'd get a decent kiss.

Eventually he pulled back. Gabi giggled softly when she saw Mallory and Suzie wide-eyed, looking impressed. Darion told them he was going to the bar, and offered them all a drink. They declined in unison. As he sauntered off, Gabi was unable to refrain from watching his firm ass slowly vanish through the mass of people.

When he returned a moment later, he slid on the seat next to Gabi and grabbed hold of her hand. Taking a long, slow sip of his whisky, he began talking with the girls. The way he nodded along, asking questions, Gabi could see he was genuinely interested in what they had to say. She was pleased. Having her boyfriend get along with her friends meant the world to her.

She squealed excitedly when a familiar beat filled her ears, and an intense desire to dance overcame her. "Heads Will Roll" by Yeah Yeah Yeahs was playing. She pleaded with the girls to dance with her again. When they refused, Gabi practically dragged a hesitant Darion to the dance floor.

"I told you I don't dance, Gabi," he said, his mouth curving upwards.

"You don't need to properly dance. Just hold me."

He placed his hand flat on her lower back and pulled her into him. Her breasts were pressed firmly against his chest, and her pelvis against his groin. They danced together, their stares intact. As the flashing colourful lights danced in his luminous green eyes, the soft vocals of the music filling her ears, and being so close to him, Gabi felt that warm feeling of being in love. She was smitten with Darion, and there was nothing she could do about it. She'd tried many times not to fall for him too fast, too hard, but she'd lost the battle. He was *everything* she ever wanted in a man, and more.

As he rotated his hips, rubbing his body against hers to the beat, her heart slammed in her chest. Darion's hand slid down to her buttocks, causing her to inhale sharply. He devoured her hungrily with his stare, a ghost of a smile playing on his lips. Moving her hips in sync with his, she felt her body burning up. His hands roamed all over her, cupping her behind, skimming up her waist, and snaking around her neck. He pulled her in for a kiss.

Gabi was unsure whether it was the heat radiating from Darion, or the busy room, but her body became moist with perspiration. She brushed a strand of hair away that had stuck to her forehead.

As she circled her hips continuously, she could feel that Darion had become aroused. With each soft kiss he placed on her neck, her skin tingled in its wake. Goosebumps raced across her skin. She closed her eyes and moaned softly. Her knees trembled slightly as a needy ache loomed between her legs. She was drunk, and *so* turned on.

"Gabi…" he murmured softly into her ear. Then he said the words she would never tire of hearing. "I want you now."

His fingers trailed up her leg, slowly aiming for underneath her dress. Gabi's chest tightened. The touch ignited a spark in the pit of her belly. As his fingers crept higher, almost between her legs, her eyes shot open. She instantly came to her senses. Not there. Not in full view of everyone. She tried to pull away, but the soft strokes which were now between her legs tantalised her, sending an involuntary excited thrill up her body. He circled his fingertips with delicate precision. She squirmed again, trying to free herself. It was no use. Darion's other hand was around her waist, holding her captive, pinning her against him. She glanced over her shoulder, to see if anyone had noticed his brazen fondling. Luckily they hadn't.

"Stop…" she ordered, her voice stern, however her treacherous body betrayed her, straining toward his touch.

She snaked her fingers in his hair, bringing his face to hers, and slipped her tongue in his mouth, massaging it, needing some sort of release— anything. He pulled back with a low, dirty sounding laugh. Gabi pushed toward him, as her body rippled with tendrils of ecstasy. The room seemed to be spinning. Everything was a blur. All she cared about was his touch, and the naughty obscenities he whispered in her ear.

She felt his tongue trace along her neck, and then he was kissing it firmly, hungrily. When his teeth dug in, she cried out in frustration. Her nipples stiffened, desperate to be touched. Her core burned and ached, needing more.

As his skilled, dominant fingers continued to tantalise and tease her clit, she was lost in the sensations coursing through her body. She writhed in excitement. The need to be relieved of the teasing was torturous.

"Darion, let's go somewhere…" She panted. "Now…"

"Aren't you enjoying it?" his voice was rough, his expression dark and possessed.

"Yes, but not here."

"We've done stuff in a club before," he reminded her, challenging her with a lift of his brows.

Yes, they had, although it had been on the second floor, where entry had been forbidden. They'd been caught and humiliatingly thrown out by the bouncers. Not that it had fazed Darion. To him, getting caught was part of the thrill. If it happened, so what?

Even though people were dirty dancing around them, grinding against one another, and were probably way too drunk to even notice, it was too risky.

"You like it, Gabi?" Darion's hot breath was back in her ear, enticing her, urging her to be a risk-taker, like a devil on her shoulder.

"You've no shame, have you?" Her voice came

out in breathy pants.

"You like that about me." He tugged her earlobe with his teeth.

"I can't take it anymore." Her voice was low and needy.

Darion removed his hand and smoothed down her dress. He snaked his arm around her waist, and indicated for her to follow him. As she wove through the crowd, she was relieved to see that not one person had been paying any attention to them. Darion led her toward the booth where Mallory and Suzie were sitting.

"Gabi's coming outside with me for a smoke," he told them.

"Sure." A drunken Mallory giggled. "Take your time."

"Oh, we will," Darion muttered so that only Gabi heard.

He entwined his fingers with hers and set off for the bathroom. They entered the women's room, Darion hasty and impatient in his manner. She knew he wouldn't care if the room was occupied. He didn't embarrass easily. Gabi felt her muscles relax when she noticed it was empty. With his hands still greedily exploring her body, Darion wasted no time in leading her inside a cubicle.

She noticed that when he pushed the lock on the door, his pupils were glinting dangerously, full of longing. A slow smirk crept across his face. Gabi could hear the sound of his heavy breathing. Hooking his fingers in her underwear, he dragged it down her legs, and tossed it to the floor. He then lifted her up in one swift movement, and sat on the toilet lid, settling Gabi on his lap. Her legs were positioned around his waist.

Unzipping his jeans and releasing his erection, Gabi wrapped her fingers around it. She slid her hand up and down the shaft repeatedly. He grew thicker and harder in her palm. With the other hand, she massaged his balls gently. Darion's features contorted in pleasure. He hissed through clenched teeth, his hands curling into fists. She increased the pressure and speed until he was rock hard and ready.

Pulling her dress up to her waist, Gabi guided the slickened head of his erection to her moist entrance. Arching off his lap a little, she carefully slid down onto him, taking him inch by inch. When she was fully filled, she instantly melted into the feel of him. Her head dropped back as she whimpered in ecstasy.

Darion bucked his hips upwards, his length sliding in and out of her, hitting her inner walls, her sensitive G-spot.

"Ah, Darion…" she murmured, grabbing fistfuls of his hair. "You feel so good."

As his thumbs circled her nipples through the material of her dress, she felt them harden and strain against the fabric, wanting to be freed. As if sensing her desire, Darion pulled her dress straps down, and eased her breasts out. He massaged her acutely sensitive nipples before welcoming a tender breast into his warm mouth. His tongue swirled over the nipple, causing it to stiffen. He licked and sucked greedily, letting out rough, frustrated grunts. Gabi whimpered as he cupped her other breast with his free hand. She tightened the grip on his hair as she arched her back, crying out with overwhelming pleasure.

"So…beautiful…Gabi," Darion murmured.

Needing stimulation along with Darion penetrating her, Gabi took hold of his hand and placed it between her legs. His thumb met her throbbing clit. He stroked over it back and forth tenderly. His gaze was intense on her, and she knew he was watching her every squirm, listening to her every moan, and taking in what movements of his pleasured her. She knew Darion wanted to press *all* of her buttons, satisfy her like no other man had, or ever would.

She closed her lids tightly, shutting everything out to concentrate on the sensations pulsing through her. Darion rocked his hips upwards, sliding in and out. She felt herself contracting around him, her inner muscles pulsing.

"I love you, Darion." Gabi tugged at his hair, now gauging his reaction.

He was silent for a moment. She was almost certain she saw a flash of worry cross his face. She saw his Adam's apple dip as he swallowed. Surely he could say it. He had said it before. Gabi averted her gaze, feeling the burn of shame in her cheeks, which she knew probably matched the colour of her heels. She felt foolish. Did Darion remember saying he loved her in the playrooms? Did he remember asking if she loved him whilst in the shower? Had he meant those words or had they been said because he'd been lost in the throes of passion?

"Gabi." He seized her face with both hands. He

thrust upward without cease, his breathing loud pants. "Sometimes it's difficult for me to express how I feel."

"Why?"

He shrugged a shoulder. His teeth clamped his bottom lip as he threw his head back, close to losing it. "I need to love you *my* way." It wasn't a plea, or a question. His tone was firm, as if that was all he could offer her.

"Okay." She nodded in agreement, hoping not hearing the words often would be enough for her to still feel secure in their relationship.

Before she dwelled on the matter, and probed him with further questions, he grabbed hold of her wrists. He slung her arms around his neck. She used him for balance as she resumed sliding up and down.

Darion's tongue met hers as he licked with long, firm strokes. His mouth absorbed her cries. Gabi felt an orgasm building as her stomach coiled with tension. Slowing her pace, she froze on the spot at the sound of a door opening.

She looked at Darion, awaiting further instructions. When he shrugged a shoulder, and continued to plunge into her, she attempted to disentangle herself. As she smoothed her dress down, Darion grasped her by the arm, pulling her into him.

"Don't stop," he commanded.

The sound of the door to the cubicle next to them flung open. Gabi didn't dare move a muscle through fear of being heard. Darion, however, resumed rocking his hips, sliding in and out of her. His thumb circled her clit again. She had to bite onto his shoulder to suppress her moans. Darion chuckled lightly, clearly amused by their situation.

Sensing she was close, he changed the pace of his thrusting and slowed down. The pleasure between her legs built higher. Darion slid his hands up her sides again to cup her breasts. When he flicked his tongue over her nipple once more, she whimpered.

"Fuck…" Darion clenched his teeth.

Gabi felt a burning sensation in her loins; unsure whether she could hold the release off any further. She prayed silently and desperately that the person in the room would leave. She heard the cubicle door open, and then the sound of footsteps. Water gushed from a nearby tap. *Please leave, please leave.* Darion's thrusts were relentless and as his fingers gripped her waist tightly, slightly painfully, she knew he was about to fall apart. It was literally a second after the sound of the door opening and closing, that silence descended upon the room.

With Darion slamming into her violently, and now tonguing her nipples, she climaxed in sharp, intense waves. Throbbing and convulsing, her heartbeat was so erratic, she felt as if it'd explode through her chest. Before she got a chance to catch her breath, Darion followed close, his features contorted, his body rigid. She could feel the pulsing of him inside her. His body stiffened and she felt the powerful orgasm engulf him as he emptied into her, grunting and shaking.

"Fuuuuck…"

They sat in a shattered heap for a moment. Gabi

squeezed her lids shut, willing her body to return to normal, for her pulse and breathing to slow, for her achy limbs to strengthen. She then focused on Darion, and together they burst into hysterics at the craziness of the scenario.

"I needed that, Gabi," he told her, pinning her with a serious look. "Gina left for London today. I don't know how long she'll be gone."

Oh. Gabi tried to keep her face straight, to not show any emotion. It wasn't the worst news she had heard—one less past conquest of Darion's to worry about. She was shocked, nevertheless. Gina had worked at the club for years. Not only was she Darion's employee, but a close friend whom he trusted and confided in. "Why did she leave?"

"Her mom's not well."

Gabi swallowed. Guilt twisted her heart, as she then felt sorry for Gina. Darion rubbed at the stubble on his chin. She could tell he was distressed.

"Are you okay?"

"I will be." His brow furrowed as he wiped the back of his hand across his forehead to remove the slight sheen of sweat. He tentatively eased his now flaccid, but still impressive length from out of her.

"Anyway." She climbed to her feet. "We need to stop having sex in public."

"Impossible." A slow smirk surfaced on his face, a naughty glint shimmering in his eyes. "When I want you, I can't control it. I have to have you."

"You're a sex addict," she teased.

"I've been called worse."

"I bet you have."

"I'm keeping these," he said, scooping up her

discarded underwear and putting it in his pocket.

"Darion…"

"Let's get back to your friends." He ignored her, standing up and readjusting his clothes. "They'll be wondering where we are."

Her gaze lifted to accommodate his height—her sexy boyfriend. She embraced him, burying her head in his chest, wanting to feel his big protective arms around her. Planting a kiss firmly on her forehead, he took hold of her hand, and led her out of the room.

Back in the bar, Gabi found Mallory and Suzie laughing hysterically at something. Gabi slid into her seat casually and picked up her drink. As she sipped it, she avoided eye contact, knowing the girls' intrusive stares would send a heated blush through her cheeks. She felt a gentle breeze up her dress. As she glanced at the people all around her, she did in fact feel a little naughty and mischievous by holding the secret that she was commando.

"How long is your cigarette?" Mallory asked Darion. Gabi could see her friend was trying her hardest to keep a straight face.

"About eight inches," Darion teased as he sat down.

Suzie almost choked on her drink, whilst Mallory's lips formed into a grin. Gabi slapped Darion on the arm lightly.

"What?" He leant back in his seat, a mischievous grin on his face. "I know a euphemism when I hear one."

"Gabi." Suzie turned to face her. "I want you to be Godmother."

"Really?" She put her palm against her chest, surprised but touched by the request.

"Yes!" She squeezed her hand. "Mallory doesn't mind. She'll have her own before we know it."

"I'd be honored, Suze."

Gabi watched as Darion gulped back his whisky. When he set his empty glass down on the table, she noticed him taking in Suzie's stomach. "When are you due?"

"Eight months and approximately two weeks," Suzie informed him, her face lighting up, looking like she'd burst with excitement.

"Yeah, and she'll probably be one of those lucky women that doesn't show until they're ready to pop," Mallory said.

"My mom was like that," Gabi informed her.

"I know it's a long way off, but I'd like you to come to the christening." Suzie was now focused on Darion.

Gabi swallowed the lump that had lodged in her throat. She waited with bated breath for Darion's response. Would they still be together in eight months? Did Darion think that far ahead?

With a tight smile, Darion asked, "Are you having a boy or girl?"

Despite knowing he liked to live each day as it comes, Gabi couldn't help disappointment deflating her from his clever avoidance of giving an answer.

"We won't find out until I'm further along."

"Well, congratulations." Darion rose to his feet. "Anyone want another drink?"

"Sure. I'll have a G&T," Mallory responded.

What the hell, Gabi thought, deciding she wanted

something strong. She all of a sudden felt too sober for her liking. "I'll have another Cosmopolitan."

Darion leant down and brushed his lips against hers. Gabi watched after him as he plunged through the crowd. Feeling the weight of Suzie's stare, she turned to face her.

"I'm pleased for you, Gabi," she gushed. "He seems perfect."

It was exactly what an outsider would think. Little did they know there was certainly more to Darion than met the eye. Gabi knew the other surprises he had in store would soon be revealed. An invitation to the playrooms at The Black Door was near. She had a feeling.

Chapter Twelve

Gabi popped two paracetamols in her mouth and washed them down with water. When she'd returned the glass to the table, she stretched her aching limbs with an inward groan. She flopped back on the bed and massaged her throbbing temples with her fingertips. She wondered how she'd ever be able to drag herself out of bed. She didn't usually suffer from hangovers, but she supposed it was inevitable with the amount of alcohol she had consumed last night. A whole day in bed seemed extremely tempting. A romantic comedy was playing on the television and Darion was next to her.

Not really focusing on the movie, Gabi rolled onto her side and offered him a small smile.

"Tell me about your family," she asked softly, wanting to know as much as possible about Darion and his life.

He leant back and chewed his bottom lip for a second. "I don't like to talk about my family, Gabi."

"Why not?" she pried, sitting up.

Darion rubbed the heel of his palm against his chest as if in discomfort or pain. "My childhood wasn't anything to rave about."

Gabi pursed her lips, her mind racing. She opened her mouth to speak but Darion cut her off.

"I told you before; my dad was a drinker, and my mom worked two jobs to keep everything together." He raked a hand through his hair. "As a kid, I was either in strip joints or at home, alone."

Gabi threw him a sympathetic look. "What are they like, though?"

"Bitter. They both hate their life."

"Why?"

"My mom dreams of a career she never got to have, and my dad's making up for lost time, gallivanting with different women."

Gabi's mouth fell. "Does she know that he cheats on her?"

Darion shrugged a shoulder. "If she does, she doesn't care. There's no intimacy between them. She got pregnant at twenty...they got married."

Gabi hugged her knees to her chest. Darion had obviously not had a good role model to look up to. Throughout his life, he had witnessed or experienced infidelity. His dad cheated on his mother, and Darion had been betrayed by several girlfriends in the past, not to mention his ex-wife Eva. No wonder he had fears of commitment. Did he even know what a 'normal' relationship was like?

She wondered if there were any good points about his parents, whether he looked like them, whether she'd ever meet them. Curiosity niggled away at her. Was Darion's inability to share his feelings for others a fault of his parents, or Eva? Judging by him being dragged along to strip joints as a child whilst his father downed beer after beer, it was clear Darion had been neglected. He must have been lonely. Did that have any bearing on his enjoyment for swinging, the fact that he liked being the centre of attention, that a lot of women wanted him? Or was it because polygamous relationships were all he'd mostly ever known?

Rolling onto his side, he leant on his elbow. "What about you?"

"I'm really close to my parents." She pressed her lips together to prevent herself from grinning like an idiot. "I should visit them more, really. They go on holidays a lot so I never know when they're home."

"And your brother?"

"Samuel's in the army." She felt herself swell with pride. She realised that she missed her family. She paused before asking carefully, "So, what about your sister?" She silently prayed that he at least had a close relationship with her.

"Dion?" He stretched out his legs, as a grin appeared on his face. "She's a pain in the ass."

"Why?"

"We fight all of the fucking time." He laughed. "We haven't spoken in a while, but we will."

"What's she like?"

"Surprisingly, she's a good girl. She has a daughter. Odelia." He shook his head. "Another reason we fought…what a name."

"It's different."

"I call her Jane just to piss her off."

Gabi giggled. "Do you want children one day?" *Please say yes, please.* She waited with bated breath for his answer. Gabi adored children. Becoming a mother was something she looked forward to.

"I haven't given it much thought." He paused. "Me and Eva never discussed it. We were too wild, too crazy for children."

Gabi bowed her head. "But you're still wild and crazy."

"You could say that."

A heavy uncomfortable silence hung in the air. Gabi couldn't help but wonder if Darion would ever grow up one day, take life seriously. Did they even want the same things in life? *Stop overthinking things, Gabi,* she scolded herself. *Take things one day at a time.* It was still early-ish days.

Darion leant over, grabbed a box of cigarettes, and lit one. She watched as he took a puff, blowing the smoke out of the side of his mouth. His jaw was shadowed with more stubble than usual. Gabi liked it. She ran her fingers through his hair, openly admiring him.

"Anyway." He held the cigarette between his fingers as his lips curled upwards. "Last night was good. You should go commando more often."

Gabi didn't speak.

"Next time you can dance with other men...commando...whilst I watch." His voice had taken on a low, seductive tone.

She rolled onto her back. Last night, it'd felt a little thrilling having had no underwear on. To dance with other men, to grind against them, to have their hands on her waist, perhaps even on her buttocks—she wasn't sure how she'd feel about that. Darion would be sitting back, enjoying the show, wanting her all hot and bothered. He'd want her ready for him. Would Darion studying the scene make her want to put on a little show, or would it make her feel dirty?

If the tables were turned, and it was Darion dancing with other women, with his hands roaming, she doubted she could handle it.

"How can it turn you on watching me get close to other men?" She turned to face him once more. "I don't get it."

"Gabi." He took a final drag on his cigarette, then stubbed it in the ashtray. "It turns me on knowing that men want you, that they want to fuck you, that they're hot for you…and only *I* can have you." He skimmed the back of his hand along her cheek gently. "Mild jealousy triggers something in me."

Mild jealousy? If the time came in the playrooms at The Black Door, and he'd want her to sleep with other men, she definitely didn't class that as *mild*.

Sensing her confusion, Darion explained, "You know how some people get a thrill with having an affair, or the risk of getting caught doing something forbidden?"

She nodded.

"The thrill is similar. When I see men flirting with you, I feel smug, I get competitive. I get these intense emotions, and I want you then and there."

"Yeah, but you want them to have me…in the playrooms at the club."

"Having your body…" His finger now traced

down to her collarbone, "and having your mind, your heart…" He trailed down to her chest, "are two different things." His gaze was intent on her. "I don't want an open relationship, Gabi. Emotionally, I want you all for me, but sexually, I like to take it to the top." His tongue wet his lips before he smiled slowly and wickedly. "The playrooms don't count as infidelity."

"I don't think I'm ever going to understand it, Darion."

"Gabi, you show me a man that doesn't want to fuck loads of different women, and I'll show you a liar…but it doesn't mean I don't care for you. I would never cheat, and I would never go behind your back." His eyes were so sincere she sort of believed him. "Okay." He sat up straighter, the covers falling from his chest. "Tell me an addiction of yours."

She traced her finger along her bottom lip, deep in thought. She adored clothes, shoes, handbags, chocolate, but she could live without them. "I don't know," she responded honestly.

Darion smoothed his hair back. "Well, whatever it is, this addiction of yours, imagine spending most of your life succumbing to this addiction. You love everything about it, the taste, the smell, the rush, the way it makes you feel. You can't go on without it." Darion paused to reach for his water, and gulped half of it back. "And one day, someone tells you that you shouldn't do it ever again, because of their own personal opinion. Could you do that? Could you give up something you enjoyed because someone else didn't share the same enthusiasm for it…because they couldn't understand it?"

Gabi could see how Darion sold the playrooms to people so easily. He certainly was persuasive. "It would be hard," she confessed. "But I'd do it if I had to."

"But I don't feel I have to give up swinging." Darion inhaled a deep breath. "I'm not hurting anyone, Gabi, and believe it or not, I know when to draw the line."

Gabi twiddled with her nails.

He gently guided her by the chin, so that her eyes met his. "Does the lifestyle I lead hurt you?"

It hadn't, as of yet. Neither of them had swapped partners in the playrooms. Gabi, although fearful of the playrooms and what could happen, was also consumed by curiosity. She guiltily found herself wanting to know more, to see more. Would she ever become comfortable with the lifestyle Darion was accustomed to? Darion always said, *'How can you knock something until you've tried it?'*

Would she eventually be hurt by it all? Averting her stare, she said, "I don't know. We haven't reached that stage yet."

"And when we do…" He leant down and placed soft, lingering kisses on her lips. "You let me know if it hurts you. Do you understand?"

"Yes." She nodded, before sliding down under the covers. Resting her head on Darion's lap, she closed her eyes.

***

Darion

Darion ran his fingers through Gabi's soft blonde hair repeatedly. He breathed out a sigh of relief. Gabi seemed open to continuing to give the playrooms a try. The Black Door was his professional *and* personal lifestyle.

Some women in his past, nothing but brief encounters, had been disgusted by the club. It agitated Darion a little when people were close-minded when it came to swinging, when they were judgmental, believing it was seedy when it was far from it. Who said by not sticking to the one person, that you couldn't possibly love them? Society had been brainwashed into believing that people should commit to one person, get married, bed that one person for the rest of their existence. Why? Sexual attraction was part of human nature.

The ancient artwork, whether it was paintings, scrolls, tapestries, or statues showed that orgies were not uncommon amongst the Egyptians, the Greeks, the Romans, and the Celts especially. Sexual freedom and frolics wasn't frowned upon then. Then there was the 'free love' of the sixties and the 'swinging seventies' era. It didn't matter what gender, nationality, religion, job, beliefs a person had, they were all drawn by sex. Besides, if the world needed anything spreading, it was love.

When it came to steady relationships, Darion had realised he could separate sex from feelings. He could get intimate with a hundred other women, and know that it was for nothing more than his own sexual gratification. The way he felt about Gabi, the feelings he had for her, as far as he was concerned, wouldn't be tarnished in any way.

He glanced down at her. She was snoring lightly. Even though she was sleeping, he could see a frown on her face. His little worrier. He leant down. His lips claimed hers. She didn't stir when he then placed tender kisses along her cheek.

"I love you, darlin'," he whispered into her ear, although he knew she wouldn't hear.

It seemed to be easier that way. It had taken him a long while to finally say those words to another woman. He prayed he'd never regret saying them.

Chapter Thirteen

Darion sat at the bar, enjoying a glass of whisky, watching Lexi and Wendy work the poles on the stage. "Porn Star Dancing" by My Darkest Days was blaring from the speakers. He focused on their seductively moving bodies. They writhed slowly, their fingers teasing the sensitive parts of their bodies, down their collar bone, skimming their nipples, running down their stomach, and between their legs.

Their come-to-bed eyes swept over the audience, naughty grins plastered on their faces tempting customers into paying for private dances. They twirled around the poles, their flexible bodies twisting into shapes that made him groan inwardly in torment. He averted his stare. It was too much to handle. His dancers were hot. Although he trusted himself, he didn't want to sit there frustrated, whilst being prick-teased. He stood up and made his way toward the bathroom.

Once inside, he cupped cold water in his hands and splashed it on his face. Slowly rising, he confronted his reflection in the mirror. His disheveled hair was hanging loose. Oh well. Some women seemed to go wild for the rough and rugged look anyway. He stroked his jaw, the stubble rough on his fingertips. He could have done with a shave. A haircut wasn't a bad idea either, but Gabi begged him not to. She couldn't get enough of him.

Feeling flushed and a little dizzy, he stripped off his jacket. He was pleased to see that he was still in good shape. His shoulders and arms had always been a decent size, even though he'd never exercised a day in his life. God had blessed him, and he'd blessed him well.

Leaving the bathroom, he returned to the bar. Taking his usual seat in the corner, Marnie approached him with a grin. Her dark hair was pulled into a high ponytail. Her breasts burst out of the tight top she was wearing, and her tanned, firm stomach was visible.

"Everything okay, boss?" she asked, pouring a glass of whisky.

"Yeah, darlin'. Everything's good." When she slid the glass toward him, he eagerly took a long swig. "How's it going?"

"Not too bad."

"How's the new boyfriend?" he asked, not particularly caring about Marnie's boyfriend's well-being, but wanting to know if he was taking care of her.

"Things are actually going great." She grinned.

"Well, anyone's an improvement from Nick."

"Hey, Darion," Wendy purred, approaching them and helping herself to a drink.

"Hey." He took in the black haired beauty before him. He'd asked her to dance downstairs until Gina returned. He had no idea how long she'd be absent.

"It's nice to see you not in the office for once." Marnie ruffled his hair. "We miss you."

Darion couldn't stop from smiling as the girls lavished him with attention. They certainly made him feel popular. If only Gabi knew how difficult it was being in his line of work. Temptation was thrust in his face on a daily basis.

"Shit…looks like someone's getting an ear-bashing." Marnie jerked her head upwards.

Darion glanced over his shoulder. Lexi was marching toward him, a thunderous expression on her face.

"Don't tell me." He groaned. "Eva's on your case again."

"Aren't you the genius?" She crossed her arms across her chest. "I take it you didn't talk to her?" She shook her head, as her lips tightened into a thin line. "Look, Daz, I don't wanna cause problems, but if this shit isn't solved and quick, I'm doing a Gina and I'm leaving."

He knew Lexi would never really leave, but he doubted he'd ever seen her so mad. "What's she doing now?"

"Earlier she was in the stock room assessing everything, what we were low on, and barking orders on calls I needed to make." She took a deep breath and Darion knew from her blazing eyes that she was on the verge of losing it. "And then she was criticising the dressing room, saying it needed a decent clean." Her mouth fell open. "The dressing room is fine. You can go and look for yourself."

"I believe you, Lex," he said quickly. He rubbed his palms over his face in exasperation. "I'll handle it."

"I hope you do, because there is only so much I can take."

Leaning back on his stool, he let out a heartfelt sigh. "Look." He glanced at each of the girls. "You fancy a lock-in tonight? It's been a while."

Marnie's hand flew to her chest. "You mean like the crazy parties we used to have?"

Darion's laugh came out louder than expected. "Not that crazy. But yeah."

Marnie and Wendy excitedly agreed to it.

"Suppose it's about time we had some fun around here." Lexi twisted a red strand of hair around her finger. "I'm in."

Marnie lined shots on the bar when Wendy tended to customers. "Absinthe!"

Darion shook his head, amused. "You trying to get me drunk, Marn?"

"Maybe." She giggled, filling the glasses.

Darion took the glass between his fingers and downed it quickly. The liquid burned through his throat and chest, making him cough.

"Eva should be upstairs now," Lexi reminded him, nodding toward the wall clock. "Go and see her. No excuses, Daz." With that she swiveled on her heel, her ponytail almost hitting him in the face.

He chewed his bottom lip. "Pour me another shot, Marn. I'm gonna need it."

Chapter Fourteen

Darion had been sitting on the sofa upstairs of the club for fifteen minutes when he felt someone's presence—*her*s. He hadn't been able to find her despite checking the bathrooms, playrooms, and booths. He watched her surreptitiously out of the corner of his eye. He felt a stabbing pain pierce his heart. He obviously wasn't as strong as he thought he was. *Shit.* He'd avoided a confrontation with her purely because he wasn't ready to deal with her yet. If only she remained upstairs, and kept her nose out of the girls' business, then speaking with her wouldn't have been necessary.

He inhaled and exhaled deeply, flexing his fingers until his knuckles cracked. His throat tightened. Memories of the past came flooding back—the bad and the good. He squeezed his eyelids shut for a moment in an attempt to regain his cool.

Opening them, he saw her run a hand through her sleek, black hair, and her red, full lips curl into a smile. Her green eyes locked with his, and as she neared him, it was like she was moving in slow motion. The red glow of the spotlights cast over her, making her look like a dream and a nightmare rolled into one.

He had a sudden desire to move closer to touch her. He didn't know whether it was the alcohol playing with his feelings, or whether he was still in love. With trembling fingers, he removed the cigar from his mouth, the smoke escaping, creating a swirl around him, obscuring his view for a second.

When she was before him, Darion was overwhelmed with emotions, too choked to speak. She slid on the sofa next to him, and he saw sadness flash in her eyes, which must have mirrored his own. His muscles ached with tension, and he felt bile rise in his throat. *Get it together,* he thought, the shame creeping up his neck. *She betrayed you whilst swinging, fucked someone else in a locked room, and made you turn to drink and meaningless sex, a path of self destruction.*

"I heard you were looking for me. To what do I owe the pleasure of your company?" she asked in a nonchalant tone, like all was well between them.

Was there no remorse on her part? Did she not have an ounce of guilt in her for all of the hurt she had caused? He felt his body temperature rising. His feelings for her crystallised into hate.

He cleared his throat after mentally reminding himself that he was there to talk business, nothing else. "I gave you one simple instruction, Eva. Leave the gentlemen's club to me. Leave the girls to me."

She rolled her eyes. "I was only trying to help. Whenever I go downstairs, they're standing around gossiping and drinking. They're losing you a lot of money, Darion. They're losing *us* a lot of money."

"They make me a lot of money. Back off, Eva." He shot her a warning look.

Her focus lingered on his mouth, and a small smile surfaced on her face. Darion shifted uncomfortably in his seat. He remembered that look of hers. She liked seeing him angry. In the past she'd purposely rile him up, start some stupid argument just so they could have explosive make-up sex afterwards. They fought as much as they fucked, the intensity equal for both. When she brought a hand up to stroke his cheek, Darion jolted backwards, as if she'd burnt him.

"What are you doing?"

Her features softened. "I miss you, so much."

He shook his head. "Don't do this." He hated the way his tone sounded like a weak plea.

"I can't help it, Daz."

"Goodbye, Eva."

He took a final puff on his cigar before dropping it in the ashtray and climbed to his feet. He shoved a hand through his hair and made his way to the exit. As he descended the stairs, he heard the clacking sound of Eva's heels behind him.

"Can we talk about us, please?" she pleaded, her voice shaky with emotion.

"I've got nothing to say."

"But I have."

"I don't wanna hear your bullshit," he said through clenched teeth.

"I made a mistake. I'm sorry. I love you, Darion!" she roared.

Oh, so there was the guilt, complete with apology. Years later! Rage swept over him. He turned on his heel, and before he could think straight, he slammed her against the wall.

"The only person you ever loved was yourself!" he screamed, feeling his blood reach boiling point. "And if you say those words one more time," he brought his face closer to hers, "you will *never* set foot in this club again."

"It scares you to know it's the truth," Eva fired back, freeing her arms. "I love you, Darion," she repeated, clasping his face tightly in her hands. "I made a mistake. I fucked up." Her expression was of pure desperation. "Whether you love me, or hate me, I want you to know how I feel…how I'll always feel."

Silence hung heavy in the air. It was as if he was momentarily paralysed for he was unable to move her hands from his face. When her fingers brushed tenderly against his cheek, he swallowed, as it ignited all of his senses. It took all of his willpower to stop his eyes from closing, and further inviting her touch. *Fuck.* He'd missed it. The lust he felt outweighed his sense of reason. His body was flushed with immense heat as her body was pressed against his.

He focused on Eva, hypnotised by the mischievous grin that presented itself on her face. Her mouth was so close that her breath tickled his skin. The smell of Apple Sourz invaded his nostrils. Studying him intently, she slowly leant closer. Her tongue darted out like a poisonous snake, and she flicked it across his lips. She laughed a low, naughty sounding laugh.

"Does she excite you the way I did?" she challenged him in a low, sultry voice.

Darion wanted to defend Gabi, however exciting memories he had with Eva invaded his mind, like an erotic movie. Eva's lips parted, and her eyes closed. He hated himself for still finding her so beautiful. His trembling hands wanted nothing more than to grab hold of her, and greedily claim every bit of her body.

Remember what she did.

He shook his head and blinked rapidly, as if coming to his senses. Taking a step back in a huff, he mentally scolded himself for being so stupid, for almost losing control and falling for her devious ways.

"You're here for one reason, and *one* reason only." He turned his back on her. "To help make this club the best it can be."

"Whatever."

He glanced over his shoulder when he heard movement. As Eva slowly made her way up the stairs, he was transfixed on her ass as it swayed in tight leather trousers. Her hair flew out behind her.

"Darion." She paused at the door. "You can lie to yourself all you want," she began. "But I know you still love me."

Before he could retaliate, she vanished. Darion cursed under his breath. He needed fresh air, desperately. He made his way down the stairs and out of the club. Glad to be alone, he leant against the wall. He brought up both of his palms to rub his temples. He felt the throbbing of a migraine. He was more confused than he'd ever been in his life. What was happening to him?

Chapter Fifteen

Gabi

Gabi picked up her mobile again, and touched the screen, causing it to light up. Darion hadn't responded to her text message. She leant back in her chair with a soft sigh, wondering what he was doing. She was unable to stop paranoid thoughts from invading her mind. Was he losing interest? Had Eva got her dirty paws onto him yet? She tapped her nails on the desk anxiously, willing herself to stop making a mountain out of a molehill. Perhaps he was occupied with work, or still sleeping. If the latter was the case, it being 3 p.m., then he must have had a late one at the club. Jealousy surged through every cell in her body. In her mind she prayed he hadn't been beyond the black door without her.

She silently scolded herself. She was driving herself crazy. Darion was driving her crazy. She was never usually this jealous. She couldn't bear the thought of Darion seeing Eva every day.

She picked up a folder and took out a manuscript. She willed her brain to focus on work. She needed to edit one hundred pages by the end of the day. Slipping into her heels that she'd kicked under her desk, she stood up. First, she needed a big cup of coffee.

"Hey, Gab," Mallory greeted her warmly in the kitchen. "How's your day going, sweetie?"

"Slow." She added a coffee capsule to the machine, and switched it on. "What about you?"

"Not bad." Mallory leant against the counter. "Nice shoes."

Gabi glanced down at the cream Jimmy Choo stilettos she was wearing. "Thanks, Mal. I've had these a while. Speaking of which, I could do with a new pair."

"Well, let me know when you go shopping. I'll join you."

"I will." When her cup was full, she switched the machine off and took a long desperate swig, wincing when it burnt her tongue. "How's Steve?"

"He's great. He's just got a promotion at work."

"Brilliant." Gabi smiled. "Send him my love."

"How's Darion?"

"He's okay as far as I know."

"Good." Mallory beamed, rinsing her cup under the tap.

Gabi was pleased Mallory didn't pry further. The last thing she wanted was to bombard her friend with her problems all the time.

"I'm so excited for Suzie and Marcus. I cannot wait for the new arrival."

"And the christening."

"So, will we have the pleasure of Darion's company?"

Who knows? I can never get a straight answer out of him. "I expect so," Gabi said instead.

"Oh good." A cheeky grin surfaced on Mallory's face.

"What?"

"I bet Darion looks hot in a suit."

Gabi threw her head back with a laugh. "You know, I've never actually seen him in a full suit." She gulped some of her drink back. Her mind wandered into pleasant thoughts of Darion Milano in a black suit and crisp white shirt, his hair gelled back. She presumed he would look sexy, powerful. *Yummy.*

"Gabi."

She blinked out of her daze. Judging by Mallory's amused expression; she knew she must have had a dreamy look on her face.

"You've got it hard for Darion."

"I have not," she denied, although she knew her feelings could be detected a mile off.

Mallory opened a cupboard and reached for the biscuit jar. Twisting the lid, she took out a digestive. "So, apart from Darion's impeccably good looks and being skilled in the bedroom, what else do you like about him?" Mallory cocked her head to the side. "I'm intrigued. Me and Steve have been together for so long that I've forgotten about the freshness and excitement of a newish relationship."

Gabi pursed her lips whilst in thought. She hadn't had many serious boyfriends in her life. Lawrence had mistreated her, and at first, when it came to Darion, she thought she'd grabbed desperately onto the first person that had lavished her with affection, listened to what she had to say, and made her feel special. Darion was an extremely persuasive man, and she knew that if he wanted something, he probably got it. She wished she could have said it had been just him doing the pursuing, but it hadn't. She had been attracted to him on first sight. The more she had gotten to know him, the more she knew he was a good man. Deep down he had a kind heart.

"He's a good man, Mal. He'd do anything for me and the girls at the club. I know he would."

Mallory continued to chew on the biscuit.

"I like that he's real. He's himself regardless of what people may think of him. He doesn't pretend to be anything he's not. I like that sort of honesty."

"I like Darion." Mallory brushed the crumbs from her hands and put the jar back in the cupboard.

Gabi drained the last of her drink. Darion was one of two things: extremely good for her, or devastatingly bad. Gabi wished she had some sort of crystal ball to predict the future. If only she knew the road she was heading for—happiness, or disaster.

Chapter Sixteen

After Gabi finished her dance lesson, she still hadn't heard from Darion. She flung her bag over her shoulder, and made her way out of the building. It was unlike him not to call or text her throughout the day. It was even more unusual for him to completely ignore her text messages and phone calls. She hoped nothing bad had happened to him.

Out in the street, she peered up toward the dull, grey sky. A cold shiver swept up her spine as she began to feel cold specks of rain on her skin. She groaned inwardly, having forgotten her umbrella. As she proceeded in the direction of the car park, the rain got heavier, until it was lashing down, drenching her clothes. She held her handbag over her hair to prevent it from further getting wet.

As she rounded the corner, she slammed into a body with force. Muttering her apologies, she lifted her head, to take in a smart black Armani suit. She then caught a whiff of the familiar smell—the Calvin Klein aftershave that she'd been so used to smelling each day.

She drew in a shaky breath. "Lawrence…"

"Gabi." He appeared as stunned as she was, although bumping into one another eventually was inevitable. They both worked in the same town centre, and used the same salon. Although Gabi had been relieved, she was a little surprised they hadn't run into one another until now.

"How are you?" she asked, half from politeness and half with interest.

Although Lawrence had slacked big time on the fiancé front toward the end of their relationship, she knew he had loved her, and would never have left her. He'd wanted marriage and children, although he had neglected his duties caring for her. Gabi hadn't wanted to risk the struggle of perhaps bringing up children alone whilst Lawrence was working away, or out drinking. Growing tired of the arguments, and suspecting him of cheating, she'd then met Darion.

"You fancy getting out of the rain, going for a quick coffee?" Lawrence asked, wiping the rain from his face, and looking up at the sky, whereby lightning bolts were flitting through the grey clouds. "It's been a while, Gabi."

Gabi bit her lip, contemplating it. She knew deep down it probably wasn't a good idea, but she found herself agreeing. She was slightly curious to see how life was working out for him.

"There's a coffee shop at the next corner."

"I know." Gabi half smiled. "I've worked in this town for years," she playfully reminded him. She paced with him toward the end of the road, desperate for shelter. "It's unlike you not to have an umbrella." Lawrence was usually super organised in every aspect of his life.

"I've had a lot on my plate lately."

Inside the warmth of the shop, the sweet aroma of coffee instantly filled Gabi's nostrils. She peeled off her coat when they found an empty table. It didn't take long for a waitress to take their orders. Wiping her wet hair from her forehead, Gabi pulled it into a ponytail.

She took a sip of her hot drink when it arrived, gasping in delight as it went down—just what she needed.

"It's nice to see you, Gabi." Lawrence regarded her intently. "Even though things didn't exactly go smoothly with the break up," he added.

Gabi felt her heart thudding against her chest. Guilt flooded her. "Look, Lawrence." She rested her elbows on the table. "I'm sorry for the way I left you. I didn't plan any of it. It just wasn't working out for either of us."

He shrugged, prior to gulping back some of his drink. "It was mostly my fault. I put work first, was away a lot. I guess I did neglect you, Gabi. I can see that now, and I'm sorry."

Gabi was silent.

"How are things with him?"

She prevented the sigh of exhaustion from escaping her lips. She wasn't about to confess her worries to Lawrence, firstly because it wasn't his business, and secondly because she didn't want to give him satisfaction that karma could catch up with her. When they had split up, Lawrence had said, '*I just hope he doesn't do to you what you did to me.*'

Cheat. The very thing Gabi feared.

"Things are fine," she lied with a tight smile. "How are things with you?" She wanted the subject changed before Lawrence sensed her agitation. "I bet Lorna is busy planning the wedding."

"I take it Mallory told you we got engaged? Well, me and Lorna split."

Gabi was surprised to hear his future appeared to be as uncertain as her own. She'd believed he'd had it all mapped out. She'd expected him to be married, with a house full of kids within five years.

"I'm really sorry to hear that, Lawrence," she said, and meant it.

"We both agreed to call it a day. Lorna was offered a career opportunity in Hong Kong. I didn't want her to lose out on something that fortunate, and neither of us wanted the strain of a long distance relationship."

"It makes sense." Gabi ran her finger along the rim of her cup, anything but meet Lawrence's stare.

"Are you happy, Gabi?"

She met his intrusive stare. The question caught her off guard. Of course she was happy. Sure, she had obstacles to overcome in respect to Darion's life and past, but she was sure they could get through it. "I'm fine, Lawrence." She arranged her expression into one of happiness. "Are you?"

He nodded. "I've cut back on work a bit. You were right; I did work myself into the ground. I'm going out more with the guys from work, meeting new people, and enjoying things that I usually took for granted."

"That's great."

She watched as he downed the last of his drink. With his blond hair, blue eyes, and kind face, he was handsome. She was sure he wouldn't be single for long. Someone who shared the same aspirations as he did would soon snap him up.

"Well…" He neatened the collar on his crisp white shirt. "I suppose I better get off."

Gabi finished the remains of her drink and pulled her coat on. "Me too."

Lawrence paid for the drinks and walked with her outside. Luckily, the rain had stopped. They stood in the doorway for a moment, an awkward silence looming between them.

"Well, Gabi, you take care of yourself."

"You too, Lawrence."

He offered her a gentle smile. "I just want you to know, Gabi, that although our relationship was boring at times; I meant what I said before. You will never find someone who loves you as much as I did."

Before Gabi could respond, he'd turned on his heel and set off down the street. His words echoed in her mind.

Chapter Seventeen

Darion

Darion rolled onto his side with a loud groan. Slowly peeling his heavy eyelids open, it took them a moment to adjust to the daylight pouring through the open door. Surveying the room, he realised that he'd slept on the couch in his office. He ran his hands up and down his face, before dragging himself into a seating position. He grunted at the throbbing pain that shot through his aching limbs. He felt fragile, like he had zero energy. How long had he been out for? The last thing he remembered was having a lock-in with the girls, and the doormen Lennie and Travis. They'd talked, played cards, and drank until they'd all passed out. He had definitely overdone it. He licked his lips, which were dry and cracked. Desperate for a drink, he slowly rose to his feet. It took him seconds to drain a bottled water from the fridge.

A knock at the door startled him.

"Hey, Daz. You're alive." Lexi poked her head

around the door before walking in.

"What time is it?"

"Half six."

Setting the bottle on the side, he leant against the desk. "You should have woken me, Lex."

"I tried, but you were dead to the world."

"Must have been some session."

"Oh, it was."

"Where's Len and Trav?"

"They crashed in one of the booths. They've just woken up."

Silence filled the air for a moment. Darion then remembered the confrontation with Eva. "Eva shouldn't bother you anymore," he informed Lexi, stroking at the stubble on his jaw.

"Good."

"Let me know if she steps out of line."

"Oh, I will." She swayed toward the door. "I better get back behind the bar. Get yourself cleaned up, Daz. You look like shit."

"Glad I can always rely on you to be truthful."

"Anytime." She grinned and left the room.

Darion headed for the couch, where he dropped down. He closed his eyes for a brief second before his mobile bleeping disturbed him. It sounded near. He dug his hands in the creases of the sofa and found it. He touched the screen. He had two missed calls, and three text messages. Gabi. His head dropped back as he focused on the ceiling. He'd forgotten to contact her. Knowing Gabi, she'd probably be driving herself crazy with worry. He knew she was a little uneasy about Eva's return. Tapping his foot anxiously on the floor, he decided it was probably better if he spoke to Gabi in person.

Sliding the mobile into his pocket, a grin surfaced on his face. Flashbacks of the night before invaded his mind. Apart from the Eva situation, he had had fun. He'd been so stressed out lately, especially with Gina leaving, that letting loose had been long overdue. *Work hard, play harder,* was Darion's motto. Losing one hundred pounds at blackjack didn't even dampen his mood. He shuffled down the sofa until he was lying down.

***

It was two hours later when Darion left the club. He flung on his jacket and headed toward his Jeep, another of his beloved boy-toys. Once inside, he glanced at his reflection in the rear-view mirror. He screwed up his face in distaste as he realised that he did look like shit. His eyes were hazy, and his usually slightly tanned complexion seemed paler. Shoving a hand through his hair, as his fingers skimmed through the length, he decided that it definitely did need a trim. A shave wasn't a bad idea either.

"I like this look." Nina, the stylist examined his hair, twenty minutes later.

"Just take a little off."

"Okay." She picked up the scissors and began chopping the ends of his hair. "How are things with you? You haven't visited in a while."

"I've been busy."

"How's the love life?" Her mouth curved. "A lucky lady tamed you yet?"

"Me, tame?" He smirked slowly.

"Tamer, then." She giggled.

"You could say that."

Darion felt invigorated when he left the salon. With his shoulders back and chin high, he strolled toward his Jeep. A grin hadn't stopped straining his cheeks since he'd begun talking about Gabi to Nina. He didn't know what was going on with his emotions, but he missed her a little. Climbing into the vehicle, he strapped his belt on and started the ignition. The engine purred nicely as he pressed his foot on the accelerator. He set off in the direction of Gabi's apartment.

He believed it was always best to confront problems face to face, rather than via phone. It was so easy to misinterpret what the other person was trying to say without seeing their expressions. He hoped they could resolve her being pissed at his lack of communication so he could kiss her pretty face, not to mention having his wicked way with her. He pictured her gorgeous body, bashful smile, and big brown eyes. He couldn't wait to get his hands on her.

Switching on the stereo, he nodded his head along to "I Feel You" by Depeche Mode that was playing.

Tightening his grip on the steering wheel, he sped down the main roads. Coming to a stop at red traffic lights, he watched as a group of girls made their way into the crossing. Their eyes met his, and they giggled coyly. One of them braved a wave to which Darion nodded his head in acknowledgement before averting his stare. Gone were the days of securing women's phone numbers and introducing them to the big bad world of Darion Milano.

He stared up at the sky. It was beginning to get dark, the moon almost visible. Pressing his foot on the accelerator, he sped off, causing the tyres to screech on the tarmac. The group of girls had come to a standstill and watched until he was out of sight.

Chapter Eighteen

Gabi

Gabi tightened the white robe around her body and hurried to answer the door. She expected it to be Mallory. They had plans to go shopping in an hour. The indoor shopping centre was always open until 10 p.m. They preferred not to shop on weekends, as the centre was usually far too busy for either of their liking.

Yanking it open, she saw Darion leant casually against the wall. He looked up at her through his dark lashes and examined her intently. His eyes darkened with desire, his lips curling in a small smile. Gabi didn't return it. She stepped aside, allowing him to enter.

Before she closed the door, she spotted a silver Toyota Yaris slowly pass. Her throat and chest tightened as that same creepy feeling washed over her. She mentally ordered herself to stop being ridiculous. It probably wasn't even the same Toyota she had previously seen. Shutting the door, she strode down the hallway, remembering she was annoyed with Darion.

Shoving his hands in the pockets of his jeans, he strode confidently toward her, exuding a cocky air of arrogance. She got an overpowering whiff of aftershave.

"What do you want, Darion?" she asked sternly, ensuring he knew she was annoyed. She entered the living room; he followed.

His stare locked with hers. "You."

"Oh." She crossed her arms across her chest. "Well, you certainly make that clear. Did you forget how to use a phone?" She glared at him.

"Don't be mad, Gabi."

She shook her head. "It takes all of five seconds to text me back, Darion." What kind of relationship was she in? She wasn't a teenager anymore. She didn't do game playing, chasing, waiting by the phone for a response. They were a couple. Sometimes she felt Darion forgot that. "Would I ignore you like that?"

"I wasn't ignoring you." He stepped toward her, towering over her. "I was out cold. I'd *never* ignore you, Gabi."

"What do you mean you were out cold?"

"I had a drink with Lennie and Travis."

Gabi tilted her head to the side. Was he omitting something? His tone didn't sound so confident. "Who else was there?"

Darion's eyebrows pinched together, as if in disbelief. "The girls," he said. "My *employees*." He emphasised the word 'employees' as if to drum into Gabi's mind that they weren't anything other than that. "Gabi," he said softly. "I lost track of time."

She rolled her eyes. "I'm sure I've heard that somewhere before."

"Don't take everything to heart. It's not that big a deal."

It is to me, she felt like yelling. *It's always push and pull with you. One minute, you're all over me, and the next, you're distant.* Instead she remained silent, sticking her bottom lip out like a petulant child. She didn't do well with feelings of insecurity. Couldn't handle it.

His tongue darted across his top lip, prior to a slow dangerous smirk crossing his face. "I like it when you're angry."

Ignoring him, Gabi turned on her heel to get dressed. She jumped, startled, when Darion quickly caught her around the waist. Twisting her around, he said, "You wanna show me how mad you are?" His hot breath tickled her neck, sending a tingle down her body. He took her earlobe between his teeth and tugged on it hard.

She pushed his arms off her. "I have to be somewhere. Sorry."

"Don't do this to me, Gabi," he pleaded.

"I'm meeting Mallory."

"It won't take long."

Before she could protest, he lifted her swiftly into his strong arms. His fierce eyes—full of longing—swept slowly over her body. Gabi felt her heart swell at the way he openly desired her. Her insecurities vanished for a moment, and she reminded herself that it was her he loved, her that he was with.

Regardless, she attempted to push him off, even though her body strained toward his. There was a powerful magnetic pull between them, which Gabi was helpless to stop. As he laid her against the cold wooden surface of the table, Gabi swallowed, waiting for his next move. She couldn't deny that she was extremely frustrated.

She felt her muscles relax when her mind realised there was no point in fighting him off. It was out of her control. She wanted him. She could never resist.

Taking hold of the cord of her robe, Darion slowly pulled it loose, his stare not leaving hers. She gasped in surprise when he grabbed hold of her wrists. Carefully and slowly, he wrapped it around her wrists, binding them together. He forced her arms above her head, demanding that she stay put.

"Darion…" She wriggled her wrists. "I want to touch you…it's not fair."

"I'm the one that needs to make it up to you." His tone was low and husky, seductive as always.

She took in the stubble that shadowed his defined jaw and cupid's bow. His full lips. So kissable. So tempting. His hair hung down his neck, but it was a little shorter than she'd last seen it. She wanted to bury her hands in it, to grip it roughly, to pull him into her for a rough, passionate kiss. She felt a pulsing sensation between her legs, and a stirring in the pit of her stomach. She squeezed her lids tightly shut for a moment, hating that everything about him so thoroughly aroused her. She was desperate to be angry at him, but like always, she'd lost that battle.

The silk of her robe brushed against her skin as he whipped it open. His black pupils dilated as he took in her naked body. He ran his hands gently and slowly up her legs.

She inhaled sharply, feeling herself melt under his touch. He was now caressing her thighs, parting her legs wider. She felt a blush heat her cheeks and bit her lip, willing herself to not feel so vulnerable and exposed. His desire clouded gaze locked on hers as he positioned himself between her legs.

His thumbs skimmed back and forth over her nipples, making them tingle and stand to hard peaks. Gabi squirmed slightly as heated pleasure tore through her. He continued to circle, tease, and taunt her nipples, a look of dark hunger covering his face.

When he lowered his head, he kissed a nipple prior to taking it in his mouth. Gabi threw her head back, clenching her fists. His breath was hot on her skin, his tongue warm and wet as it flicked over it. He was gentle at first, and then his suction was fast and greedy as he got carried away, low grunts of appreciation escaping.

He moved across to her other nipple, lasciviously taking it between his teeth, and tugged. Gabi felt herself moisten as pain collided with pleasure. Her legs stretched, and her toes curled when his fingertips now met her swollen clit, rubbing it in gentle circular movements. Her sex throbbed, bringing on internal muscle spasms with the need, the desperation to be filled.

"I could lick, suck, touch, and fuck you for hours," Darion said, his voice firm and ferocious.

Dangerously gleaming eyes stared up at her, his mouth parted, letting free soft pants of desire.

"I could let you," Gabi murmured breathlessly as he carefully inserted a tantalising finger.

She writhed against the table as another finger plunged in. Her hips circled onto them, wanting more. He slipped his fingers in and out repeatedly, making her gasp and arch her back. She was so wet, so hot with arousal. When his fingers burrowed in deeper, moving in and out even faster, she cried out. Darion smiled at her lewdly.

"Come here, Darion." Impatiently, she tried to break free from the cord around her wrists. "Untie me."

"Not yet."

He withdrew his hand and whipped off his top, tossing it aside. Gabi marveled at his strong physique. His jeans hung low, revealing the perfect sculptured V below his abdomen, and the top of his Ralph Lauren boxer shorts.

His hand reached down and unzipped his jeans. His irises, full of salacious longing, fell on hers as he pushed himself forward and into her. Gabi felt herself slammed against the table as her body accepted his thickness and length. Gripping her by the waist, he anchored her body to his as he plunged in and out slowly.

Gabi swiveled her hips, matching his rhythm. He picked up the pace, pounding into her powerfully, filling her completely. She pressed her lips together to muffle her moans. His fingers circled her clit at the same time, leaving it pulsing and tingling. Heat surged through every cell in her body. She felt flushed and light-headed when he worked his hips faster, unable to take the pleasure that overwhelmed her. It was too much. Her muscles throbbed around him, and she knew she was on the verge of exploding.

"Darion," she cried out in frustration, trying again to free her wrists.

He ground his teeth as torment twisted his face. Gabi wriggled, wishing she could reach out and pull him in for a kiss. Her inner muscles gripped his cock, a delicious burning sensation filling her. She pushed her body closer into him. Aching and needy, she took in a deep breath as intense waves rippled through her, an orgasm building.

"Gabi." Small guttural cries eased from his throat.

Her breathing became erratic as her thighs clamped around his waist. She clenched her fists, her nails digging into her palms as they rocked in synchrony. It was heavenly. When Darion leant forward, his tongue finding hers, she knew she'd be unable to hold out for much longer. As his tongue brushed against hers hungrily, possessively, their teeth clashing together, her stomach tightened.

"Ah..." She threw her head back.

"Gabi." Darion pressed his forehead against hers. His jaw twitched, and she knew he was struggling to keep in control, on the verge of falling apart. He seized her face in his hands. "I care about you so much," his tone was stern. "I hope you know that." She felt exposed, like he could see right into her soul—her fears and insecurities of losing him. Instead of feeling reassured by his words, she felt even more afraid of losing him.

"I do," she responded breathlessly.

As he drove into her one final powerful time, she was filled with tendrils of ecstasy. She screamed out, her stomach clenching, her sex pulsing around him, her body shaking. An orgasm exploded through her, making her body tremor.

She heard Darion cry out incoherently as he climaxed deep inside her. His fingers dug into the delicate skin of her waist. After a few more grinds into her, he stilled and collapsed.

With his head resting against her bare chest, she could feel the soft blowing of his breath, which tickled her skin. She could feel the beating of his heart against her own. She breathed in his masculine scent, and savored the moment; all feelings of anger she had for him long vanished.

"That was so good..." she managed to say, whilst trying to catch her breath. "Shit! Mallory's here." She sat up abruptly at the sound of the doorbell.

Darion pushed himself to his feet, tucking himself away and zipping up his jeans.

"Quick, untie me."

He unhooked the cord, releasing her. Gabi hastily wrapped the robe around herself. She watched as Darion pulled his top back on. She frowned; disappointed she couldn't spend longer with him.

"Let Mallory in. Tell her I'm just putting my jacket on." She hurriedly headed for the bedroom.

"Hey," Darion called her back.

She turned around.

He didn't even have to speak and she knew exactly what he wanted. Shaking her head in amusement, she stepped forward and planted a kiss on his lips. Snaking his hand around her waist, he deepened the kiss, his tongue meeting hers, wrestling with it. She moaned out as he kissed her roughly, savagely.

"Behave," she warned.

"Never."

"Oh, Darion?" She stilled, suddenly remembering the Toyota and needing peace of mind. "What car does Eva drive?"

"A mini convertible. Why?"

"No reason."

She scolded herself again. Why would Eva be following her, anyway? It made no sense. As if anyone would be following her. Her life wasn't *that* interesting. Her emotions were getting the better of her again.

Dismissing it, she fled to her bedroom. She heard the sound of the front door opening. Mallory was a little early. She flung open her wardrobe, scanning over the rails of clothes, unsure of what to wear. Glancing out the window, she guessed the air would probably be bitter. English weather was deceptive, as even the times when it appeared bright, you never knew what you were getting.

After a quick body wash in the shower, she pulled on a black trouser playsuit, and teamed it with white Manolo Blahniks to match her handbag. Gabi liked wearing heels. It made her feel glamorous, lady-like. She was so used to wearing them that she must have desensitised herself from the pain they often brought.

Rushing into the living room, she found Mallory sat on the sofa, Darion making an attempt at small talk. She could tell Mallory was quite taken with Darion. His gaze met Gabi's, holding the secret of what they had just done. Gabi felt her cheeks flame. She smoothed her hair down, hoping Mallory didn't suspect anything.

"Are you ready?"

"Sure am." Mallory stood up. "I'll see you soon, Darion."

He nodded. "Yeah. You more than likely will." He grinned slowly. "Drop by the club some time. We'll make a night of it."

"I'll hold you to that offer."

They exited the apartment together, making their way to the cars. Gabi gave Darion a quick peck.

"Call me later."

"I will, Gabriella Woods," he teased her. "Don't you worry about that."

Chapter Nineteen

The shopping trip with Mallory was successful. Gabi purchased several new dresses, sexy lingerie, and a pair of heels. She also bought a new sim-card and placed it into her mobile, not wanting Lawrence to be able to contact her, should he ever feel the need to. He was single again and she knew what he could be like—forceful, and maybe he'd even try to persuade her into trying again. She quickly sent a text message notifying everyone she knew of the new number.

The rest of the evening had been pleasant. She and Mallory had been gossiping and laughing whilst browsing almost every store in the town centre. They'd then hit the nail shop and had a French manicure, plus pedicure.

Gabi even decided to get a piercing in the top of her ear—a silver stud which glittered in the light. She was pleased. She'd always admired piercings, but Lawrence had put her off each time, as he didn't like them, the same went for tattoos. He believed women should remain au natural, untouched.

Once she'd packed away her new purchases, she made herself a salad sandwich. She remained in the kitchen whilst she wolfed it down hungrily. As she brushed the bread crumbs from her fingers, she realised she fancied a chilled glass of wine. Removing a bottle of white from the fridge, she filled a glass to the rim. She took it into the living room and made herself comfortable on the sofa.

As she sat there, her mind drifted to Lawrence. She wondered whether Darion loved her as much as Lawrence claimed he did. At the start of their relationship, Lawrence had always been declaring his love, whether it was by words, or actions. He never ever let her down at the start. He surprised her with romantic trips, dinners, and presents. And then he'd proposed in the most romantic way possible—in Paris in front of the Eiffel tower.

Gabi would be lying if she said she didn't miss romance. But she couldn't expect romance from Darion. Not yet anyway. He found it difficult to show that side of him. She knew he was afraid of getting hurt. He feared that if he got too close, gave it his all, then it would hurt him more if the relationship didn't last. She needed to get him to take a risk, to jump into what they had headfirst, and properly enjoy it.

Her mobile ringing dragged her back to reality. She answered without even looking at the caller ID.

"Hello…"

"Gabi. What are you doing tonight?" his laid-back drawl came through the line.

"Not much."

"You fancy coming to the club?"

"Maybe. What's going on?"

"There's a live band on tonight. You know how we have people in sometimes."

"Oh. That sounds good."

"Do you want me to pick you up?"

"I can drive."

"On the bike?" he cut her off.

She bit down a smile. *Hell yeah!* "Um…sure," she responded coolly. A shiver of excitement ran up her spine. She'd wanted to get on that bike since she'd first seen it. It was a beast. And even better, Darion looked *hot* on it.

"I'll see you in about an hour."

"Okay."

She entered her bedroom and pulled out her new black body-con dress. It was all cotton except for the waist area, which was leather. She dressed and applied make-up: black smoky eye shadow, with lashings of mascara, and pink glossy lips. Ruffling her blonde waves, she added hair grips to one side, to reveal her pierced ear. She checked her reflection for the final time and slipped into flat, pointy shoes.

Back in the living room, she cradled her glass of wine, waiting eagerly for him to show up. She focused on the television in a bid to calm the butterflies in her stomach. Why the hell did Darion still make her nervous after all this time? She put it down to the attraction she felt for him, and his seductive, dangerous aura.

It wasn't long until she heard the roar of a powerful engine. Climbing to her feet, she switched the television off. She stilled for a moment, wondering what she needed to take with her—coat and mobile. She sauntered into the hallway and unhooked her long coat from the wall. Slinging it on, she then placed her mobile in the pocket. She glanced down at her appearance, and feeling satisfied she looked okay, she headed outside.

Darion had a black Yamaha R1 between his legs, and his hands were firmly gripping the handlebars. He was wearing black jeans, matching top, and jacket. His helmet was nestled in his lap. Her pulse began to race, and she felt a heated blush spread through her chest. How she wished she could fan herself without it being obvious. She pulled at the collar on her coat. He looked sensational.

As she neared him, he looked up. His gaze swept over her slowly, making her feel exposed in the intensity of his stare. A ghost of a smile played on his lips. She inhaled a deep breath, willing her heart to slow its frenetic racing.

"Hey," his voice was low and silky.

"Hi." She smiled, twiddling with her nails. *Get a grip, Gabi.*

He leant back to evaluate her. "You look amazin'."

"Thanks." She laughed softly. "You don't look too bad yourself."

"I aim to please," he said, the humour apparent in his tone.

"Um…" She stepped forward. "Do you have an extra helmet?"

He pulled a large black rucksack off his back and tossed it to her. "This is the surprise I told you about. It almost slipped my mind." He slapped a palm on the shiny black body of the bike. "I knew you'd like a ride on the bike."

"How did you know that?"

"All women do."

Gabi shook her head in amusement. She unzipped the bag. So the surprise didn't include some sexual fantasy, or visiting the swinging rooms of The Black Door like she'd suspected. She took out a helmet. It was black with a pink swirl on the side. Turning it over in her hands, she noticed that her name was engraved inside.

"My own helmet?" She beamed. She never thought she'd see the day when she, almost permanently heel-clad and girly, would own a helmet, let alone ride on the back of a motorbike. Before Darion, she had never even met anyone who owned one. "Thank you. I love it."

She placed it on her head and fastened the straps. She was touched by Darion's gift. She could definitely get used to his sweet side. She zipped the rucksack up and slung it over her shoulder. Climbing onto the bike, she hooked her arms around his waist tightly. Anticipation ran thick and heavy through her veins.

"Hold on tight."

"Go slow...I'm a little scared," she confessed.

He shot her a look over his shoulder. "You're in safe hands."

The engine screamed to life as the bike took off. Gabi gripped onto him tighter. Her face was pressed against his back, the smell of his musky aftershave filling her nostrils. She took in the row of houses on the streets, as they went by. Then Darion was speeding, until the scenery became a blur. Gabi bit her lip, her nails digging into his waist.

It was only when they were amongst nothing but grassy fields that she started to feel herself relax. The gentle breeze cooled her face. She sucked in the fresh air. As the engine got louder, and the bike moved faster, Gabi grinned. Her heart slammed against her chest. The adrenaline rush from the speed warmed her from the inside out. She was unable to stop giggling. She closed her eyes and allowed the open road to take her. At that moment, nothing and no one mattered. She felt as free as a bird.

Chapter Twenty

The excited emotions Gabi had felt from the journey on the motorbike diminished rapidly as she neared The Black Door. She dug her nails into her palms as she allowed Darion to lead the way. She wasn't overjoyed about seeing the girls, knowing that Darion had slept with most of them. Lexi, however, was someone she classed as a friend, having met her on the first visit to the club.

Once inside, she and Darion settled on stools at the bar. The atmosphere was lively, and the room held quite a busy crowd. Gabi took in the band on the stage. There was a drummer, guitarist, and a lead singer. She sat up in interest, smiling. She liked the music. Stealing a glance at the stage, she noticed Wendy was occupying one of the poles.

"What can I get ya?" Marnie asked.

"A white wine, please," she responded.

"How are you, Gabi?" She poured the most expensive bottle of wine she had into a glass, and handed it to her.

"Great, thanks. You?"

She shrugged one shoulder. "I'm all right."

Gabi noticed Darion was talking to Lennie. "How are things here without Gina?" She resumed her attention to Marnie.

"Quieter." She grabbed a cloth and began wiping the surface of the bar. "I'm counting down the days until she comes back. It's not the same without her." She straightened her posture. "Plus, she was the only one really who had the balls to put Eva in her place."

As Gabi downed a quarter of her wine, she realised she'd forgotten all about Eva. She instantly felt her spine stiffen. She surveyed the club, feeling anxious. The last thing she wanted was a run in with her. She contemplated asking Darion of her whereabouts, and then decided against it, not wanting to ruin the night. Maybe Eva would obey Darion for once, and stay where she was meant to—upstairs.

"You okay?" Darion asked her once Lennie had gone, running his fingertips slowly up her leg, causing her stomach to tighten hard with desire.

She nodded.

His gaze, full of salacious longing, lingered on her lips for a second, and then his hands reached into her hair, pulling her head forward. As his engorged lips sealed over hers, his tongue parting her mouth, she closed her eyes, savoring the sensation. She gave in to his deep devouring kisses, feeling her pulse quicken and her body heat with pleasure.

"Gabi," his voice was hoarse and needy. "You wanna take these drinks to the office?" His pupils were dilated, almost glowing.

"Later," she told him, wanting to enjoy the show.

Reluctantly, he tore away. "You got a piercing?"

She touched her earring. "Yes. Do you like it?"

"I do." He squeezed her thigh.

"Darion?" Lexi appeared from the door behind the bar. "Call for you."

"Who is it?"

"A potential client, I think. Carl Johnson, or something."

Darion rose to his feet. "Gabi, he's a friend of mine. I gotta take this."

"Okay."

He leant over her, brushing his lips against her temple. Both girls then watched him vanish to the corridor which led to his office.

"How's it going, Gab?" Lexi asked, finally dragging her hard stare from Darion.

"As good as can be. What about you?"

"I've been better," she said.

"Can I help with anything?" Gabi asked, throwing Lexi a sympathetic look. Lexi was usually upbeat and always smiling. It was odd seeing her somewhat wound up.

"No." She smiled tightly. "For what is my problem is your problem."

With that she stalked off in the same direction Darion had taken. Gabi chewed her lip, feeling confused, not knowing what Lexi had meant. She was obviously referring to a problem linked with Darion, for they didn't share anything else in common. What other problem came with Darion that irked Lexi? Gabi held her glass to her lips and took a small sip. *Ah, that was it. Eva.* She realised then that Eva's return must have bothered Lexi as much as it did her.

Placing her glass down, she turned her attention to the dancers, and tried her hardest to concentrate. She absorbed how their flawless bodies writhed to the music, how their fingers teased their hair, and their eyes seduced their observers. As many times as she'd seen them dance, Gabi was in awe every time she saw the girls put on a show. Gabi had danced privately for Darion in the past, after a few too many drinks. It made her feel daring, alive, and confident.

Ten minutes later, she managed to tear her focus away from the stage and made her way to the bathroom. She touched up her make-up and tidied her hair. As she did so, she couldn't help but hear a commotion coming from Darion's office. In the corridor, Gabi paused near his door, contemplating knocking. When she heard him shouting, she decided against it, however she hovered for a moment, wondering what to do. Should she go in and help?

"She needs to stop interfering," Darion's stern tone filled the air. "And you need to ignore her. How many times do I have to tell you, Lex?"

"Just sort it out, Darion," Lexi's voice was impatient, demanding. "She obviously hasn't listened to a word you said."

Gabi heard a loud bang, like the sound of a fist hitting the table. "I can't handle this."

"It's your job to handle it, Daz."

Gabi felt her skin go eerily cold, and

goosebumps prickled her arms when she felt someone's presence. She slowly lifted her head, her breath catching in her throat. The familiar green eyes bored into hers, the same knowing smirk plastered on her face. Gabi clamped her now damp palms together, taking a couple of tentative steps backwards to put space between her and the woman before her. She hadn't even heard her approaching.

"You must be Darion's girlfriend," Eva purred, a perfectly arched brow rising. Unlike Gabi, she didn't appear in the least bit uncomfortable.

"You must be the *ex*-wife," Gabi tried to keep her voice steady.

Gabi examined Eva intently. She was even more beautiful up close. Her pupils held a mischievous twinkle. If they weren't slightly slanted and cat-like, it'd be like looking into the eyes of Darion, for they were a light green, the same colour. Her glossy black waves framed a face which consisted of perfectly defined cheekbones and full, upturning lips. Gabi swallowed as she took in her body. Her silicone implants appeared huge compared to her tiny frame. She managed to make out a few of the tattoos that adorned her arms.

"You're different." Eva cocked her head to the side. "Darion doesn't usually do prissy."

"No." Gabi smiled. "He did tacky. Luckily, he went up in the world." Gabi was surprised at the words that tumbled from her mouth before she had time to think first. She really did have an inner-bitch. *Wow*. She really was protective over Darion. She was almost certain she saw a hint of a smile on Eva's face, as if she was impressed with her little comeback.

Disturbed by another of Darion's outbursts, they both glanced back toward the door.

"Someone's moody," Eva confirmed. She stepped toward Gabi and brushed a strand of hair out of her face. Gabi could feel the warmth radiating from her. "If you don't keep your man happy, sweetheart," she whispered close to her ear, "someone else will." Her tone was threatening. Her eyes glittered dangerously, like she knew the secret to Darion's happiness and Gabi didn't.

Gabi was about to respond when Eva darted into the bathroom. *Shit!* She sighed heavily. What did Eva mean by that? Was she implying that *she'd* take Darion from Gabi? Or that another woman, more adventurous and fun would? Storming back into the bar, Gabi necked back the remainder of her wine. Eva must have meant keeping Darion happy in a sexual way.

Jealousy crawled over her. Images of Darion and Eva tortured her mind—their perfect bodies writhing together, their gazes locked, their dangerous smiles and dirty sounding laughs combined. She knew she'd probably never compare to Eva. She feared she'd lose Darion. Could she give him what he wanted?

One thing was for certain, she was sure going to try.

Chapter Twenty-One

"You wanna head off?" Darion asked Gabi once he'd returned.

She nodded, peering over his shoulder, wondering if Eva would make another appearance.

"Are you okay?" He regarded her cautiously.

"I'm fine." She grinned, feigning happiness. "What about you?"

"Yeah," he replied, rubbing his jaw, averting his gaze, an indicator that he too was lying. He slung his jacket over his shoulder. "Let's go."

Once outside, Darion led her to his Audi. She was relieved they weren't riding the motorbike back, for she was exhausted. She needed the comfort of a car seat. Darion veered around the car to hold her door open for her. Gabi thanked him. She admired Darion's impeccable manners. He may have had 'bad-boy' written all over him, but he could be quite the gentleman at times.

Before she climbed in, she paused to glance over

her shoulder. She felt someone watching her. Were they? Or was she being paranoid again? She contemplated telling Darion about her suspicions of being followed, but didn't want to worry him, or for him to think she was crazy. She had no concrete evidence either. She'd seen a silver Toyota twice. That was it.

Entering the car, she made herself comfortable in the leather seat. She focused her attention to Darion, knowing something was also worrying him. She opened her mouth to speak. She was blocked out by the sound of rock music as he switched the stereo on. Hastily turning to face the window, she linked her fingers together. He was shutting her out, trying to avoid her questions.

"I know you're not okay. I wish you'd talk to me," Gabi said softly when they were eventually lying in bed, a gentle light sweeping over the room from the street lamps.

"There's nothing to say, Gabi." He hooked his hands together behind his head.

Gabi rolled onto her side, her back facing him. She didn't want him to see the disappointment on her face.

"Gabi." He let out a frustrated groan. "It's nothing I can't handle. Just some minor issues at the club. Eva and the girls aren't seeing eye to eye, that's all." He shifted toward her, wrapping his arms around her waist. "I don't wanna drag you down with my problems."

She turned to face him. "Darion, I want to be here for you."

"I know you do, darlin'," he soothed, and half

smiled. "But there's nothing you can do. Only I can rectify this."

Gabi closed her eyes for a moment, thinking, gearing herself up to find out what she needed to know—whether they had a future together, whether Darion believed in them, or whether she was wasting her time. "Do you think you'll come to the christening with me?"

"Gabi." Darion stroked her cheek. "It's a long way off. Let's talk about it then."

"It's a simple question, Darion." She hadn't meant for her tone to sound so tight with agitation.

"Okay." His features softened. "If you want me there, then I'm there."

Before she could respond, he silenced her with a kiss. Gabi reciprocated, opening her mouth to allow his tongue access. She tasted the liquor he'd sipped. His lips crashed against hers urgently, desperately, possessing her. She heard the sound of his muffled grunts, and then his hands were exploring her body.

She reluctantly pulled back. "I need to ask you something."

She saw a flash of concern cross his face. "What is it?"

"Do I make you happy?"

"Yes." He nodded. "You do."

Gabi wasn't sure whether to feel comforted by his answer. How could he be happy when she wasn't fulfilling his every need?

"Do I make you happy?" His voice tremoured with obvious nerves, uncertainty showed on his face. She noticed he was studying her expression. Gabi felt a little relieved to know that Darion could sometimes be unsure of her feelings, as she could of his.

I've never been happier with a man in my life, she thought, *on the good days, anyway.* "Most of the time," she teased instead.

"Is that so?" He tickled her ribs, causing her to wriggle and laugh.

"Stop," she cried out. "I hate being tickled."

"Am I making you happy now?"

Involuntary giggles continued to escape her mouth as she tried to push him away. He kneeled on top of her, his body weight pressing her against the mattress. His fingers began to tickle under her arms.

"Get off," she pleaded, writhing around. "Stop! Please."

"On one condition." A playful smile teased his face.

"What is it?" She grabbed his arms, trying to remove them from her body.

He stopped tickling her as he leant in to her ear to whisper, "You let me fuck you...*all* night." His voice was smooth sounding, so sexy it was almost enough alone to persuade her. Grabbing the bottom of his top, he then lifted it from his head, and tossed it to the floor. Gabi hungrily studied him, taking in every inch of his firm, smooth body. As he raked a hand through his hair, his tongue darting out to wet his bottom lip, Gabi felt her heart skip a beat. Darion Milano. With the white sheets wrapped around his legs, his fitness-model-like physique, and slow mischievous smile, Gabi knew he wouldn't be out of place in GQ magazine. Women worldwide would lust over him, and that was a fact.

She grinned in delight and answered, "I'm sure that wouldn't be a problem."

***

Darion

Darion tightened his hold on her fingers. Eva looked sensational in her wedding dress. It looked like it had been made especially for her, to accentuate every inch of her perfect body. The white bodice lifted her bosom. The flowing white skirt clung to her hips, and the tail flowed behind her beautifully. Her eyes peeked out from under her veil, twinkling mischievously. She had whispered that underneath her dress, she was wearing a black bra with slits in, and a crotchless G-string, complete with a garter on her leg. He couldn't wait to get his hands on her.

"I love you, Mr. Milano. Here's to the rest of our crazy life." She giggled in his ear. "May every year get better and dirtier."

"It will," he'd promised. "We're gonna live the high-life, baby."

As they wove through the crowd, he felt his ego swell. He noticed that others openly admired his girl. As they stood next to their boring wives and girlfriends, he had something they didn't—a prize. Eva was everything men wished for, lusted after from afar—probably someone they pictured as they got intimate with their partners.

All of those years of having nothing, he now had everything. People were actually jealous of him.

They wanted to be him. It made a change from being the lonely, insecure boy. The one that watched the world go by, wishing for a better life, desperate to be loved, to be wanted. With his shabby clothes, two-year-old trainers, and not even a pot to piss in, he had enviously watched the older boys on his street. They had fancy cars, clothes, and different beautiful women every week. He remembered the words like he'd heard them only yesterday, 'Dream on!' One of the boys had caught him admiring a stunning blonde climbing into their car.

It was a dream, all right. If his own parents didn't love him, then how could anybody else? He had begged them to say they loved him. 'Mom, do you love me?' 'Dad, I passed my GCSE's.' 'Mom, I'm gonna make something of myself when I'm older, I promise.' 'Dad, I'll open my own bar, and you can come there every single night.'

And nothing.

The feeling of rejection had usually hit him at night. He'd sit on the windowsill watching families and couples stroll by, laughing, hand in hand, and wonder what it felt like to be loved, and to give love. He knew how it felt to be lavished with attention. At the gentlemen's clubs' with his dad, even as young as the age of seven, the dancers had fussed over him. As they ruffled his hair and pinched his cheeks, they were forever telling him how cute he was, how one day he would be a heart-breaker.

And so in his late teens, he made his time at the clubs valuable. He questioned the bosses constantly, wanting to know how the business ran. He listened to the dancers whining about things they hated about the club, and bragging about things they loved. He bugged the customers to see what they felt was lacking in the club, and how it could be improved.

At eighteen, Darion moved away from the rough parts of London. He stayed with his aunt in Westhaven. At first it took a while to get used to. Whilst Westhaven was beautiful to look at with its historical churches, grassy parks, and quaint shops, it was boring. There was only one nightclub in the whole town, Sky Bar. It needed livening up. Darion made it his mission to become an entrepreneur. He'd make his parents proud, make them love him. What better way than to open a gentlemen's club? He could be surrounded by stunning women every day, and his dad would like visiting.

He ensured he got a job in a call centre where he saved every single penny. He'd had his eye on a building down a backstreet. There was something about it that drew him in. It had character. He knew he'd own it one day. He knew that it'd be popular with people queuing in the street to get inside. Men could enjoy private dances, whilst women could have a nice cocktail with their friends without getting hit on and harassed by men all the time.

When he'd visited the empty space of the upstairs, he'd spotted a door to another section of the club. The door looked lonely, wasted. The room was bare, cold, the walls crumbling, and the one window that looked out onto the street took his breath away. It was arched; the dark wood surrounding it looked expensive. It seemed out of place, like the view of the street wasn't enough. One would expect to open that huge window and look out onto the cerulean Mediterranean Sea. As Darion ran his fingers along the glass, he didn't know how, but he would make certain that the window was remembered, that when people saw it, they knew that beyond it was something special. The same went for the door. The walls even. And if they could talk he wanted to ensure they had secrets and stories beyond anyone's wildest imagination.

As he left the room, he glanced at the door for the final time. The Black Door.

"Dream on!"

No thanks. I'd rather make it a reality.

Darion's breathing accelerated. He kicked the covers off and jolted into a sitting position, gasping for air. Digging his fingers in his hair, he cursed under his breath. Eva! Her laugh, her smile, her body, her eyes haunted his mind. Ever since he and Eva had split, he hated sleeping alone. It was then when flashbacks seemed to force their way into his brain. The comfort of Gabi sleeping next to him hadn't stopped the nightmares. *Shit.* He had assumed that he'd stop obsessing over Eva now that she had returned. He rubbed his palms up and down his face. Maybe he still needed closure after all. Maybe he needed the questions swimming around his head answered. Why she cheated. Why she ruined his whole fucking life. *Calm down, Darion.* He couldn't ask her yet. He didn't want to dredge up the past. He shouldn't. Couldn't.

He shifted around to watch Gabi sleeping. Her

blonde waves were splayed out across the pillow. Her lips were parted with her soft breathing. Her olive complexion was free of make-up. She looked pretty. So natural. So opposite to Eva.

He felt an urge to stroke her cheek, but decided against it, not wanting to wake her. Lying back down, he closed his eyes again and silently prayed that he could sleep.

After a few minutes of tossing and turning, he made his way to the kitchen. Opening the fridge, he took out a bottle of vodka. Adding it to some orange juice, he swigged half of it back, before settling in the living room, taking the bottle with him. He switched the television on, pleased to find an episode of *Dexter* playing. Taking another large gulp of his drink, he placed it on the table and shuffled down on the sofa. He needed to find another way to de-stress that didn't involve alcohol and gambling.

Hearing Gabi enter the room, he looked up. Her wide, seemingly worried eyes fell on him.

"Are you okay?" she asked softly.

"Got a bit of a headache, that's all."

He noticed her take in the bottle of vodka. "Well, drinking that won't help." She walked toward him and sat down, placing her hand on his. "You want me to watch some television with you?"

"If you want."

She lay down, hooking one arm and leg over him, her head resting on his chest. He stroked her hair gently until his arm began to ache, and his eyelids were too heavy to keep open. Soon they were both in a deep sleep.

Chapter Twenty-Two

Gabi

"One, two, three, four…that's right…get those muscles really working."

Gabi stretched her arms above her head until she felt the pulling ache on her muscles. A hip-hop song was blaring from the stereo. Gabi's forehead was slicked with sweat from the brutal exercising and the lack of air in the stuffy room. Her heart was racing a million miles per hour, and her breathing was sharp and heavy. Grabbing her towel from the floor, she dabbed at her face, and resumed to dancing.

"Okay…watch what I'm doing here, and then copy me."

Her attention was focused on the tutor as she moved her feet in intricate patterns. Gabi then mirrored her actions, as did the other people in the room.

"I'm exhausted." The pretty brunette next to her giggled. It was Kalli, a girl that Gabi had met at her very first dance class.

"Me too." Gabi licked her dry lips, desperately needing a drink. She didn't want to reach for her bottled water and break her dance imitations.

"How's things with you?" Kalli asked whilst jogging on the spot.

"Great." Gabi beamed. "You?"

"Yeah. I enjoy these classes. It's nice to get some peace away from the kids and hubby."

"How old are they?"

"Five and eight." Kalli spun around, her hair flying out behind her. "Do you have children?"

"No," she responded, not intending for her tone to come out as glum as it did. "Maybe some day," she added cheerily.

"Ah, you've got plenty of time." Kalli waved her hand in the air, dismissively. "You're a brilliant dancer, Gabi."

Gabi ducked her head with a soft laugh. "Thank you." Was she? The compliment made her feel as if she would burst with joy. *So I am good at something,* she thought. She realised how sad that sounded. Apart from her job being a brilliant editor, with a fine eye for detail, Gabi hadn't really found a hobby in which she excelled. Lawrence would have been happy having her stay at home, raising children, and washing dishes. Gabi didn't agree with that. Motherhood didn't mean that any hobbies or interests should be abandoned. *A happy wife makes for a happy life,* she had read once. Maybe if she ever did have children, that she would find other things she was good at. Would she be a good mother? If her own mom was anything to go by, she had no reason to doubt her abilities. Her childhood had been nothing but good memories to reflect back on. Her heart twisted in her chest as sadness overcame her at Darion's childhood. For adults to steal that away from you was cruel. It was a time to play, to be silly, to make mistakes, and most of all, to be cared for and loved by the most important people in your life—parents. She swallowed the lump that had lodged in her throat. Some people didn't have a close relationship with their parents. She was pleased that at least Darion had Dion.

"Gabi?" A yell broke her thoughts.

"Yes?" She blinked rapidly, not realising she had stopped in her tracks.

"Everything okay?"

She nodded. "Sorry," she muttered. "I was in my own little world there."

"Glad to have you back." The tutor grinned. "That's all for today, folks. You all did brilliantly. I am immensely proud."

Gabi grinned.

"I'll see you all next lesson. Have a nice evening." The tutor strolled toward the stereo, which she switched off.

"See you next lesson." Kalli slung her bag over her shoulder and waved at Gabi.

"Bye." She waved.

Gabi grabbed her water and drained half of it in several gulps. Taking her bag of clean clothes, she headed toward the shower rooms. Once inside, she was relieved to see that it was empty. Setting her bag on the sink, she stripped off her leggings, crop top, and underwear. Not wanting anyone to catch her in the nude, she quickly tied her hair into a top knot and scurried into the shower.

When she was under the showerhead, she switched on the water. Her tense muscles relaxed from the warmth. Tearing open a packet of shower gel, she began lathering it over her body, making it foam. She closed her lids, luxuriating in the silence and heat of the room.

It was 8:30 p.m. when Gabi got home. It didn't take her long to prepare some pasta. She took it with a book to the living room, and made herself comfortable on the couch. She ate whilst she flipped through the pages, reading. It was a romance novel, her favourite genre. Like most girls, Gabi had been brought up watching and reading fairytales. Wasn't everyone after the happy ending? She laughed to herself, thinking of her prince. He was a far cry from the knight in shining armour she thought she'd end up with. Maybe Darion wasn't the prince. Maybe he was the beast yet to turn into the prince. She tucked her legs under the cushions for warmth. A self-congratulatory smile appeared on her face. Yes, that was definitely it. She had to peel back Darion's layers to find the sweet, romantic prince.

But how to tame the beast was the question that spun around in her head. Damn Disney. Can't a Belle, Cinderella, Ariel, and Jasmine come with man management instructions? How much easier life would be.

Chapter Twenty-Three

Darion

It was mid-week and Darion was perched at the bar, keeping Marnie company. Glancing down at his watch, it displayed that it was 11 p.m. The girls had informed him that Eva hadn't arrived yet. It wasn't like there was much for her to do anyway. The staff was more than capable of doing their jobs just fine without being under her watchful eye. However, Eva said she would ensure the club made more money. He'd wait to see the day.

He tapped his fingers anxiously on the bar surface and surveyed the room, landing on the entrance door. He couldn't sit still. He was agitated, fidgety. Lately, he ensured that he got to the club early enough to get everything done, and was able to leave before Eva arrived. Alternatively he locked himself away in his office. He hated feeling on edge all the time.

"It's busy in here tonight." Marnie jerked her head toward the tables, most of which were occupied.

He nodded in agreement. He was about to reach for his cigars when he noticed Marnie's eyes widen before she scampered off. Darion licked his dry lips to moisten them, knowing exactly who was standing behind him. Slowly twisting around on his stool, there she was. Eva. Dressed in a white vest and black leather skirt, hair curling down her back. He noticed the murderous expression on her face.

"Can we go somewhere to talk?"

"What do we have to talk about?"

She flashed him a slow saccharine smile which didn't reach her steely eyes. "Everything." She barged past him. She indicated for him to follow her to the office. Darion's shoulders sagged as he let out a long, low sigh. How important could it be? Knowing he wouldn't get any peace otherwise, he rose to his feet and followed Eva.

As he unlocked the door to his office, she was standing so close to him that he could smell her perfume, and the minty gum that she must have previously been chewing. Stepping into the room, he flicked on the light, and dropped down onto the sofa. Eva towered over him in her black platforms. He waved his hand in the air, as if to give her permission to speak.

"What's going on, Daz?"

"What do you mean?"

"The club." She shook her head, an incredulous look on her face. "Is this all just one big party to you?"

He chewed his bottom lip, feeling his pulse speeding. She had some nerve.

"Okay." She folded her arms across her chest. "For starters, the girls have got no respect at all for me. They're obviously clueless in respect of their job roles, and what they get paid for," she spat. "The website design is dated, not to mention that it states *nothing* whatsoever about the playrooms. I mean, how will we attract new customers?"

Darion rose to his feet, his nose only inches away from hers. "The playrooms are detailed on the website, with photographs, rules, and what the club offers," he fired back. "But you have to register first. You'd know that if you looked properly." His body brushed past her as he headed toward the mini bar.

"Well, that's no good, Darion. We're competing against other clubs. Some people haven't got time to complete lengthy fucking registration forms."

"It's been fine until now." He carefully selected a glass from the shelf and took hold of a bottle of Jack Daniels.

"Well, what about the girls?" She approached him, glaring. "They don't know what the heck is going on. One minute they're twirling around a pole, and the next minute they're pulling pints."

Darion filled his glass, and then twisted the lid back on the bottle. "We like to shake things up around here."

"Shake things up, or fuck things up?"

He remained silent. He didn't need to explain himself to Eva. The girls liked interacting with the clients, and being behind the bar when they weren't dancing. It saved them from sitting around bored stiff waiting to be called for a lap-dance. They got sick and tired of doing the same thing for hours on end, they liked a bit of variety.

"They could sue you, ya know," she told him. "They could say you're underpaying them. I mean, are they being paid to dance, or to bartend, or both?"

He took a large swig of his drink.

"I wanna see their contracts. They choose which job they want, and that's it." She shifted from one foot to the other. "What did you do to this place?"

"Careful, Eva."

"Oh, and the cleaner is useless." She shook her head. "You need to get a new one. Do you know I found a condom in the shower room?"

Darion felt his chest heaving. He pressed his lips together to regain control. He wasn't having anyone badmouthing his employees. He had never known Rita to make mistakes in her job before. Ever. The whole place was usually immaculate. The laundry was always done on time, the clothes baskets and bins in the playrooms empty, the bathrooms stocked with soap, and tissues, the condom dispensers full, and she even went above and beyond by doing tasks that weren't even in her job description. If she had missed something in the shower room, then she must have had an off day. It was life. Shit happened.

"The leaflet designs need sprucing up. The dressing room needs a good coat of paint. You say you love this club, and yet you've neglected it."

I wonder whose fault that was, he thought

bitterly. His nostrils flared at the way her gaze swept over him. As she continued to slate the club, he marched toward her. Gripping her tightly around the wrist, he yanked her toward the door.

"Get out. Now."

"I'm not going anywhere." She pulled her arm away.

"I'm not having this conversation with you."

"These things need addressing. Work with me on it," she yelled. "Please. I really could do with making some money, Daz, and I know you could too."

He rubbed his hands up and down his face, inhaling a deep breath. More money certainly sounded appealing. He did need to pay off his vehicles. "Ten minutes, Eva."

He crossed the room until he was before the desk. Pulling out the leather chair, he sat down, and indicated for her to do the same. They had once been business partners, and had made a decent profit. Personal issues aside, surely they could get the club booming again.

"So what do you have in mind?" he asked, picking up his drink again and taking a small sip.

Eva helped herself to bottled water from the fridge, and took up residence on the chair opposite him.

He hated the way she obviously felt at home in the club, that she was comfortable to swan around, barking orders, and helping herself to things. He cursed the day he ever allowed her to have joint ownership of the club. *Oh well. You make your bed, you lie in it.*

"I was thinking of hiring a web designer. I think it could do with a new look. We also need to implement the playrooms on the homepage. People should be able to browse before deciding whether to register, or even better, becoming a member."

He leant back casually on his chair. "Fine. If you think it will improve business."

"I also think we need to update the leaflets. Everything should be the same design."

"Agreed."

"We should pay for magazine advertisement space, like we used to do. Are the leaflets still being distributed to businesses in and around London?"

He nodded.

"Good."

He ran a finger gently across his bottom lip, and then straightened his posture, leaning his elbows on the desk. "I've been meaning to renovate the club for a while."

"Nothing too hasty, I hope. We need to bring in the money before we spend it." She crossed her leg over the other causing her skirt to ride up, revealing the spiral of tattoos.

Darion averted his stare quickly. He'd almost forgotten what he was about to say. "I want every wall painted in black with a glittery sheen, *including* the dressing rooms," he added, hoping it'd shut her up. Pulling open his drawer, he retrieved an interior design magazine. It was folded in half, displaying a bar he liked the look of. He dropped it on the desk and slid it toward her.

"Very glam." She nodded, examining the image. "I like it. The colour scheme would look great with the chandeliers and the hundred mirrors throughout the place."

"About the contracts," he began. "Marnie, Lexi, and Wendy are my best dancers. They remain downstairs, dancing. If we need to hire a couple of barmaids, then so be it."

"What about a replacement for Gina?"

He shook his head. "We've got more than enough dancers upstairs. We don't need them there. People are more occupied with other things going on in the rooms."

"Okay."

"Rita is staying and that's not negotiable," he said firmly.

She shrugged a shoulder. "Whatever."

"Anything else?" He wanted her out of the office so he could massage the crick out of his neck.

"Apart from me organising a masked themed night in the playrooms once a week..." She shook her head. "I can't think of anything."

"Good." He linked his hands together. Smirking at her he said, "We're done."

He saw Eva's shoulders droop in obvious disappointment. She groaned before lifting herself to her feet. Jamming her hands in the pockets of her skirt, she stood before the wall of photographs. "Wow." She giggled. "We made some amazing memories, didn't we?"

The wall was adorned with pictures of Darion fishing, skiing, skydiving, swimming with dolphins, and other adventures, not to mention the swingers' resorts and parties he'd visited, surrounded by beautiful women. The photographs of Eva had been taken down the day she had betrayed him.

He felt a sick acidic feeling in his stomach as his mind recalled that torturous night. *Vin, don't stop.* He inhaled a deep gust of air. Rising to his feet, he rolled up the sleeves of his shirt, all of a sudden feeling flustered.

"Yeah. They're just that." He stood behind her. "Memories."

She swiveled around to face him. Her gaze lowered to his mouth for a moment. When her tongue darted out to moisten her full red lips, he swallowed to rid the lump that had lodged in his throat. He unfastened another button at his collar, feeling claustrophobic. The room was so quiet that if a pin dropped, it would be heard.

Eva lifted her hands, aiming for his face. He knew she was about to slide them past his cheeks and bury her long fingernails into his hair, like she used to do. She'd then roughly pull his face to hers and catch his lips with her teeth. She'd nibble at them first, naughtily, before diving her skilled tongue inside, where she'd twirl it around the tip of his, teasingly. She'd then take his whole tongue in her mouth and suck on it hard and fast like her life depended on it, kissing him like she owned him.

Catching both of her wrists tightly, he said in as menacing a tone as he could muster, "Eva. The meeting is over."

Chapter Twenty-Four

Darion ran his hand over the smooth velvet of the red sofa. He inhaled the scent of the room. It smelt like a mixture of alcohol and sex. His jeans suddenly felt uncomfortably tight across the fly. Deep down in his core he felt a desperate need for release. He groaned inwardly. Everywhere he looked, he was filled with an erotic memory. Images flashed through his brain like the naughtiest porn movie he'd ever seen.

As he neared the private VIP booth, he recalled the time when he'd told Gabi about everything the club had to offer—beyond the actual black door were rooms consisting of swings, whips, toys, mirrored walls, dancer poles—the lot.

He remained rooted to the spot for a moment, enjoying the silence of the place. The club had closed half an hour ago. After his meeting with Eva, he'd lain on the sofa in his office, and before he knew it, he'd drifted into a deep sleep. Lexi and

159

Marnie shouting goodbye to him had jolted him awake. Darion was no stranger to sleeping in his office. Before he had met Gabi, he had made quite a habit of it. The music and the sound of chatter and laughter from the bar seemed to help him nod off. The majority of the time it succeeded in preventing him from having any flashbacks of Eva.

Before ensuring the electrics were all switched off, and locking the place up, he had had a sudden urge to visit the playrooms. It had been a while. Now inside, he slowly made his way down the strip of red carpet. He passed the rope to come face to face with the black door. Next to it were rows of lockers and rules were pinned to the wall. He knew what they said off by heart.

No mobile phones. No cameras. No recording devices. No weapons of any kind. No smoking. No use of drugs or prostitution. You may bring your own toys. Lockers and use of showers are at no charge. Rules will be strictly enforced. Any violation of the rules will result in ejection from the club.

Privacy in the playrooms was paramount. It saw the likes of doctors, teachers, judges, celebrities, people who wouldn't want their reputation tarnished in any way. Westhaven, being a small quiet place an hour away from the city, was convenient for many people. They could escape to The Black Door and not have to fear being recognised by anybody they knew.

Hooking his fingers around the gold handle, Darion pulled the door open and stepped inside. He felt his ego swell with achievement. *His* creation. He was like a kid in a candy store, his mouth watering at everything that was on offer. *Every* fantasy could be fulfilled. Home to the sexually adventurous and liberated, Darion had ensured that when finalising the rooms, they provided everything one could need to make their fantasies a reality. He had even hired girls to dress up and role-play with clients. If they wanted a kinky dominatrix, a sexy nurse, a naughty teacher, or whatever, then for a reasonable price, they got just that. It never went further than acting for them. Darion would never condone prostitution—ever.

He smiled to himself when he remembered the steamy sessions he had had with those girls. He had denied them for months, trying to keep things professional. It must have spurred the girls on even more, made them see him as a challenge, as they never tired of flirting with him. Just like he had warned Gabi that he was no good for them, to stay away, they had teased and seduced him until he had eventually caved in. It hadn't been just the one who had wanted him, either. It had been all four of them. So like any hot blooded male, he went for it. Although it was well over a year ago, he could remember the orgy like it was yesterday. He had never felt so adored, so wanted, so secure in his entire life. The way those girls had looked at him with longing, and fussed over him like they couldn't get enough of him had been as addicting as any other session in the playrooms. He couldn't explain the rush he got from it. Being in a room where almost every single person wanted him was a huge help to his self-esteem, the years he had been neglected, refused love, ignored even in conversation. Darion would have been stupid not to have taken advantage of what was on offer. As far as he was concerned, what was the difference with a man bedding different women every single night, to a man who bedded perhaps the same amount of women in one weekend, at once? People could judge him, but they knew not his reasons.

Continuing to survey his surroundings; his eyes had to adjust to the dim red light. The left side of the room held areas, separated by walls, but the playrooms had no doors, specifically for voyeurs and exhibitionists, those that got off on others watching them, and by receiving attention. The rooms along the right-hand side were more private, consisting of doors, but with round glass windows. Nude but tasteful portraits hung along the walls of the corridor, and small condom dispensers were positioned outside every room.

Darion passed the first room on his right and peered in. The walls were mirrored, and a hot tub was in the centre, surrounded by black loungers. Another flashback presented itself of when Gabi had kissed another woman for the first time in that tub. Audrina. He wondered if she'd visited the club recently.

The room on his left contained a king-size bed, and a ceiling mirror. He continued to make his way down the corridor. Arousal fired in the pit of his stomach. He needed a fuck—desperately. He readjusted himself in his trousers, so he felt a little more comfortable.

Focusing his stare on another room, he leant toward the glass window. Huge red cushions were sprawled all over the floor, making it look like one big mattress, and again, the walls and ceiling were mirrored. That room was the best for a perfect orgy. Turning to a room on his left, a low groan escaped from his lips. The dungeon suite—one of his favourites. He took in the leather cuffs hanging from the ceiling, the leather swing, bed, rail of garments, and table holding whips, paddles, and toys. BDSM was amongst his top ten sexual desires. Although he had participated in a bit of soft bondage with Gabi, he was yet to introduce her to the hardcore stuff. A part of him really believed she'd like him taking charge.

The next room held a bed in the corner, a dancing pole near a mirrored wall, and a rack of outfits for men and women. Darion liked to see a woman in uniform or sexy lingerie. He sauntered inside, settling before the women's outfits. His fingers skimmed over each one: schoolgirl, maid, army, police officer, and nurse outfits. Each outfit brought back special memories with several different women. He wondered what most of them were doing now. He hadn't seen some of his past lovers for years. Perhaps they'd gotten married, had kids, settled for the vanilla lifestyle—more fool them. Or maybe they'd kept up their kinky activities in private.

He drew in a sharp breath as his fingertips felt the smooth material of the final outfit, a PVC cat-suit. Eva had rocked this one perfectly, her breasts protruding over the zipper, complete with six inch thigh-high boots, and a whip in hand. He'd knelt naked at her mercy. She'd pleasured and tortured him simultaneously, and he'd had probably one of the most intense orgasms of his life. Then the roles had reversed, and she had hung from the ceiling whilst he'd dominated her. He scratched his head, turning his back on the outfit quickly.

He examined the glass cabinet full of brand new packaged toys, available for purchase. Again, he'd used all of those types of toys on Eva. Why not stimulate all of the erogenous zones?

Exiting the room, he tried to block everything out involving Eva. There was no point in reminiscing. He willed his heart to stop its frenetic pace. Throwing his head back, he closed his lids for a moment. Once he'd regained his composure, he continued on his tour.

The next room to his left wasn't that kinky, allowing his excitement to decrease. A large king-size bed faced a wall-mounted television which always played an erotic movie. Candles and red roses adorned the shelves, creating an intimate romantic feel. Darion rarely ever went in that room—his romantic side had been ruined by Eva. Never would he be weak, too giving, too loving, and too open to a woman *again.*

Another room he entered had no glass window to peep in. A sign hung from the door stating **'couples only.'** It was where most of the partner swapping took place. There were round gigantic beds in each of the four corners, which automatically rotated for great viewing pleasure. Two dancer poles occupied the middle of the area.

Stepping out, he didn't bother visiting the last rooms. One was a shower room with hot-tub area, and the other used to be a room for complete privacy. Even to this day it pained him to enter that room, so he avoided it as much as he could. It had been the ultimate private room for the swingers—no disturbances or interruptions, the ability to do as they pleased. Ever since Eva had locked herself in it with Vinnie whilst he fucked her behind Darion's back, without agreement beforehand, he'd changed it into a dressing room. The sign above the door stated:

'For assistance in role-play, please request a price list and choose a member of staff in this area.'

Darion's employees liked being able to get ready in the room, doing their hair and make-up, and changing into provocative outfits. They were extremely popular with the clients.

Turning on his heel, he made his way back down the corridor. He took in the rooms briefly for a final time.

He couldn't wait to explore them all with Gabi.

Chapter Twenty-Five

"*Don't stop,*" *the hot, breathless pleading in his ear further aroused him.*

He kissed her ankle tenderly, followed by another as he slowly worked his way up her long, slim leg. When he got to her thigh, he bit into her skin roughly, causing her to giggle. God, her body was amazing.

Spreading her legs invitingly, she gripped his hair, and yanked him up. Burying his head in her shoulder, he inhaled her sweet scent. She writhed in excitement when he guided himself into her. He closed his eyes on a soft sigh, in pure ecstasy. Sliding his hands under her buttocks, he marveled at the perfection of it. It was firm, and her skin was smooth. Every plunge into her sent him closer and closer to the climax that ached his stomach.

"*How good does this feel?*" *she purred.*

"*So good,*" *he responded with a groan.*

Digging his fingers into her flesh, he rocked her

up and down, to move with him in sync. A perfect, controlled rhythm that had them both moaning, sweating, and panting. He kept his eyes clenched shut, but felt her lips searching for his. When they pressed against his firmly, he wasted no time in swirling the tip of his tongue around hers. It started off slow, soft, but then the kiss became harder, faster, trapping the sound of his grunts.

He grimaced, and clenched his teeth when he felt her long nails tear at his back. It hurt and pleasured him simultaneously. Punishing her in return, he slammed into her with all of the strength he had, filling her with his full length. In and out. In and out. Her muscles gripped his erection, sending him closer to the edge.

"Oh yes..." she cried in agonising pleasure, obviously as desperate as him for release.

Their sweaty, heated bodies continued to glide together, the pace and pressure building. Her legs hooked around his waist, and she yanked him even closer, pushing her hips up, meeting each and every one of his powerful slams.

"Oh god, Darion..."

He fondled her breasts, licking her hardened nipples before burying his head in the crook of her neck again. He tried to control his breathing, but he knew he was close. He continued to push in and out, and then he sucked in air. His body shivered as spasms of pleasure shot through him. It was coming, so close, so good...

"I always knew we'd get back together."

Darion bolted upright, his chest heaving, his

throat tight, unable to breath. He couldn't see straight, couldn't think right. Frantically scanning the room, his mind started to register familiar objects. He sucked in a lungful of air and collapsed back down onto the bed. He was in his bedroom, in his apartment. His body was drenched in sweat and his heart felt as if it would explode through his chest. He rubbed it in circular movements, slowing his breathing, and trying to focus. What the fuck was that? As if the nightmares and flashbacks of Eva weren't enough, he was now fantasising about her. Balling his hand into a fist, he punched the mattress hard. *No, no, no.* He was with Gabi. He should be fantasising over Gabi, not a scheming bitch like Eva.

Kicking the sheets off, he clambered out of bed. He needed air. It felt as if the walls were closing in on him, and there was no escape. Eva would forever be embedded in his mind, anchoring him to a past he wanted to forget.

Trudging toward the balcony, he pulled open the door, and dropped onto one of the chairs. He didn't care that he was only in his boxer shorts. The cool, gentle breeze felt like heaven. He parted his lips and drew it in before closing his eyes. He didn't want to fuck Eva. No, surely he didn't. It was probably the playrooms bringing back all sorts of memories, playing havoc with his emotions. He couldn't forgive Eva and give the relationship another try, and more importantly, he didn't want to. Did he?

You're with Gabi now, he sternly reminded himself. *She's everything you need. Isn't she?*

His mind and his heart wanted Gabi. It seemed

that, at times, his body craved someone else.

Chapter Twenty-Six

Gabi

Gabi stabbed her fork into her tomato-drenched pasta and put it in her mouth. Only when she'd swallowed did she thank Darion for taking her to the restaurant. It was a favourite of his, tucked away in the hills. With floor to ceiling windows, they had the stunning view of the leafy nature that surrounded them, not to mention the city's lights dotted under the night sky.

The working week had flown by, and Friday evening had come around. Darion had called her to see if she fancied going out for dinner. Wanting to spend some time with him and not fancying one of her bland meals, she'd agreed.

"You're welcome," Darion responded, gently placing his fork down, having finished his meal. He downed some of his water, the ice cubes rattling in the glass.

"Last time we were here, we barely finished our drinks." Gabi toyed with the stem of her glass, biting down a smile.

A grin surfaced on Darion's face. "I remember."

Unable to ignore the sexual tension between them, they had fled to his jeep. They had pleasured one another on the backseat. Gabi felt her lower inner muscles warming at the thought, excitement building just thinking about it.

She pushed her plate away and took hold of Darion's hand. It sat in hers unmoving, when usually he would caress her fingers in affection. He straightened his posture, as if trying to relieve himself from a stiff spine. Gabi couldn't help but feel that he was on edge. Most of the evening, his brow had furrowed to the point where it was noticeable, as if his mind was constantly wondering and worrying about something.

She knew he couldn't be overly thrilled about Eva's return, or about Gina's departure. Whether his concerns lay with his business, or that of a personal nature, she had no idea.

"Darion," she said as softly as she could, "is everything okay?"

"Yes, Gabi." He smiled but it didn't reach his eyes.

Rather than feeling close to him, she felt he was pushing her away, hiding something from her. There was distance between them that left her stomach swirling and feeling unsettled.

"Do you still feel the same way about me that you did the last time we were here?" She tucked a strand of hair behind her ear with her free hand. She hated how needy and insecure she probably sounded, but she needed reassurance.

"Yes, Gabi. I do." He brushed his lips against hers. "I can take you to the car now and prove it to you."

Gabi lowered her head with a soft laugh. She knew he was dead serious.

The waitress sauntered over to collect their empty plates. "Can I get you anything else?" Her focus was on Darion as she openly admired him. Wearing a navy long sleeved top and matching jeans, Darion's hair hung loose, free of product. His appearance was casual, rather than smart, and he still looked as handsome as ever.

"Just the bill, please." The woman's face flushed a little red as Darion gave her his killer smile.

"I'll be right back," she mumbled with a giggle, and hurried off.

Darion turned to face Gabi. He cupped her face in his hands, skimming his tongue teasingly across her lips. "What do you fancy doing now?"

"Anything you like." She moved back and placed a hand over her mouth to hide her yawn.

"Anything?" he asked. His pupils gleamed wickedly, as if he had something particular in mind.

"Sure." She finished the last of her wine and scrambled to her feet.

She followed Darion toward the front of the restaurant so he could settle the bill. Gabi shook her head in amusement at two of the waitresses that seemed to be talking about Darion and giggling. Darion was oblivious to it. The way he carried himself, exuding confidence, the way he smiled wickedly, the way he moved gracefully, she understood it. One would never think that beneath the mask was obviously an insecure man who doubted himself. One would also never think that his constant search for sexual thrills and swinging was how he lived his life.

As they strolled alongside one another toward the car, Gabi grabbed hold of his hand and squeezed it. She was just about to hook her arms around his waist when she heard a rustle in the bushes. She came to an abrupt halt. Even when she lifted her head to get a better view, all she could see was darkness.

"Are you okay?" Darion asked, his voice laced with concern.

"I keep getting this weird feeling that someone's following me."

"Why would someone follow you?"

"I don't know." She laughed at how ridiculous it sounded. "It's probably nothing."

Darion's expression turned serious, and he said firmly, "Nothing will happen to you whilst you're with me."

Her muscles softened when he pulled her into his protective arms. Perhaps he was right. She knew he would never let anyone hurt her. Feeling a little safer, she followed him to the car.

The drive back to her apartment didn't take long. They were silent the entire time, appreciating the music. As soon as they were in her bedroom, Gabi unzipped her dress, wanting to reveal the surprise she had for him. She stepped over the fabric when it pooled at her feet. She was wearing a black, lace halter neck corset and matching underwear. It was completely see-through. Keeping her black, shiny Louboutin heels on, she leisurely strolled toward the bed. Darion's head shot up to attention. A low, frustrated grunt came from his lips.

"Gabi," his voice was hoarse. "You've been wearing that the entire time?"

She nodded. "Do you like it?"

He shifted into a kneeling position. "I more than like it."

He wrapped his arms around her back, pulling her closer to the bed. Although she could tell he liked what he saw by the wandering of his hands, his eyes seemed empty; his expression devoid of emotion, instead of the darkening look of longing he usually gave her. His sensual lips didn't twitch upwards as they usually did with that satisfied smirk of his. She had no idea what he was thinking.

Quickly lifting her, he laid her on the mattress. Her breath caught in her throat as he traced a finger down her neck. He then stroked down to her nipple. His circular movements brought it to a hard peak. Gabi felt herself relax, and she sighed softly. Why did his touch have the power to take over her mind, her body, to heighten her senses and make her lose her ability to think rationally?

She felt the weight of his stare as he said, "You're so fucking beautiful, Gabriella Woods." He tweaked her nipple between his thumb and forefinger. Gabi arched her back as tingles of pleasure swept over her. She was so sensitive to his touch. Her body craved more and all feelings of tiredness and the need to question his mood diminished. She couldn't bring herself to ruin the moment, wanting to be close to him.

"You're gorgeous too, Mr. Milano." She sat up and ran her palm across his jaw. His stubble felt a little rough, but she didn't care. His green eyes were so wide and captivating. His lips were full, so kissable and tempting. She lowered her gaze to his large biceps and smooth, firm chest. The flimsy bed covers hung just below the perfect V below his abdomen. His appearance alone sent spasms of desire between her legs.

"How about a little music?" Darion grabbed his mobile from the bedside table. They both believed there was nothing better than getting intimate to sexy music. It seemed to make it that much more pleasurable. Darion scanned through his playlists before settling on one. "#1 Crush" by Garbage was the first song. Placing the mobile back on the side, he turned to face her.

Gabi swallowed when his fingertips trailed slowly up her leg. She heard the creak of the bed as he then knelt before her. Before she knew it, he attacked her corset, tearing it from her body. She didn't get time to gasp before he pushed her legs apart. It took all of her willpower not to close them when he tilted his head, a smile crossing his face. She gripped the bed sheets as his hands stroked up each of her trembling legs slowly, and began massaging them firmly. She stifled a moan as his strong hands worked the tension and knots out of her muscles. It felt heavenly.

"I love your body," he murmured, his gaze travelling upwards, scrutinising her intently. "I hope you've more lingerie like this?"

She nodded. Ever since meeting Darion, she'd stocked up on sexy outfits.

He removed her underwear and tossed it to the floor. She drew in a breath and tensed when he stroked her clit in gentle, circular movements. She felt the blood rushing to it, causing it to swell and throb. Her abs tightened in sexual frustration, greedy and desperate to be pleasured. She felt arousal pool between her legs. Hearing a husky groan from Darion further turned her on.

In one swift movement, he flipped her onto her front. Gabi pressed her lips together to prevent herself from scolding him for being so rough.

"Get on your knees," he said in a low, authoritative tone.

She swallowed and did as she was told. She was unsure whether she liked his bossiness, or whether she preferred his gentler, endearing side.

He hooked his hands around her waist, pulling her buttocks higher. With her face pressed against the mattress, her legs quivered as he spread them wider. As his fingers met her wetness, plunging in and then withdrawing, she felt the cool air in absence, making her sex flutter. She glanced over her shoulder to see that he was crouched down. Then she felt the flicker of his wide, wet tongue meeting her clit. With slow, firm strokes, he licked her repeatedly. When the rhythm increased, Gabi gasped, squirming impatiently, pushing her behind upwards.

"Gabi," a strangled cry met her ears. She liked the sound of her name spilling from his lips. He had a way of making it sound erotic.

She tensed for a second when she felt his finger slip inside. Before she had time to properly welcome it, another finger spread her wider, and then another. Her breath caught in her throat as his fingers pummeled in and out of her several times. It felt so good. When he stopped, she shot him a questioning stare. He sat on the heels of his feet, openly admiring her.

She felt her sex throb, a needy ache swirling in her stomach. She hated how he always tantalised her, making her wait, to plead to be pleasured. Resuming his position between her legs, he parted her with his thumbs. Gabi threw her head back as his tongue dipped in. The tip of it met her inner walls, lapping her up, feasting on her. His satisfied grunts sent vibrations through her.

"Oh, Darion…" she whimpered. She didn't know whether it was him or the mind-blowing sex that had her hooked. She decided it was probably both. She liked the way he made her feel. Without him she knew she'd feel empty, knowing what she'd be missing out on. In the short time she'd known him; he was an expert when it came to her body. He knew exactly which buttons to press. Rather than foreplay simply being a lead up to sex, to get her ready, Darion enjoyed it. He liked exploring her body, every inch of it.

He sucked harder and faster, basking in her taste, and she knew that by pleasuring her, it pleasured him. He inserted his fingers again deeply. Gabi clamped her lips together as he pounded in and out relentlessly.

When she heard frustrated moans coming from him, she noticed that he had gripped his erection. He tugged on it, jerking up and down. His features screwed up in what was obvious ecstasy. She could see the muscles tensing in his broad shoulders with each pump of his hand. Her body writhed in delight as his fingers continued to fill her. Her breathing was now erratic, and judging by his groans, which had become louder, she knew that he was close.

Her body trembled, urgently needing release.

"Darion, come here."

When Darion plunged into her powerfully, she screamed out, gripping the bed sheets. His length made her sore as it slammed against her inner walls. Her body finally accepted it, stretching, widening, wanting more. His cock was smooth, and she could feel it pulsing inside her. As he pounded fast, gripping her hips, she whimpered involuntarily. He then released one hand to grip hold of her hair roughly so her head was forced back, an ache persisting in her throat. She swallowed. How could something feel so good but so bad at the same time? She experienced moments of discomfort as he slammed in deeper.

Low satisfactory grunts came from him as he pleasured himself selfishly, wanting release. With a hand still grabbing fistfuls of her hair, his other hand cupped her buttocks with his nails. Then he let go to land a slap on her behind. Gabi gasped at the sharp sensation. She didn't get a moment to brace herself for the next one. She heard the sound of him whacking her again, this time more forcefully, causing her cheek to sting and burn. Another slap came into contact in the same area. She clenched her teeth. *Ow!*

"You like it rough, Gabi?" he panted, knowing full well she did—at times.

He thrust in, then out, in, and then out. Gabi rocked upwards, her sex meeting his cock. She gripped the edge of the bed, her chest heaving with her heavy breathing. Her whole body was slammed forwards continuously as he ravaged her.

"Fuuuuuck," he growled, slamming into her so hard and fast as if he was punishing her. Gabi clamped her lips together to muffle her cries. "So...fucking...good," he said hoarsely, in between each and every thrust.

Gabi's insides throbbed, clenching around him. She writhed fervently, before stilling on a few deep breaths. As delightful spasms spread through her, she came fiercely with a mournful sob.

"Ahhh..." Darion threw his head back with a groan. He continued to grind into her until he came with a roar, coming violently inside her. He gripped her buttocks, pulling her into him, and she felt the pulsing of his cock.

When he'd finally finished, she collapsed onto the bed, needing her heartbeat to resume to normal, for her body to stop tingling, and the soreness on her buttocks to subside. She was physically drained. Darion rolled her over so that she was on her back. His body dropped onto hers, and she liked the naked feel of skin on skin. She could feel the thudding of his heart against her own. She was breathless, aching.

After five minutes of lying there, Gabi broke the

silence. "Darion, do you ever think about the future?" When he disentangled himself, she lifted the bed covers and clambered underneath their warmth.

"I prefer to live each day as it comes."

"I like to plan things. I like to have an idea of where I'm headed." *Otherwise I worry and I'm restless.*

"Gabi, an idea and the reality of that idea can be two different things. The future is uncertain for everyone." He swept his hair back with his hand. "We could get hit by a bus tomorrow, discover a life-threatening illness, lose someone we know. Enjoy every moment whilst it lasts." He buried himself under the covers. "And don't take life too seriously. None of us get out alive." His mouth curved upwards, humor twinkling in his irises.

Gabi lay down. At first she had been attracted to Darion's outlook on life. Sometimes though, she believed it was irresponsible and careless. Yet he must have been responsible at some point in his life. The man owned his own business. Maybe he was now afraid of making future plans incase they went wrong, or didn't live up to his expectations. Or maybe he was confused about what he actually wanted in life.

She had craved excitement and hadn't minded Darion's unpredictable nature. She had escaped her previous relationship, which had made her rethink the whole marriage and kids thing. Yet it just proved that Lawrence obviously hadn't been the right man for her, because if he was, she would have wanted those things with him. She knew she wanted those things with Darion if their relationship lasted, and they overcame certain obstacles. But did he want all that?

Gabi wanted nothing more than for Darion to open up to her. Until he did, she would forever feel in limbo. She prayed he wouldn't start neglecting her, like Lawrence had. She did need the security. She needed to feel they were on the same page.

Turning to face him, she saw a glazed, faraway look in his eyes again. He was focused on the wall before him. She called out his name, which didn't break his gaze.

"Darion," she repeated, even louder, squeezing his arm lightly.

He met her stare and rubbed the back of his neck, as if in discomfort, to alleviate the pain.

"What's the matter?"

"Nothing's the matter."

"Darion, you've been distant all night. Talk to me. Is it work? Is it Gina leaving? Your ex-wife? What?" She exhaled heavily, losing her patience.

He leant back slowly. "It's all of those things."

Oh. "Well, can I do anything to help?"

"No, darlin'." He cupped her face in his hands, causing her lips to pucker up. He pressed his mouth firmly against hers. He kissed her a few times before pulling away. "Everything will be okay in the end." His tone shook with emotion, not at all sounding confident.

The end would be okay for whom? As his fingers entwined with hers, she wondered whether it was just a matter of time until she got her happy ending, or whether Darion would become bored, and move onto his next conquest.

Chapter
Twenty-Seven

Gabi sat in her office, a doughnut to her lips, and a steaming coffee before her. Her day had been productive so far, although her troubled mood hadn't subsided. Placing the doughnut on a napkin, she rested her head against the back of her chair, inhaling and exhaling slowly. The rest of the weekend with Darion had been pleasant. They'd watched a movie at the cinemas on Saturday night, and Sunday afternoon, they had strolled around Westhaven checking out the sights it had to offer. She'd just closed her eyes when a tap at the door disturbed her.

Tara, the receptionist entered. In her hands was a beautiful bouquet of red roses. As she placed them before Gabi, the sweet aroma filled her nostrils. Gabi thanked her, and picked out the card. Unfolding it, she read it. She couldn't refrain from smiling as warmth filled her.

She shoved the card in her top drawer and lifted

the roses closer to her nose. She breathed in the scent again. Her fingers ran across the smooth petals. Was this Darion showing his romantic side, or were they flowers to say sorry for his distant behavior?

She was about to call him when Mallory entered. Closing the door behind her gently, she dropped down onto the seat opposite.

"Oooh. Is Darion showing his sweet side?" she teased.

"Or his sorry side." Gabi softly laughed.

"What would he have to be sorry about?" Mallory tore a corner off the doughnut and popped it into her mouth.

Gabi's pursed her lips. "It's nothing major. He's just really quiet lately, like shutting me out. I know there's something on his mind, but he doesn't tell me anything, Mal." She rested her elbows on the table. She hadn't realised she'd been tapping her Louboutin-clad foot until Mallory regarded her suspiciously. She stopped instantly. "Does Steve tell you everything?"

"Honestly, Gabi…" She nodded. "Pretty much, yes. If something is bothering either of us, we share."

"Why does Darion feel that he can't open up to me?" She folded her arms across her chest.

"Darion's obviously a private person."

Gabi shot her a look.

Mallory laughed. "You know what I mean." She picked up the top page of a manuscript and examined it. "Has he got problems at the minute? Or do you think he's hiding something?"

She shrugged a shoulder. "Both, I think."

"And you've tried talking to him?"

"Yes."

"I don't know what to suggest, Gab. Maybe the longer you're together, the more he'll let you in."

"Maybe." Gabi touched a key on her computer keyboard to check if she had any new emails. "So, how's everything with you?"

"Everything is great. Steve's new job is perfect for him. The extra money doesn't hurt." She beamed. "We're thinking of going to the Maldives some time this year."

Gabi groaned. "What I would do to be lying on a beach with a cocktail."

"Maybe you and Darion could go to one of those swinger resorts abroad. A nudist beach," she teased.

"You're a cow." Gabi had to laugh or else she'd cry. *My crazy fucking life,* she thought.

"Have you seen his slutty ex recently?"

"No." Gabi shot up in her seat, suddenly remembering Eva's warning. "I forgot to tell you what happened."

Mallory sat up straighter, eager for gossip, as always.

"I saw her at the club, and guess what she said to me, Mal?"

"What?"

"She basically said that if I don't keep my man happy, then someone else will."

"What a bitch," she spat. "Well, fortunately for you, you do keep your man happy."

Do I really?

Mallory glanced at the wall clock, and eased

185

herself off the chair. "Anyway, we better go visit Suzie again soon, drop some baby gifts around."

Gabi grinned. "Baby clothes shopping," she squealed excitedly. "I'm up for that, just let me know when."

"I will. I better get back to work before Phil does his rounds and fires me."

"He would never. He's too sweet."

"To you, yes. Our parents can't all know the boss and ensure we have a cushy little office." She laughed.

Gabi stuck her tongue out playfully. "See you later."

"Bye, sweet cheeks."

When Mallory left the office, Gabi couldn't stop from grinning. She was genuinely pleased for her friends. Suzie was soon to be a wonderful mother, and Mallory was planning a romantic getaway. She knew she would be as broody as hell when she saw Suzie's baby for the first time, and she'd be desperate for a holiday when Mallory shared the thousand photographs she would definitely take in the Maldives. Grabbing hold of her pen, she chewed the end, deep in thought. Maybe she and Darion could take a trip somewhere. Explore London or something.

Leaning back on her chair, she caught sight of the telephone on her desk. She abruptly sat up and reached for it, forgetting that she hadn't thanked him for the flowers. Cradling the telephone in the crook of her neck, she tapped in his number. The sound of the dialing tone filled her ears, followed by Darion's smooth sounding voice.

"Gabi."

"Hi." She swiveled in her chair to face the window. The sky was blue for a change, without any clouds to spoil it. The sun was beaming, flooding through the office. She could feel the heat of it on her face. Summer was upon them, and she prayed it would be a decent one, weather-wise. England could be so unpredictable, raining for weeks, and then bright the next, and then back to rain. She wanted to wear summer dresses and flip-flops, take leisurely walks in town, and visit new places. The Lake District sounded appealing with its picturesque hills, lake, and quaint little shops. Then again, she knew it was about time she visited her parents in Mayfair, London.

"Hello?" Darion's voice broke her thoughts.

"Hi." She smiled. "I wanted to thank you for the flowers. They're beautiful."

"You're welcome." She heard a harsh blowing sound and guessed he was smoking.

"What's the occasion?"

"They were going cheap at the corner shop."

Gabi threw her head back with a laugh. "Seriously?"

"I'm joking, Gabi. There's no particular reason."

"So, how's your day going?"

"Not bad," he responded.

She chewed her lip. Darion and his short answers. She'd probably have more luck getting blood out of a stone. "Busy day?" she pried.

"Yeah. We've revamped the website, had a delivery of new leaflets, sorted advertising, booked a decorator to paint the club. It's all coming together." The enthusiasm in his tone was apparent.

"I'm glad to hear it." She meant it regardless of her dislike for the club. At least he was putting his attention on other things, rather than dwelling over Eva and Gina. He sounded a lot more positive, which was an improvement from being withdrawn lately.

"So, what do you wanna do this weekend?" he asked.

"I don't mind. We have all week to decide." As long as she was with him, that was all that mattered. She could be at a bar with him, watching a movie, or eating out and she would feel blessed.

"What are you doing later?"

"I'll probably have a relaxing bath, read a book. You?"

"I might cook up something nice and watch a film." He was quiet for a moment before adding, "Well, I'll leave you to get some work done."

"Okay."

"See ya, Gabi."

"Bye."

She rose to her feet and stood before the window, taking in the busy street below. The sound of cars, talking, and laughter filled the air. She watched as a couple walked by, hand in hand. They paused to kiss one another, and then embraced. Eventually going in different directions, they turned to look back at one another a final time, huge smiles plastered on their faces. Gabi's heart swelled.

She returned to her desk when her mobile bleeped. Darion. As she read the content, a shiver ran down her spine, her stomach twisting in knots.

Collapsing on her chair, she tossed the rest of her doughnut in the bin, having lost her appetite. Her mood instantly plummeted. She felt sick, although she didn't know why she was surprised. She knew it was only a matter of time before Darion wanted to liven up their relationship, let loose, and make her a part of *his* world.

Darion: *We could have fun at the club this weekend? ;) D xx*

So he was craving swinging, craving the playrooms, craving other women. She swallowed the bile that rose in her throat. She knew he'd never force her into doing something she felt uncomfortable doing, but she also knew he'd be disappointed if she wasn't willing to try new things. Would he think she was boring, unadventurous? Could she step out of her comfort zone and give Darion what he wanted? Could she satisfy him enough?

Fuck! She scratched her head. If there was a button to switch off her feelings for him, she was pretty certain she'd press it at that moment in time. But there wasn't. Her feelings for him were too strong. She was still at the stage where she couldn't get enough of him, and enjoyed every single second spent with him—even the times when he pissed her off royally.

She hated that love made her weak. It made her consider doing things that she never usually would.

She wished he could be happy with visiting the playrooms, and them soft swinging—not agreeing to penetration with other people. She could just about handle getting frisky with others whilst he observed. But to actually have full sexual intercourse with someone else in the same room with Darion, whilst he did the same, it didn't even bear thinking about.

It was her worst nightmare.

Chapter Twenty-Eight

Darion

Darion placed a card on the table, and looked at Lennie and Travis, trying to read their expressions, to see if they were winning or losing. Several cards were placed on the table before them, along with wads of cash, and bottles of beer. They were seated at the club, near the stage, too engrossed in their game to even notice the new barmaid Jasmine appear. Eva had hired her.

It had been a while since Darion had properly enjoyed Travis and Lennie's company. He'd been so concerned with other issues going on in his life, or too infatuated with Gabi, that he'd neglected his friends.

He felt his tense body slowly start to relax as the game continued. *That's it,* he thought, swigging back half of his beer, *keep your mind occupied and you won't dwell on Eva-problems.* Placing a card down, he snatched up his tin of cigars and offered one around the table. They accepted. Darion stuffed a cigar in his mouth, lit it, and handed Lennie the lighter.

Jasmine stood near their table, swaying her hips, and running her hands through her ash-blonde hair. Darion hated being disturbed in the middle of a game.

He placed a card down. Jasmine stepped closer to him, leaning into him, her cleavage mere inches away from his nose. Her blue eyes sparkled at him, a cheeky smile sweeping across her face.

"Are you winning or losing?" she asked, picking up some empty bottles.

He leant back, evaluating her. She was pretty. Before he got the chance to respond, he felt his mobile vibrating in his pocket. Glancing at the screen, he realised it was Gabi. He pressed the decline button quickly. Jasmine laughed loudly, turning away from him so he got a view of her firm ass in a tiny black skirt.

"Daz, let's finish the fucking game, yeah?" Lennie snapped, growing impatient.

"Jasmine," Darion said softly. "How about you get back behind the bar?"

"Sure. I'm just collecting the empties, boss." She shook the bottles in front of his face before sauntering off.

His mobile rang again. Gabi.

"Call her back," Travis told him. "I'm close to beating your ass. I can feel it."

"We'll see. I reckon I've got you, Trav." He grinned confidently as he checked over the decent hand that he'd been dealt.

Five minutes later, Darion kissed a hundred pounds good-bye. Lennie walked away a winner. Finishing the last of their beers, Lennie and Travis returned to working on the door of the club as it began to slowly fill with people.

At the bar, Darion pulled out a stool, and ordered a bottle of Corona. As he waited for Jasmine to get his drink, he scanned the club. It was fairly busy. The customers all seemed to be enjoying themselves, and there weren't any lousy drunks he had to chuck out. Maybe it'd be a smooth night. He hoped so. When Jasmine handed him his drink, he downed a quarter of it back.

"Lex, have you heard anything from Gina?" he asked her as she approached him. He realised that he missed Gina.

"Nope." She pulled herself onto the counter of the bar and sat on it. "I thought she would have called you."

Darion took out his mobile and clicked on Gina's name. Holding it to his ear, he was surprised to receive an automated voicemail message stating she was unavailable. He ended the call, shoving the mobile back in his pocket.

"It's not working." He ran his hands up and down his face. "I hope she's okay."

"She will be."

He was silent, his fingers drumming on the bar. "What's she like?" He nodded toward Jasmine.

"She's a hard worker. She's sweet."

"Good. Eva did something right for once."

He rose to his feet with a yawn and stretched his

limbs. His body was aching. He'd been nonstop working lately, catching up on emails, membership applications, and organising private party bookings. He knew that a cool shower would do him a world of good.

Hearing a familiar loud laugh, he stopped in his tracks. He felt goosebumps trail across his body, his heartbeat quickening. He thought he'd told her to stay upstairs.

As suspected, he saw Eva propped on a stool, talking with Jasmine, who was behind the bar, cradling a glass of liquor. Noticing him, she straightened her posture, and flicked her hair back. Apprehension filled her eyes. Jasmine scrambled away, leaving them to it.

"What are you doing here, Eva?"

"I thought I'd come in early today," she replied.

"I mean, what are you doing here…downstairs." His tone was stern as he felt himself getting agitated.

"Don't be like that, Daz." She stood up, towering an extra six inches in her heels. "Can we just be civil, please?" she pleaded.

He removed his cigarettes from his pocket. Feeling for a lighter, he grumbled when he realised he'd forgotten it. Stepping behind the bar, he took the club's personalised black strip of matches and retrieved one. Lighting his fag, he took a long, slow drag, the smoke then drifting from his lips. He felt Eva watching him.

"Don't you have work to do?" Inside he felt a sick, acidic feeling in his stomach. He pulled out a stool, fearing he'd lose control any moment, and pick a fight, the hateful words he had for her spilling out.

"Like I said," she paused, taking a sip of her drink, "I'm early."

"Whatever," he grunted. "Like me, you pick and choose your shifts."

"Darion," she said sternly. "Whether I come here in the day, or night, I ensure I do my eight hours, like you do. Don't worry about that."

"Well, take your drink upstairs. I told you, I run things down here."

She shook her head, an expression of disbelief on her face. "I was getting to know Jasmine. As joint owner, don't I have the right to get to know my staff?"

He remained silent, smoking his cigarette.

"Look." She sighed heavily. "We got off to a bad start when I returned. Can we start over?"

Stubbing his cigarette in the ashtray, he made his way behind the bar again, pouring himself a large whisky. Back on his stool, he surveyed the room. He noticed Lexi on the stage, and Marnie leading a client into a private booth. Wendy was on the stage, slowly removing her top.

"Whatever."

"Don't be so grouchy. By the way, did you check the club's bookings?"

"No, why?"

"We're fully booked, Daz...for the next five months. Every single weekend is jam packed with no less than a party of fifty."

"How did you manage that?" He hid the surprise from his face.

"The new distributor I hired has five years' experience. He added like ten businesses in addition to the ones we already had to stock the leaflets."

He nodded slowly.

"We have an ad in five magazines, which have weekly releases. And the website now has a video tour of the playrooms, and it's had thousands of views. People like it."

"Sounds like it's all coming together."

"It is." She swept her hair off her face. "I'm looking forward to this month's fucking paycheck." She giggled.

"Solo Dancing" by Indiana now boomed from the speakers. Eva squealed and jumped to her feet. She rocked her hips from side to side, dancing. She stated that it was one of her favourite songs, her stare fixed on Darion. For some strange reason, he couldn't tear his eyes away. As she ran her fingers down her collarbone, her chest, her stomach, and thighs, he found himself mesmerised. That familiar body. That familiar dance. The way she used to strip for him, teasing him, slowly removing her clothes item by item. As if seeing right through her clothes to the tattoos that he used to run his tongue along, he swallowed, hating what his raging hormones were doing to him.

Eva took a few steps forward until she was before him, still dancing. He found himself leaning back slightly to evaluate her, devouring every inch of her body. Eva's smile turned dangerously sexy. She was the sort of woman that knew she was a catch, and didn't mean to let anyone forget it. She had an air about her exuding trouble.

Leaning into him to create a bond of intimacy, she kissed her hand, and blew a kiss at him. His heart was galloping in his chest, his palms becoming damp with sweat. He shifted on the stool when she spun around, giving him a full view of her firm, shapely behind. Darion licked his lips to moisten them, trying to ignore the leaping sensation in his stomach, and his cock that was straining against his jeans.

When the song ended, he blinked a couple of times, feeling himself being pulled back to reality. Rubbing his forehead, he stood up, a mixture of rage and panic returning.

"Get to work, Eva," his voice came out sharp, vicious sounding as heat flooded his face.

"Relax." Eva giggled, flinging her arms around his neck and pressing her body against his. "Everything is running smoothly upstairs. I checked."

He removed her arms and glared at her. Turning his back, he drained back the last of his drink.

"Don't be so uptight, Daz. What happened to that fun, carefree man I used to know and—"

"Don't." He held a palm up, indicating for her to be silent.

"Fine. Suit yourself." She shrugged. "I really wish we could get along," she said, shaking her head vehemently. "For the sake of the club, at least."

He didn't respond.

"Things would be so much easier if only I could work out what was going on in that head of yours," she purred, with a little wink.

Darion felt the blood rushing to his face. The way she observed him made him feel as if she really could see right into his head, like she knew he'd fantasised about her. Feeling his chest tighten, he felt a sudden need to leave the room. Turning on his heel, he made his way toward the exit.

"Yeah, you keep running, Darion," he heard her yell after him. "One day you're gonna realise that me returning was the best thing that ever happened!"

As he stepped out into the chilly evening air, he took out his mobile to call a taxi. Now he did need that cool shower more than anything. He wanted to wash away the smell of Eva's perfume that he was sure was lingering on his clothes. Maybe he was just imagining it. He didn't want to take any chances. If only washing traces away of her was as easy as getting rid of her.

Chapter Twenty-Nine

Gabi

Friday night appeared faster than Gabi had expected. Usually she would have been glad of the weekend being upon her; however this time she was overwhelmed with anxiety. She spritzed some perfume on her wrists and gently stroked one against her neck. Her blonde waves had been scooped up and arranged into a messy pile, with a few strands hanging loose. She'd decided to wear a short white dress, with buttons all the way up the front. The colour complimented her golden skin. It made her look almost pure, virginal.

She supposed she was virginal when it came to the antics in the playrooms, for she could bet that Darion would be ensuring she tried everything once. Taking her red Mac lipstick from the dressing table, she stained her lips with it, making them instantly appear fuller, sexier.

Although she looked as if she exuded confidence, inside she was a nervous wreck. She willed her hands to stop shaking, and her burning cheeks to cool. She'd helped herself to a quarter of a bottle of wine, hoping it'd give her Dutch courage. Taking a massive breath, she grabbed her white clutch bag, and made her way to the living room.

"If you don't keep your man happy, someone else will." Eva's words echoed in her mind. She could do this. She could give swinging a good go. She could satisfy Darion's needs. She could prove Eva wrong, that she was more than capable of keeping her man happy, especially sexually.

She was relieved when Darion called her to say he was parked outside. The quicker she got to the club, the quicker she could down another strong drink, and face her fears. She exited the apartment, locked the front door, and climbed into Darion's Audi.

She got an instant whiff of his masculine aftershave as soon as she sat beside him. She took him in. He was wearing black jeans and a black shirt. His hair was gelled back, and he'd shaved, so only a millimeter of stubble shadowed his jaw line. He always made more of an effort on his appearance when it came to participating in the playrooms.

Her stomach tightened hard with longing, her pulse quickening. She linked her fingers together in a bid to stop herself from grabbing him and kissing him greedily. She had all night for that.

She felt the weight of his intense stare, as if he

were undressing her with his sweeping eyes, a raw and animalistic lust in them. Gabi could feel the chemistry between them thick in the air. The admiration and desire was apparent on his face.

As if by a magnetic force, he possessed her with his mouth, his tongue crashing against hers, exploring. Her pleasured moans met his. Gabi massaged his rock-hard erection through his trousers, whilst Darion slipped his hand under her dress, rubbing firmly between her legs.

"Mmmm…" he murmured breathlessly.

Gabi rocked against his hand, silently screaming inside for him to push her underwear aside and penetrate her with his fingers. Delicious shivers ran through her body. She felt her sex quivering as it became moist with arousal. She fumbled with the zipper of his jeans, desperate to stroke her hand along his smooth shaft.

"Darlin'." He withdrew his hand, a dangerous smirk crossing his face. "Let's continue this at the club."

Feeling herself sink into her chair, she removed her hand and sulked. Why did he tease her and get her so worked up if he wouldn't give her the pleasure of immediate release? Her core tightened, and she felt the burning, needy ache between her legs, unsure of how she'd manage the journey. She was so turned on she feared she'd explode.

"Let's go inside," she pleaded. "We can do it again at the club."

He snagged his lower lip between his teeth. "It'll be better if we hold it off…trust me."

She knew he was right. Their climax would be

more intense if they waited. Darion turned his head to focus on the road, and started the engine. The stereo screamed to life, "I Get Off" by Halestorm came from the speakers. The song heightened her raging hormones, making her want to ravage Darion to the sexual lyrics.

As they made their way through the darkness of the night, both of them were silent, taking in the music. Darion's eyes were dancing with merriment, obviously eager for what was to come. Gabi drummed her fingers on her clutch bag, doing anything but keeping still. With a sharp intake of breath, she opened her window a little, desperate for the coldness of the air. Her whole body was heated, and she was unsure whether it was because she was dreading the playrooms, or because she was sexually frustrated.

"Gabi?"

"Yeah?"

"If we decide to go all the way…don't forget the rules in the playrooms," he began, his voice stern.

"I know, I know," she cut in. "No separating, and no sex unless we both agree, and safe sex *always*."

"Good girl."

He was now gripping the steering wheel. Gabi studied him. He was chewing on his bottom lip. She'd never betray him and break the rules in the playrooms like Eva. She wished he could trust her.

"I don't think I'm ready to go all the way."

He looked at her, his features softening. "We'll do whatever you're ready for. This is for *both* our pleasure."

"I need to take it one step at a time."

He nodded in agreement. "You can lead the way, Gabi."

She slouched in the chair, backing her head against the headrest, and stared at the road ahead. What room should she choose? Which people should she get intimate with? Same-sex, singles, or other couples? Her mind raced with hundreds of thoughts. Perhaps she should just go with the flow, try and relax, and enjoy the experience.

"I wonder if Audrina will be there." She perked up a tad. She'd felt comfortable with her, and a rematch could be the best way of escaping getting intimate with strangers.

"Maybe."

She noticed Darion's lips tilt into a smile, making her flush with jealousy. There were the uneasy thoughts again—wondering if he fancied other women more than her, whether they were better sexually, more experienced, better looking. She rubbed her forehead, trying to dismiss it. She was the woman he was going home with, the woman he was in a committed relationship with, the woman he said he loved.

"It's gonna be weird to eventually see you with another man," he said, his face unreadable.

She watched as he straightened his posture, as if stretching out a stiff back. Gabi felt herself relax a little, knowing that he could be as worried and unsettled as she was made her feel better. Giving her up to other men obviously wasn't as easy as he'd thought. It must have panicked him a little, although he got off on it simultaneously.

"Yeah," she agreed. "It will be weird to

eventually see you with another woman." She concentrated on the road once more.

"Our relationship is strong. We'll get through it. We'll enjoy it."

She doubted he even convinced himself, let alone her.

Chapter Thirty

Darion

Darion tightened his hold on Gabi's hand. They were mounting the stairs at The Black Door. Eva had been warned to steer clear that night, so he felt nothing but an excited rush at having some fun with Gabi. Having a loving relationship and being able to sexually explore and be open with his girlfriend, and still do as he pleased, no restrictions, was most men's fantasy, he believed. He really did have the best of both worlds.

He pushed open the door and stepped inside. Rock n' roll music filled his ears. A red erotic glow cast over the room, over the luxurious décor, the bar area, and dance floor. The newly painted black walls with specs of glitter shimmered glamorously. The crowd was relaxed and lively at the same time, with people either sitting and chatting, or dancing, complete with drinks in their hands. There were couples, singles, people of all professions, all ages, shapes, and sizes. He noticed a couple of rich A-list celebrities in one of the VIP booths.

The magazine advertisements, revamped website, marketing strategies online, and in public *had* obviously worked wonders. Eva had been right. He hadn't seen the place so busy in years. The profit turn over would be decent, he knew it. In respect of entrance fees, single women had the lowest fee, couples slightly higher, and single men the highest price. Then there was the money coming in for the beverages, and he could see that every single table was loaded with beers, cocktails, and expensive champagne.

Darion could feel the sexual tension in the air, as one thing everybody was doing was flirting.

After he'd greeted Tiana at the door—his employee who monitored the membership list—he made his way toward the bar. Hungry, predatory eyes from both women and men swept over him. Darion instantly felt his ego swell. Some of them knew he owned the club, and some didn't. Darion didn't like to make a big fuss about it, as it sometimes had the affect of intimidating people. He didn't want that. He wanted everybody to feel at complete ease.

Turning to look at Gabi, he flashed her a smile, and noticed she was curiously eyeing the room. He slipped an arm around her waist and ordered them drinks at the bar.

"It's busy tonight."

"Yeah. It is," Gabi agreed, eagerly reaching for her glass of white wine.

Darion turned back to face the crowd. He took in women: brunettes, blondes, redheads—the lot. He noticed several that he wouldn't have minded getting up close and personal with.

"Shall we go and sit in a booth?" he asked Gabi.

"Why not?"

He wove through the bustling crowd. The booth in the corner, which was a small seating area, was always kept reserved for Darion. He grinned at the bartender that rushed over, asking if he wanted any other drinks. He asked her politely to fetch a bottle of champagne. He felt like going all out.

Dropping onto a red velvet sofa, he placed his whisky on the table and reached for his tin of cigars. Gabi sat next to him, and he couldn't help but notice that she was tense. Wasn't she as excited as he was at what the night would bring? He took a long puff of his cigar.

"You okay?" he asked, prior to blowing smoke from the corner of his mouth.

She nodded.

"If you feel uncomfortable we can go. Remember, I will *never* pressure you into doing something you don't wanna do."

"I'm fine." She beamed. "Just need a few drinks to calm my nerves first."

At that moment, the bartender returned with a bottle of champagne in a silver bucket of ice, complete with four glasses. She knew it was certain they'd soon have company. Darion poured himself and Gabi a generous glass. Then he sat further back on the couch, relaxing, super proud of the club. He wondered which room to visit. Maybe he and Gabi would visit them all. He had no idea how far she was willing to take it.

Taking another drag on his cigar, his eyes locked with those of a beautiful redhead. She flashed him a flirtatious smile. He took the cigar between his fingers, and grinned back at her slowly. He felt the pace of his heartbeat grow faster. His breath caught in his throat as lust jolted through him. He sat straighter, intrigued, when she seductively skimmed her collarbone with her fingers, prior to landing on her breast, teasingly.

He continued to stare at her, silently daring her not to avert her gaze. Placing the cigar between his lips, he took another puff, and blew the smoke out slowly, causing it to swirl around him, obscuring his view. When his line of sight was clear again, she was gone.

He doused his cigar in the ashtray, picked up his drink, and turned to Gabi. He'd expected her to be focused on him, either insanely jealous and aroused, or furious, revealing her sexy, dark side. She was neither. She was laughing at something an attractive man was saying to her. On closer inspection, Darion noticed he was an actor he'd seen on television a few times. He felt himself grow a little faint with envy. Taking a sip of his drink, he put it down and slicked back his hair with his hand.

"Who's that?" he asked, sliding his fingers up and down Gabi's leg possessively, warning the man that Gabi was *his*. Then he felt ridiculous. It was a swingers club, it was what they were there for—to mingle and all do as they pleased sexually. He couldn't keep Gabi to himself. It was not only hypocritical of him, but completely out of character. He'd never had a problem sharing before.

"It's Jayce Carter," she replied. "He's from that show, *Those Were The Days*."

"I see."

"He's asked if he can join us." Gabi's expression was blank and he had no idea what she was thinking. "He's with his girlfriend," she added.

He felt his muscles relax a little, and told Gabi he was fine with it. Jayce welcomed him with a nod of the head, and sat on the sofa opposite them, his girlfriend following suit. Jayce was extremely handsome in a clean shaven pretty-boy way, and his brunette girlfriend was equally attractive. If Gabi was drawn to Jayce, maybe he would be the one to make her feel more comfortable in the playrooms.

"Do you want some champagne?" he asked them.

"Sure."

Gabi leant over to pour them both a glass. Darion got an eyeful of her perfect cleavage, encased in a red silk bra. He groaned inwardly. He couldn't wait to get his hands on her. He noticed that Jayce had noticed, a seemingly satisfied smile on his lips. Gabi handed them their drinks, and flicked back her blonde hair.

Darion snaked his arm around her waist, pulling her closer to him. She took hold of his hand and squeezed it, due to nervousness, or happiness, he had no idea. He brushed his lips against hers softly.

He waited patiently whilst the girls made small talk. He and Jayce knew the score, knew what they wanted. It was the women that needed to get familiar with one another in order to feel at ease. Within ten minutes, they were giggling away, the alcohol obviously having kicked in. Darion was relieved when Jayce suggested they take the conversation elsewhere.

He didn't miss Gabi's eyes widening, and a flicker of worry crossed her face. It was normal. He'd been like that the first few times he had experienced swinging. He knew that when Gabi adapted to his world, she would enjoy it as much as he did. How could she not enjoy being brought to pleasures she had never known?

"Remember, darlin'…" He leant closer to her, running his thumb gently across her bottom lip. "You lead the way."

Chapter Thirty-One

Gabi

With a sharp intake of breath, Gabi slowly rose to her feet. As she turned and took in the black door at the back of the room, she felt her stomach flip with nerves. She closed her lids for a second, regaining her composure. *I can do this,* she told herself. *Eva is wrong. I can keep my man happy.*

She followed Darion down the strip of red carpet toward the playrooms. Darion had told her she could lead the way; therefore she could choose the room. She didn't fancy stripping off to her underwear and getting in the hot tub like last time. Nor did she fancy fumbling around in the dark room, where everyone just felt around, and got on with it, trying to join in with her and Darion.

"Maybe we can check out the room with the four beds," she said to Darion softly, having made up her mind. At least the beds were widely spread apart, so

211

you couldn't really make out what the other couples were doing. It seemed a little more private as could be in that sort of place.

"Whatever you want, Gabi."

Darion nodded at the security guard, Travis, and entered the corridor which led to the rooms. Jayce and his girlfriend Leah were searched by Travis, to ensure they didn't have any recording devices or cameras, and then they were standing next to them. Gabi felt her cheeks heat, and was relieved the red ceiling spotlights would have camouflaged it. Digging her nails into her hands, she braved peering into the rooms on either side of her.

In the room to her left, a naked couple were having intercourse, whilst several others watched. The floor was also occupied with people pleasuring one another, all underneath a large ceiling mirror.

As the man pounding into the woman on the bed looked up, Gabi turned away, coyly. Meanwhile, Jayce, Leah, and Darion stood rooted to the spot, transfixed on them, the dark hunger on their faces clearly apparent. Gabi wished she had another drink to hand.

Turning on her heel, she peered into the room on her right. The hot tub was full of writhing bodies, as suspected. Continuing down the hall, she froze when she came to the room which resembled a dungeon. She was unable to stop her mouth from falling open. A man was strapped against the wall, whilst a woman wearing a PVC cat-suit whipped him forcefully. Gabi could see the red indents in his skin where the whip had lashed him. He had a ball-gag stuffed in his mouth to keep him quiet, and a leather eye-mask restricting his vision.

Gabi swallowed the lump that appeared in her throat, and licked her dry lips to moisten them. She stared at the scene before her, feeling utterly bewildered. A woman was sitting naked in the leather sex-swing, her legs apart, whilst a man penetrated her. She caught sight of another woman with her wrists and ankles tied up, on all fours, whilst several people pleasured her, hands everywhere. Her glazed eyes met Gabi's, to which she took a step back. How did she not feel degraded, dirty? But then she guessed that was the whole point—fulfilling kinky desires.

Her heart slammed in her chest. Darion startled her by placing his hand on her waist. He asked if she was ready. She nodded. Her breath held tight inside her with anticipation. Her palms were damp, shaking slightly. She tried to stop her mind racing by telling herself that she had been in the playrooms before, enjoyed them even. *Do only what you're comfortable with.*

"Gabi." Darion eyed her cautiously, his tone soft and soothing. "If you're having second thoughts, we can leave."

She sucked in air, gathering her courage. "I'm fine." She manufactured a smile.

His mouth curled wickedly, his irises darkened with desire as he destroyed her with a slow sweeping look. Gabi felt her confidence soar at the way Darion wanted her so much, the way he made her feel so sexy, so desired. She felt the stirrings of lust, and couldn't wait to get her hands on him.

A low laugh escaped from his lips, as if he knew

what she was thinking. Before she knew it, he had his hands in her hair, and his mouth hard on her lips, kissing her urgently, hungrily. As his tongue roamed in her mouth, sending her heart racing, and goosebumps spreading over her body, she felt herself being backed into one of the rooms.

As she kissed him and unbuttoned his shirt, she fell back onto a large round bed. She forgot everyone and everything around her but Darion, the feel of his smooth kiss, his warm, leisurely licking tongue, the smell of his musky aftershave, and manly hands skimming under her dress. Her stomach somersaulted as his hand stroked between her legs.

She yanked the clip out of her hair, allowing it to tumble down her back. Darion playfully nipped her lip. *How sexy can one man be?* she thought, tearing his shirt off, studying his body. She ran her tongue up the middle of his chest slowly. Then she caught his nipple in her mouth, and circled it with her tongue. Darion let out a low grunt as she flicked over it faster, sucking it. Pulling back, she placed a trail of firm kisses across to his other nipple, capturing it between her lips. Darion tensed, grinding his teeth, his senses clearly reeling, as much as her own.

I can keep my man happy. The words echoed in her mind.

When he opened her dress, exposing her red underwear, she searched for Jayce and Leah. They were lying next to them, only inches apart, also kissing and undressing one another. When Jayce unclasped Leah's bra, Gabi couldn't refrain from stealing a glance at her perfectly pert breasts. When Jayce lowered his mouth to them, Gabi's pulse quickened, heat surging through every cell in her body as she surprisingly became aroused. When actually in the playrooms, in the middle of all the action, it was like being possessed. As pleasure took over, nothing else seemed to matter. The person you were only minutes before was long gone. Every fantasy, fetish, dirty dream, or kinky thought that popped into your mind could be made true and no one batted an eyelid. The air smelt of nothing but sex—unadulterated pleasure.

The room is pretty dark. No one can see you, except for Jayce and Leah, but they're busy doing their own thing, Gabi told herself. *Give it your all. If you don't enjoy it this time, then you never have to return.*

"Darion…" She curled and uncurled her fingers. "I don't want to get fully naked."

"Then don't," he said, planting a soft kiss on her lips.

Her bra was pulled down so her breasts were resting above it. Darion's lips surrounded her nipple. With each vicious lick, she closed her eyes. She felt her tense muscles beginning to relax, and the nervousness subsiding. His hand cupped her other breast, tweaking her nipple between his thumb and forefinger, eliciting a sharp but pleasurable pain.

Darion then unzipped his jeans, releasing his cock. Guiding her, he placed her hand on his length. Gabi hesitated a moment before sliding her hand up and down his shaft firmly, but slowly. A cry left

215

Darion's throat. His erection was smooth, hard, ready…the tip glistening. Gabi massaged his balls softly with her other hand.

Darion's head whipped back, the muscles in his neck taut, his face contorted in a grimace. It pleased Gabi seeing him so turned on. Her treacherous body strained toward his, telling her she wanted him, that it didn't matter about the location, the people surrounding them, that she could surrender to the intense feelings pulsing through her body.

When Darion lay onto her, she encircled her legs around his waist. She brushed her pelvis against his rock hard length, moaning softly as she felt a throbbing sensation. A needy ache rippled through her, torturing her. She gasped as the tip of his cock slid in, making her clamp her lips together to trap her moans. Her body once more overruled her mind. She couldn't deny it. She was helpless. She wanted more. Needed more. Wanted to feel all of him.

Darion thrust his hips upwards, getting deeper. Stealing a glance at him, she saw his eyes were glowing with an alluring mix of lust and desperation. Withdrawing, he pushed back into her with soft, shallow plunges, teasing her. Gabi's sex fluttered. As his tip prodded her entrance with slow movements in and out, she gripped his ass, pulling him into her. The urgency became overwhelming; every part of her *needed* his rough tough.

"Harder," she murmured into Darion's ear breathlessly, now shutting everything out around them, focusing solely on him and her.

A slow smirk crept across his face. "You want it hard?" He ran his tongue along her bottom lip slowly, tantalising her. "Okay."

Spreading her legs further, he pushed in deeper. Gabi cried out as he slid in all the way, filling her completely. She arched her back, biting her lip, unable to take his now powerful plunges. Grinding his hips, he filled her aggressively, possessively claiming every bit of her, taking her to her limits. She felt a little light-headed at the fullness of his length, her body both accepting and refusing it. It was too much. But she had asked for it. She clawed his back, gritting her teeth.

"Darion..."

He thrust in and out of her fiercely—fast, hard—making the pressure build up inside. Desire surged through her blood. She watched him panting, beads of sweat forming on his forehead as he jerked his hips, grinding into her. Taking a fistful of his hair, Gabi pulled on it, yanking his head down.

She greedily searched for Darion's mouth, wrestling her tongue with his, licking, sucking, tasting, groaning. Her teeth clashed with his as she kissed harder. Gabi felt her lips beginning to swell.

As Darion continued rocking into her, making her writhe, and moan out, she turned her head. Leah was naked, except for a miniscule thong, which was pulled to the side as Jayce feasted on her. Leah's fingers were gripping his hair, pulling him closer. Her lips were parted with the moans he was eliciting from her. Gabi assumed they weren't new to the swinging world.

She knew Darion was enjoying the show as his thrusts became faster. As he hit her inner walls, tension coiled in her stomach. She felt her body tremble as Darion bucked his hips, grinding into her at a hurried pace. Her body was slick with sweat, her heart racing, her skin tingling.

She felt Darion's cock throb inside her. Her sex clenched as spasms of pleasure shot between her legs. She took in a deep breath, feeling herself build higher and higher. Struggling to maintain control, her body shuddered powerfully as intense wave after wave rippled through her. She orgasmed loudly, moaning with quivering lips.

Gasping for air, she felt Darion clutch her tightly as he continued to slam into her, her heart beating frenetically. Torment twisted his face. He threw his head back and climaxed deep inside her, shaking and groaning her name.

"Fuck..." He finally stilled and collapsed on top of her.

Gabi reached down and stroked his face softly. She remained in a crumpled heap as she basked in the afterglow of the steamy session. She had done it. She had managed to lose her inhibitions again and participate in Darion's kinky play. Like him she was silent, and observant, taking in the surrounding people reaching their own orgasms, watching as they fell apart, surrendering, screaming out.

After a few seconds, Darion pushed himself into a seated position. Gabi readjusted her breasts in her bra, and pulled her dress together slightly. She looked toward Jayce and Leah. He was now inside her, pounding away. He didn't stop until they both climaxed loudly, shaking and groaning.

When Jayce and Leah had obviously recovered from their orgasms, they also sat up. Gabi swallowed as Jayce's eyes travelled up and down her body. He edged toward her, and the mischievous expression on his face was as clear as day. She knew what he wanted. It was what they were there for, to swap.

She glanced at Darion when she felt him squeeze her hand. Leah was now positioned next to him. "Are you still okay with this, Gabi?" he asked.

She felt the thudding of her heart as if she had run ten kilometres. She rubbed her chest, feeling a heavy, painful ache. Darion still wanted to go ahead and swap partners. He obviously wasn't fully satisfied. Before she had time to respond, Jayce forcefully pressed his lips against hers. She tore away for a moment; catching sight of Darion's questioning expression.

"Gabi?"

"Yes, I'm fine with it," she replied. *Just go with the flow, Gabi. You can stop at any time if it becomes uncomfortable.*

She was able to witness Leah kissing Darion frantically before her head was jerked sideways by Jayce. His tongue filled her mouth. His kiss was unlike Darion's. It was gentler, definitely less demanding, and he tasted different. She didn't care that Jayce was a well known actor, and that thousands of girls would have killed to be in her position. The only man she wanted was her boyfriend and him alone. Regardless, she decided she would try and give Darion what he wanted.

Pushing Jayce onto his back, she straddled him. She kissed him with as much passion as she could force. She ran her hands through his hair, pulling him in closer. Surely Darion would be enjoying the little show. She planted kisses along Jayce's collar bone, her palms now sliding down his chest.

As Jayce wriggled beneath her and yanked her head down for another kiss, Gabi looked across at Darion. She noticed Leah stroking his biceps, her eyes glowing with delight, as if she didn't know what to do first with her precious prize. Gabi could feel her irises burning with jealousy. Even when Jayce tweaked one of her sensitive nipples over her bra, her utmost turn-on, she desperately wanted to slap his hand away. Her focus remained solely on Darion.

She watched as his lips pressed against Leah's skin, slow, lingering kisses along her neck. Leah's hands gripped her hair, her features screwed up, her body squirming, as if she was unable to take the pleasure being lavished upon her. She thrust her pelvis upwards, obviously in need of more, in need of release from the teasing, just like Gabi so often did.

His lips met hers, and they seemed to be kissing savagely, unable to get enough. Finally pulling apart, Darion's fingers caught hold of hers for a moment, where he squeezed them tightly, to remind her of the strong bond they supposedly shared.

When he withdrew his hand, his head lowered to Leah's stomach. His mouth travelled down her skin, causing her to arch her back and whimper. The kisses were going lower, toward her navel. With every kiss he landed on her, Gabi could see Leah writhing around. The hand that had held hers only a second ago was now hooking into the top of the

Leah's underwear. By the time Darion's lips were almost between her legs, the material was at Leah's knees, and she was exposed. Gabi's breathing suspended as Darion's head sunk lower, and lower. Then he looked at Gabi for a final time, in what she believed was to further seek permission to ravish Leah with his tongue.

***

Darion

Darion swallowed the lump in his throat and sucked in air. He sat back on his heels for a moment. Leah was spread out before him, trying to reach for him, a look of desperation on her face. He knew she wanted him, knew it was his tongue she urgently needed to bring her to an orgasm.

Stroking himself through his trousers, he ducked his head. Surely he hadn't gone soft, had he? Grinding his teeth, he wondered what was happening. He had never experienced erectile problems in the playrooms. Ever. What was happening?

He lifted his head to check on Gabi again. She was sitting on top of Jayce, with her arms hooked around his neck. She was in her underwear, her dress at her feet. Her lips were attached to his and she appeared to be enjoying herself, but he couldn't be certain. He wished he could see her eyes, read her expression.

He reached out and gently shook her arm in a bid to get her attention. Before he got a chance to speak with her, he caught a figure from the corner of his eye. He stopped in his tracks. He lifted his head. There she was, complete with long black waves cascading down her back, petite tattooed arms, on the verge of bringing a man to climax. She threw her head back and laughed. It couldn't be. Could it? He'd told her to steer clear of the playrooms when he was using them.

He drew in a slow, steady breath. His mouth was dry, his heart racing wildly, his hands shaking ever so slightly. *Turn around,* he thought, transfixed on the flawless naked body on the bed opposite. *Turn around.*

She did.

Her brown eyes met his, and he instantly felt his muscles soften as he relaxed. For once, Eva hadn't broken an agreement.

Chapter Thirty-Two

Gabi

Gabi brushed her lips briefly against Darion's. However he pulled her in for a deeper kiss. She could taste strawberry on his tongue. It must have been the flavour of Leah's lip-gloss or chewing gum, or something. Her stomach somersaulted, an acidic feeling appearing in her throat, and she felt on the verge of vomiting. Swallowing quickly, she held it down.

The quicker she got out of the car, the better. She wanted another hot shower so she could scrub herself clean; wash away the traces from last night and the scent of Jayce still on her skin. She was sure she reeked of sex, that sweaty, strong odour. She tried to stop replaying the antics in her mind but was failing miserably.

She'd been a different person in those playrooms, definitely a person she didn't recognise.

Now that the alcohol had worn off, she felt a little ashamed, dirty…like the guilty rush of feelings one may get after a horrid one-night stand. *Urgh.* She rubbed her forehead. She inhaled a deep breath, feeling suffocated, needing air. She grabbed the handle and pushed open the door. She was about to step out when Darion's hand gripped her arm.

"Are you okay?" He studied her intently.

She nodded. "Yeah." She manufactured a small smile.

He tilted her face up to meet his. "You enjoyed last night, right?"

"Of course." Her voice came out chirpy, just as she had intended.

Darion's face broke into a smile. "Good."

He seized her face with his hands and caught her mouth in a rough kiss. His tongue roamed deep inside, wrestling with hers. Gabi felt herself pulling back, something she'd never done before.

"I'll call you later." He kissed her temple. "Have fun, whatever you decide to do tonight."

"I will."

She dug out the keys from her handbag, and paced up the path to her apartment. As she heard the roar of the car engine, she didn't look back, wave, and watch him drive off as she usually did. When she was in the comfort and privacy of her home, she dropped on the couch, her gaze transfixed on the ceiling.

Her heart twisted in her chest as tears stung her eyes. Why couldn't she alone be enough for him? Burying her fingers in her hair, she blew out air. She was tired, worn out. The relationship was taking its toll on her emotionally. Darion had offered to take her to a restaurant, or to a bar in town, however she'd pretended that she had plans with Mallory. She needed space from him. She needed time to reassess the whole relationship.

When she looked in the mirror, she didn't even recognise who she was. Gabi had turned her back on all normality since the day she had met Darion. Having witnessed and experienced the things that she had, she realised there was no going back. She was tainted forever. How could she stay with Darion when her own identity was being stripped?

She rolled onto her side and lay there for a moment in a complete daze. She didn't know what to do anymore. Dragging herself to her feet, she caught sight of the red roses in a nearby vase. Now, instead of filling her with warmth, they were a constant reminder of Darion, and the dirty night they'd just shared.

She grabbed hold of the vase and threw the flowers against the wall with as much force as she could muster. The glass smashed, water sprayed everywhere, and the roses sank to the floor in a heap. Perhaps Darion and Eva *should* get back together. They were suited, that was for sure. They both enjoyed the same sexual swinging kicks, something she would never understand. Ever.

Trudging to her bedroom, she realised she'd never felt so rejected in her entire life. When Darion had been kissing Leah, becoming oblivious to Gabi even being there, it had not only sickened her, but saddened her deeply. The very person that she loved with all of her heart hadn't even noticed her discomfort, a result of the position that he'd put her in.

Wrapping her arms around herself protectively, Gabi sat on the edge of the bed. She needed to talk to someone. She didn't want to spend the day going over everything in her head, worrying about Darion.

Retrieving her mobile from her pocket, she decided that she would in fact call Mallory to see if she fancied meeting up.

***

Darion

Darion collapsed on the bed with a heartfelt sigh. Lately, Gabi had completely fried his brain. She'd seemed to have enjoyed it in the playrooms the few times they had visited, but judging by her actions now, he wasn't so sure. He'd noticed that she seemed standoffish when he'd dropped her home. It was also unlike her to turn down 'date night' at a restaurant, the cinemas, whatever. Usually she wanted to spend as much time with him as possible. He tore off his t-shirt, feeling feverishly hot.

He wished he had someone to talk to, seek advice. Grabbing his mobile, he scanned through his contact list. He settled on Gina's number. Pressing the call button, he rolled onto his side, the phone pressed against his ear. Wise with words, Gina would say all the right things, the things he needed to hear. He waited with bated breath as the ringing tone filled his ear. *Please pick up, G.* He tossed the mobile to the bed when he reached her voicemail. *Fuck!* He flopped onto his back. He hoped she was okay.

Ten minutes of lying there in complete silence, focused on the ceiling, he then tried to call Gina again. He felt a stabbing pain in his chest when it failed to connect. He wished he knew where her mom lived in London. Gina was a private person though. She rarely ever spoke about her personal life at the club.

Darion felt his palms growing clammy with sweat. What would he do without Gina? Regardless of them drifting apart a little, she'd been the one woman he'd turned to—about anything and everything.

He sat up abruptly and rubbed his hands up and down his face. He was being stupid. He didn't need Gina. He didn't need anyone. He was worrying over nothing. Gabi must have had fun at The Black Door on every occasion. She had orgasmed every single time. If she hadn't been comfortable then she would have told him. Wouldn't she? He ensured that he'd drummed it into her head that communication was imperative, that if she ever felt uneasy, then all she had to do was inform him. She hadn't ever said no to visiting the rooms, nor had she expressed a dislike for swinging. A lack of understanding perhaps, but that was all. He sensed that Gabi was taking it slow, getting used to the lifestyle.

He clambered to his feet and loosened his jeans, allowing them to tumble down his legs. Kicking them off, he entered the bathroom. A hot bath should soothe his aching muscles. But first, he needed to brush his teeth again. He could still taste

Leah's lip-gloss. He grabbed his toothbrush, loaded it with toothpaste, and stuffed it in his mouth. He lifted his head to the mirror. His light green eyes stared back at him. They said the eyes were the windows to the soul. Good job nobody could see his soul, for it was damaged, filled with pain he told no one about. Well, except for Gina in one of their many drunken heart to hearts. Oh and Eva. Not that she cared anyway…talk about knocking a man when he was down.

Averting his stare, he brushed his teeth and tongue, and swilled his mouth out. He then filled the tub with water, which didn't take long to fill. Darion pushed down his boxer shorts and stepped into the warmth of the water. He gasped in delight. It was heavenly. When he submerged his body in its depths, he dropped his head back and closed his lids.

"I can't believe your mom and dad didn't even say congratulations to you on your wedding day," Eva said, as she stood before the mirror, removing her earrings.

Darion remained on the king-size bed, taking in his surroundings. Although the honeymoon suite was beautiful with the flower arrangements, rose petals on the bed, candles throughout, and a bottle of champagne cooling in a bucket, it was empty, just like his heart. There was nothing personal in the room, no familiar items, nothing to make it feel homely. It was bare. Just a room that had seen thousands of newly married couples like him and Eva come and go. There was nothing special about it.

He hated the negative emotions that took over his mind, but he'd been unable to shake off his mood when his parents had left shortly after he'd said his vows. How could they not stay and celebrate the one day that meant everything to him? Did they not want him to be happy?

"Who needs them, anyway?" Eva shrugged. She slowly turned around to face him. "Your dad's an alcoholic pervert, and your mom's an old hag in dreamland." She laughed.

"Don't you dare speak about them that way."

"Why are you defending them? Look how they treat you."

"I don't wanna talk about it."

"Good." She unzipped her white, flowing wedding dress and allowed it to fall from her shoulders. "I've got something that may take your mind off everything."

Stepping out of the dress, Eva, in her skimpy, black underwear, crawled up the bed at a leisurely pace. "Tonight is your special night, my sexy, sweet husband." She straddled him. "You can do anything you want with me…anything."

Chapter Thirty-Three

Gabi

Gabi groaned inwardly, trying to push the niggling thoughts out of her head. The night at The Black Door seemed embedded in her brain. Like some dirty, sleazy secret, it haunted her. Darion touching Leah, Audrina, other women before made her lower lids burn, as she was on the verge of tears. *I can't fucking do this!* her mind screamed. What was she meant to do when he wanted her to go all the way? Her body didn't betray her this time. It agreed with her head. No amount of pleasure she was spoilt with could persuade her to continue the sexual activities in the playrooms.

She kicked the cushion off the sofa in frustration, wondering what to do with herself. Mallory's mobile had been switched off. She needed to get out of the apartment, knowing that she'd drive herself insane if left to her thoughts.

Glancing at the clock, she could see it was 6:30 p.m. Snatching her mobile from the table; she dialled Mallory's number again. She sighed in relief as it rang.

"Hey, Gab."

"Hi, Mal."

"What's up?"

"Please tell me you're not busy tonight."

"Actually, I'm not. Steve's having a night out with the boys'."

"Do you fancy going to Sasha's?"

Mallory was quiet for a moment. "Ah, go on." She laughed. "Who am I to refuse tequilas and a dance floor?"

Gabi found herself smiling. "Great. I'll get a taxi and meet you there. Say about nine?"

"Okay. What are you wearing? You going for casual or dressy?"

"Definitely dressy." Gabi needed to feel as good as possible to repair her shattered self-esteem.

"See you later, sweetie."

"Bye."

Gabi decided she wouldn't bore her friend with the details of needing a last-minute night out, and that she wanted to drink to block out the previous night's events. She also didn't want Mallory to urge her to leave Darion. She had fallen for him hook, line, and sinker, so at that moment it wasn't even an option. Her stomach lurched. Her heart ached just thinking about it.

She knew though that she couldn't allow him to go all the way and sleep with another woman in the playrooms. She needed to be honest with him and tell him she wasn't cut out for swinging. Unlike him, she didn't need further sexual highs. She didn't need variety in her sex life in the form of multiple partners regularly. She was happy with Darion and him alone.

She spent the next couple of hours having a long relaxing soak in the tub, and then taking her time drying her hair and getting ready. It was 8:30 p.m. when she was almost done. When she'd applied her make-up consisting of charcoal coloured eye-shadow, and pink lip-gloss, she stepped into her dress. It was a short, gold dress which clung to her body, and dipped at her buttocks, exposing her bare back. Slipping into her heels, she grabbed her clutch bag and headed to the front door. She was just in time to hear the taxi pull up outside.

It was just after 9:15 when she arrived at Sasha's Bar. She found Mallory at a table not far from the bar. The table was laden with several drinks. Gabi wasted no time in downing a few shots. Mallory observed her suspiciously, and asked if everything was okay.

"Yeah." She grinned. "I just fancied a night out."

Mallory nodded with a tight smile, and Gabi knew she believed there was more to it. "I take it things are still rough at the club?"

Gabi's head jerked upwards, wondering if Mallory sensed the real reason for her aim to get as drunk as possible. Was it that obvious that she had been in the playrooms? "What do you mean?"

"Eva issues?"

Oh. Her shoulders sagged as she relaxed. "Yeah. Eva issues." *That too.*

"What will be, will be," Mallory told her. "Only time will tell, Gabi, which route you need to take when it comes to Darion. Just enjoy it for now."

Gabi glugged back half of her Cosmopolitan, some of which spilled down her chin. Giggling, she put the glass down and wiped her face.

"How is everything with you, Mal?"

"Everything's great, honey. I live a pretty boring life." She laughed.

"At least you're happy," she mumbled.

"Aren't you?"

"Sometimes," she confessed. "Darion's a lot to take on, Mal."

"A complex man is an interesting man." She beamed. "At least he'll always keep you on your toes."

Ten minutes later, Mallory dragged her to her feet. Together they hit the dance floor. Waving her arms in the air and twirling around, Gabi was stumbling more than she was actually dancing. The alcohol had definitely taken effect.

She stopped laughing when she sensed someone was watching her. She scanned the bar area, knowing she wasn't imagining it. No one appeared to be paying attention to her. It did nothing to calm her hammering heart. Taking a few steps forward, she craned her neck, trying to see the bar area. She froze instantly. Her pulse rang loud in her ears. It was Lawrence. She wondered if he'd been following her all along. She shook her head as if to dismiss it. Sasha's had been his favourite bar too. It was obviously just a coincidence him being there.

"Mal," she screeched, nudging her. "Lawrence,

he's…over there." She pointed in his direction.

"Oh great," Mallory mumbled. "That's all we bloody need." She shook her head in annoyance. "Come on, Gab. Let's go to a different bar."

"No way." She shrugged off Mallory's tight grip on her arm. "I like it in here."

"Well, let's go sit down for a bit before he notices us. The last thing we want is him ruining our night with his fucking soul-destroying abilities."

Gabi couldn't refrain from bursting into hysterics. Oh how she adored Mallory. She hooked her arm in hers and led her to the seating area. Gabi was about to reach for the last of her cocktail, of which there was only a quarter left, until Mallory snatched it from her.

"Gab, you've downed three drinks already. Take it easy. How about a bottle of water…mix it up a little?" She pushed the glass out of the way. "Besides, that drink has been left unattended for half an hour. Are you looking to get spiked?"

Gabi shrugged. "It wouldn't be the worst thing right now," she slurred, meaning it as a joke.

"Gabi, what's wrong? Tell me."

"Nothing." She wrapped Mallory in her arms as she embraced her tightly. "We're having fun, aren't we, Mal?"

"Sure. It makes a change, me being the sober one," she mumbled.

Gabi scanned the room again. Leant against the bar, Lawrence was laughing and talking with a pretty redhead. He looked happy, carefree. She felt her heart twist. A pang of jealousy shot through her, and she hated herself for feeling that way. She put it down to being tipsy from the alcohol, and the music bringing out all sorts of emotions in her. The song that was playing was one Lawrence used to listen to repeatedly in his car, having liked it. She turned her head away, trying to stop herself from staring.

"Oh no." Mallory groaned. "Soul-destroying Lawrence is on his way over here."

"I forgot to tell you I bumped into him a while back," Gabi said, leaning into Mallory, so that she could hear her above the music.

"What happened?"

"He's single again."

Mallory pursed her lips. "It doesn't surprise me."

"Gabi? Mallory?" Lawrence was now before them, a big grin plastered on his face. "What a pleasant surprise."

"Or a shitty one," Mallory said under her breath, causing Gabi to bite down a giggle.

"How's it going?" His gaze flitted from Gabi to Mallory.

"Great, thanks."

"Never better." Mallory's face broke into a smile; however Gabi noticed the happiness didn't reach her icy eyes. "We were just heading for another bar, weren't we, Gabi?"

"Um…" Gabi tore her attention away from Lawrence. "I think we're okay here."

Mallory's face fell and she rolled her eyes. "In that case, I'm going to get another round." She stood up. "I have a feeling a strong drink will do me good."

When Gabi and Lawrence were left alone, an awkward silence filled the air.

"So....we meet again," Lawrence finally spoke, looking pleased with himself.

"When did you start coming back to Sasha's?" She hiccupped involuntarily.

"A couple of weeks ago. I avoided it for a long time. It brought back too many memories."

"And now you're okay with it?"

He nodded. "Mind if I sit down?"

She waved her hand, indicating that he could go ahead. He sat on the stool opposite her, placing his bottled water on the table. He was dressed in a white polo neck t-shirt and black trousers. He looked smart, as always. His blond hair was brushed to the side, and his complexion looked fresher, rosier, than the last time she had seen him. He looked younger than his thirty-seven years. Grinning from ear to ear, she knew he really was at a happy place in his life. She wished the same could be said for her.

"So, how have you been?" he asked.

"Fine," she quickly responded.

"How's work?"

"It's good." Gabi felt herself perk up. She enjoyed her job. "How's work for you?"

"It's going well." He took a swig of his drink. "Mallory looks great. How is she? And Suzie? I haven't seen her in a while now."

Gabi noticed Mallory was now being served at the bar. "She's fine." She clutched her glass. "Suzie's expecting."

"Wow. Send my congratulations."

"I will."

He drummed the table with his fingertips. "You

look lovely, by the way."

"Thanks," she mumbled. She looked for Mallory again. She was laughing and talking with a young man.

"You seem stressed. Is something on your mind?" Lawrence eyed her suspiciously.

She shook her head.

"Do you want me to leave you to it?" He began to stand.

"No," she blurted out. She didn't want to be alone. Nor did she want to be a third wheel, with Mallory and her companion.

"I miss you, Gabi," he said softly.

"Wh..what?" Gabi spluttered, wondering where that came from.

"I wish I could take back how I treated you. I was selfish. I hate myself for it."

"Lawrence, don't." She raised a hand to stop it. "It's in the past."

He drained the last of his water. "You want another drink?"

"Yeah…may as well." She hiccupped again. "Why are you drinking water?"

"I'm driving."

An hour passed to which Gabi, Mallory, and her companion were in fits of laughter, all of them drunk, except for Lawrence. When it came to the bar closing, they stood outside, trying to hail down a taxi. It was no use. There was a huge queue, and what seemed like at least half an hour wait.

"I can take you both home?" Lawrence offered.

"We're fine. We can get a taxi," Mallory responded.

"I insist."

Gabi wrapped her arms around herself, feeling goosebumps spread on her arms in the chilly air. Her heels were pinching her feet, and she desperately wanted the warmth and comfort of her bed. "Come on, Mal. We'll be waiting ages otherwise."

"Okay." Mallory groaned. "It was nice meeting you, Todd," she told the friendly man. "You brightened up an almost ruined evening." She giggled.

"Glad to be of service." He grinned.

"I can take you home too," Lawrence offered.

"Nah." He shook his head. "My friends are around here somewhere."

Mallory waved to Todd, and then followed Gabi and Lawrence toward the car park. They hopped in the back of his Mercedes, laughing hysterically at the night's events. Gabi's dress was drenched with beer, after Todd had accidentally knocked some over her. She kicked off her heels, and fell against Mallory as the car swerved around the corner. It was fifteen minutes later, when Mallory sat up abruptly, her eyes wide with terror.

"Lawrence, I thought we were dropping Gabi off first?"

"We're almost at your place," Lawrence told her. "It was nearer, Mallory."

"I wanted to make sure Gabi got home safely."

"She will." He glanced at her in the rear-view mirror. "Don't you trust me?"

"No, I fucking don't."

"Look, Mallory, I know we've had our ups and

downs, but I would never bring harm to Gabi. I messed up once already. I wouldn't go down that road again."

When the car stopped outside Mallory's house, she pulled Gabi in for a quick hug, and climbed out. Before she strode off, she said, "Lawrence, don't do anything you might regret. Believe me, you will suffer the repercussions."

"I'm taking her home. That's all."

"Yeah, that better be all."

Mallory waved at Gabi a final time before stumbling down her garden path. Gabi fell back against the seat, feeling as if she would vomit. Lawrence wound down his window, allowing a cold breeze to seep through the car.

"Is that better, Gabi? Maybe it'll sober you up a little."

"Hopefully," she mumbled.

Half an hour later, Lawrence was assisting her toward her front door. Gabi inhaled deeply. She was hit with another reminder of the night at the club, like a sharp slap in the face.

Darion unzipped his jeans slowly. As he pulled them down to his ankles and kicked them off, Gabi and everyone else in the room got a full view of his perfectly shaped, firm ass. Except for his boxers, he was fully naked—his smooth chest, tight abs and muscular biceps making him the centre of attention under the dim lights. Gabi wanted nothing more than for him to remove Jayce, who was annoyingly kissing her neck. She was only pretending to enjoy it. She'd wished that Darion would wrap his arms around her, and be only hers.

Instead he lowered his body atop of Leah's and kissed her. Grinding his body against Leah, his arse bobbing up and down, he grabbed hold of Gabi's hand once more. Their stares locked.

"Darion. I want to experience everything with you," Gabi lied. "But can we take it one step at a time?"

"Do you wanna go home?"

"I wouldn't mind having you all to myself."

"Anything you want, Gabi. Remember, I've got all of the patience in the world for you."

"I'm not ready to go in just yet." Tears steamed down Gabi's face. Although she was feeling insecure, she knew the alcohol played a part in her emotions showing so openly.

"What's wrong, Gabi?" Lawrence studied her intently, his expression displaying concern.

"I don't want to be alone…" she slurred. "I'm so tired…but I know I won't be able to sleep."

"Do you want me to sit with you for a while?" he offered.

Gabi nodded meekly as she dived into her bag for her keys. When she had them in her hands, she attempted to open the door, but failed miserably, cursing when it wouldn't work. Lawrence then tried, and when he was successful in opening it, he informed her she'd been using the wrong key. She giggled as she led him into the living room.

"Do…do you want a drink?" She kicked her heels off and flopped onto the couch.

"I'm fine." He sat beside her. "Nice place," he

said, checking the room out.

"Thanks." She hiccupped.

"Gabi." He shot her a serious look. "What was all that about at the door? Are you in some sort of trouble?"

"No."

"What are you upset about?"

She shrugged. "Sometimes...sometimes life can be a bit overbearing."

"Yes," he agreed. "It can."

When silence loomed upon them, Gabi found herself thinking of Darion again, wondering what he was doing, who he was with, whether Eva was there. She hung her head in her hands. How could she, at times, love Darion to the point where it was insane, and then at other times, dislike him for his desires—hate him even? The good points about him filled her mind, making it seem almost impossible to leave him: his gorgeous appearance, his kind heart, his ambition, and drive, his caring and protective nature, his fun, spontaneous personality. Oh and not to mention his skill between the sheets.

God. She sighed heavily. But the bad really did outweigh the good. Just that one thing alone: his love of swinging. Images filled her mind again of him kissing Leah, her neck, her chest, her stomach, grinding against her, groaning with her, touching her.

She burst into uncontrollable sobs, her shoulders bouncing. She knew she probably looked a mess, mascara streaming down her cheeks, and her hair all wild. She held her palms to her face, feeling pathetic. She felt her cheeks burning in embarrassment when Lawrence wrapped his arms around her.

"It will be okay, Gabi," he soothed. "Whatever it is."

"It will never be okay."

Lawrence lifted her head and stroked loose strands of hair from out of her face. Gabi stared at him, sniveling. She tried her hardest to stop crying, but the tears seemed never-ending. As she studied Lawrence's face, his brows that were creased with concern, she felt warmth spread through her, knowing he cared. *"Nobody will ever love you the way that I loved you,"* his words echoed in her mind. Had Lawrence been right? She inhaled air, wiping her eyes. When Lawrence leant toward her slowly, she didn't stop him when his lips pressed against hers. She squeezed her lids shut as his tongue swept in and filled her mouth. She reciprocated, desperately needing to feel loved, for someone to take away the hurt that Darion sometimes caused her.

She felt her body being lowered onto the sofa.

Chapter Thirty-Four

Darion

It was Sunday evening and Darion was sitting at his usual spot at the corner of the bar, downing whisky after whisky. He focused his attention toward the stage, where Marnie was seducing the crowd. She was toying with her bra straps whilst gyrating her hips. Darion remembered the evenings when he'd sit and watch the girls dance for hours, especially Marnie, Lexi, and Gina. It felt like a long while ago.

"Hey, boss." Lexi appeared from the store room, carrying a cardboard box. She placed it on the counter and began stocking the shelves with vodka bottles.

"Hey, Lex. Everything okay?"

She nodded. "For now."

Darion glanced back at the stage. Marnie was topless, and fondling her boobs, whilst the crowd watched on in admiration. She could sure move her body. He felt his shoulders droop a little and realised he missed Gina. She always knew how to cheer him up when he was feeling down in the dumps.

"Daz." Lexi shoved the cardboard box under the counter. "Something's up, I can tell." She rested her elbows on the bar, leaning closer to him. "What's wrong?"

He tapped his fingers on the counter. He despised talking about feelings. He preferred to keep it all in and handle any problems himself.

"Nothing's up." He forced a smile. "Everything's great, darlin'."

"I don't believe you." She straightened her posture. "Are you sleeping better lately?"

"I'm mostly always with Gabi, so yeah."

"Have the nightmares stopped now that Eva's back?"

"Yeah," he said, not wanting Lexi to worry about him.

"So, how's things with you and Gabi? Eva told me you were using the playrooms."

"She shouldn't be discussing my private business."

"Oh, give it up, Daz." She shook her head. "How did Gabi find it? You don't want to push her too far. She's not like the other women you've dated. Even I know that."

"I think she enjoyed it," he said and meant it. "She's asked to take it slow. She needs to get used to it, that's all."

"I hope you know what you're doing."

"Darion, can I speak to you for a moment?" The silky voice cut through him like glass, and he felt his muscles instantly tense.

"Sure." He reluctantly turned around to face her.

He noticed Eva cast her eyes on Lexi. She raised her eyebrow. "A little privacy, perhaps?" She hooked her arms together over her ample chest.

"Sure." Lexi smiled, which Darion knew was as fake as Eva's breasts.

"Why are you behind the bar? Shouldn't you be dancing?" Eva's voice was stern.

"I'm just giving Jasmine a hand." Lexi rolled her eyes. "You know where I am, Daz." She squeezed Darion's shoulder supportively before she sauntered off.

"The girls haven't changed much," Eva snarled. "Still interfering in other people's business."

"What do you want, Eva?" Darion pushed himself to his feet.

"I was talking to Kit—you remember her, right? She used to date your friend Lennie here."

"Get to the point." He sighed heavily, glancing over her shoulder. A man was stumbling to the bar, although he certainly didn't need another drink. Darion made a mental note to throw him out after Eva was done with him. As he was pulled back to reality, he saw her lips were moving, but her words weren't meeting his ears.

"So, what do you think?"

He shook his head. "About what?"

"Weren't you even fucking listening?" Eva snapped, raking her fingers through her long, silky black hair. Her green eyes, clouded with anger pierced through him. "I said, me and Kit decided that male strippers once a month would bring in shit loads of money. This town is lacking—"

"Not gonna happen." Darion turned his back on her and drained the last of his whisky.

"Why not?"

"I've never had male strippers, and I'm not starting now."

"This is *our* club, Darion." She stood tall in her heels. Leaning closer, she said, "You might want to remember that before you're so quick to dismiss my ideas."

He smirked, purposely trying to aggravate her. Mirroring her actions, he leant into her, so he was mere millimeters from her face. She didn't step back, didn't flinch. Nothing. In fact, Darion believed by the upturning of her red glossed lips that she liked him being so close. "You might wanna remember that I've run this club for years—*solo*."

Eva half smiled. "I see you're still afraid of a little competition." She laughed.

"No one even comes close to competing with me, Eva." He placed a hand on her hip. "After all," his voice was low and husky, "that's why you're back, isn't it?" He pushed her aside, not waiting for an answer.

"Daz! Get Lennie, or Trav!"

Darion shot around to see Lexi, backed against the wall. The drunken man was throwing his empty glasses at the bar, shattering them. As he screamed obscenities, Darion raced over. He grabbed the man tightly by his arm.

"Drop the glass," he ordered, shooting him a murderous expression.

"Who the fuck are you?" the man slurred loudly. "You don't know me," he screamed even louder. "She won't serve me a drink." He pointed at Lexi.

"I own this club. I think you've had enough for tonight." He tried to reason with him, "I'll call you a taxi, okay?"

"I'm not going anywhere." He shrugged Darion off and smashed a glass bottle off a table edge.

When he shouted in his face, Darion could feel his blood reach boiling point. Curling his fists, he inhaled a deep breath.

"Look, let's just call you a taxi...ah! Shit!" Darion grimaced as the stumbling man unintentionally cut his arm with the jagged edge of the glass. With his free hand, Darion pressed down on it to stop the oozing blood.

"I can stay where I want." The man's arms were flailing around.

"Hey," Eva said firmly, coming between them.

"Get out of the way, Eva," he roared. He may hate the bitch but that didn't mean he wanted to see her get hurt.

"I got it," she fired back. "Hey." She turned back to the man. "Let's go get you that drink, okay?" She soothed. "Tell me, you like Carling? Or is it Guinness? Or Corona?"

He shook his head. "Nah. I don't fucking like Carling, and Guinness, and fucking...what you just said?" he yelled.

"Okay, why don't you put that glass down, and come show me what drink you like."

247

The man appeared to be mulling it over in his head. "Okay." He shrugged, dropping the glass.

"That's it." Eva placed her hand on his shoulder, leading him away from Darion. "On second thought, you don't want another drink," Eva told him. "If you have another drink now, you won't want to come back tomorrow. You'll have the bitch of all hangovers."

Darion followed closely behind Eva as she seemed to be leading the man toward the entrance. Where was Lennie when he needed him?

"I am coming back tomorrow," the man roared.

"That's right." Eva flashed him her killer smile, the one that made men go weak at the knees. "So what you need is a good night's sleep, and we'll see you tomorrow, okay?"

"I—"

Before he could change his mind, Eva practically pushed him out the door. Lennie trudged down the stairs.

"Where have you been?" Eva snapped.

"A toilet break. Is that allowed, your majesty?"

"Get this man in a taxi."

"Thanks, Len." Darion gave him a nod.

Back at the bar, Eva was pouring herself a drink, a cocktail of a bit of everything. Only when she'd taken several gulps, did she offer him a drink.

"I'm good."

Silence loomed over them for a moment, and Darion hated the fact he suddenly felt uncomfortable. Rubbing at the stubble on his chin, he remained standing, whilst Eva took up residence on *his* stool. It irked him more than it should have.

"Shit! Your arm."

Darion glanced down and noticed the blood was still trickling. "It's just a scratch."

"It could get infected," she exclaimed, standing up and yanking him by the arm. "We need to get you cleaned up."

"It's fine," he repeated tersely.

When Eva didn't take no for an answer, he reluctantly allowed her to lead him into the office. He perched on the edge of the counter whilst she rummaged through the cupboard. The first aid kit was in the same place it had always been. He grimaced when she pressed an antiseptic wipe on the cut. It stung like hell. When she was satisfied it was clean, she covered the area with a cotton pad.

"It will probably scar."

"Good thing I'm not some pretty boy then."

"You couldn't be prettier if you tried." He noticed her features soften and the remorse in her eyes. "Well…" She put a hand on her hip. "I dunno about you but I could do with another drink."

She turned on her heel and swayed toward the mini bar. She took hold of the bottle of Apple Sourz. Instead of using a shot glass, she selected a large glass and filled it to the top.

"Want some?"

"Why not."

He watched as she filled another glass, and sashayed toward him. Their fingers touched as she handed him the drink. He ignored the jolt of tingles that shot up his arm and took a sip of the alcohol.

"Thanks for what you did in there," he said, referring to the drunk man that she'd handled like a professional.

"It's what business partners are for."

"Next time, leave it to Len and Trav."

"Feeling a little overprotective, are we?" Eva smiled over the rim of her glass.

"It's not in your job description to escort out drunks."

Eva rolled her eyes. "Anyway." She held her glass in the air. "A long overdue toast, but to you, me, and The Black Door."

Darion reluctantly tapped his glass against hers before finishing his drink. When Eva drained hers also, he was surprised to see her go and refill them. He accepted it. It had been a long night and he didn't have the energy to fight with her.

"You don't mind if I have one of these, do you?" She took a cigar from his desk, not waiting for his answer.

Darion crossed the room and collapsed on the sofa. He shuffled over when Eva sat too close for his liking. Lighting the cigar, she took a drag.

"Do you remember Iceland?" She nodded her head toward one of the photographs on the wall, grinning.

"Hmmm."

"We got so drunk—"

"I remember," he snapped, cutting her off. How could he forget? They had had urgent, animalistic sex in the back of a taxi.

"Trust us to get a pervert driver." She giggled softly.

"You loved the fact he was watching."

Eva blew out smoke and grinned. "Yeah." She

shrugged a shoulder. "I probably did." After a couple more drags, she held out the cigar. "Do you remember that time in Amsterdam…"

"Eva. Stop," he said sternly, before holding the cigar to his lips. He didn't need any reminders. He wanted the sensitive subject of the past over.

"We used to have so much fun." Her tone was low and sultry as she looked at him.

"We also had a lot of unpleasant times too," he said, averting his stare.

"The good times definitely outweighed the bad."

When Darion finished the cigar, he stubbed it in the ashtray that Eva held out before him. He then lazily reclined in his seat, exhaustion taking over. He felt the sofa dip and noticed Eva tucking her feet underneath her, making herself comfortable. She was close again, and he flinched when her arm brushed against him.

"Want another drink?" she asked, curling her hair around her finger.

Darion declined and leant further back, his top riding up a little, revealing his firm, tanned stomach. He spotted the dark hunger in Eva's expression, the look she used to give him when she wanted him. As she inhaled deeply, her bosom rose. Images of the fantasy he had had about Eva flooded his mind. Her erotic sounding moans, her smooth skin, her sharp nails on his back, her perfectly firm buttocks, her breasts, her long, slender legs. *Fuck.* His head rolled back on an exhausted sigh.

"Everything okay?" Her hot breath met his ear.

The feeling of unease increased when Eva stroked his hair back gently, as if trying to soothe him. Then she leant toward him, her gaze on his mouth. Darion tried to control his breathing and erratic heartbeat. When her fingers tightened on his hair, pulling his head in closer, he knew she was seconds away from kissing him. He abruptly pushed himself to his feet.

"They probably need you upstairs."

He wanted Eva out of his territory. He didn't like the way she was haunting his thoughts, how she helped herself to his things, and the way she was lounging on his sofa, looking all relaxed. He wasn't about to let her become comfortable in his space. He also didn't trust her not to try and seduce him. If she thought she could worm her way back into his life that easily, then she had another think coming. She was lucky he was even maintaining a level of professionalism with her.

"Are you sure I can't tempt you into having another drink? Make a night of it?" She flashed him a sexy smile, her luminous green eyes sparkling mischievously.

"I'm more than sure."

She groaned and stood up. "I'll see you tomorrow then."

Darion watched as she left the room. Out of her line of sight, he closed his eyes for a moment, trying to regain his cool. He wouldn't let Eva spoil his newfound happiness with Gabi. No way.

Chapter Thirty-Five

Gabi

By the time Monday came, Gabi was back in the office. She had spent two hours editing a manuscript. It took all of her concentration not to think of one of the worst weekends she had ever had. Maybe if she blocked it all out, she could pretend it never happened.

Slouching in her chair, she threw her head back, knowing that pretending was impossible. She felt tears forming on her lower lids and quickly blinked them away. So she had slipped up. So she had kissed Lawrence for all of a few seconds, before pulling away. She had regretted it instantly. She wasn't having second thoughts about Lawrence. She had simply clung onto comfort when it had been offered. Not only had she been drunk, but her mind had been a hurricane of sickened thoughts of Darion at the club, the way that his lips moved against Leah's, how his tongue had tasted of strawberry, and his eyes had searched for Eva.

Darion probably thought she hadn't noticed, but she'd seen him. In the playrooms, he'd come to a standstill, focused on a woman that resembled Eva. He had that look in his eyes again like last time, which she couldn't quite make out, a look of either anger or lust.

She blew out an exasperated puff of air. She had *cheated* on Darion. Although he didn't mind her kissing other men and whatnot in the playrooms, it was to satisfy one another, to lose their inhibitions and have fun *together*. There was nothing secretive or deceitful about it.

Yet, she had kissed Lawrence behind his back, betrayed him. Her heart ached as she was flooded with disappointment and regret. She couldn't help but feel hypocritical, having preached trust, and she'd broken it. She had to tell Darion. She needed to confess what she had done. Gabi believed there were two types of cheaters. The ones who cheated and hid it, further betraying the other and sometimes having no regrets at all. Then there were the ones who regretted it every single day of their lives, intending to come clean. Gabi was the latter.

What if she lost him?

At that moment, the telephone on her desk interrupted her thoughts. Taking hold of it, she held it to her ear. She expected it to be a client querying their manuscript, wanting an update. The voice that came through the line made her shudder.

"Lawrence." How could she have forgotten he knew her work number? "What do you want?"

"It's quite clear what I want." He paused for a second. "I want you back, Gabi."

"You can't have me, Lawrence. I'm with Darion."

"What happened last night happened for a reason."

"No, it didn't. It was a drunken mistake. Nothing more."

"I don't agree."

Gabi rose to her feet, feeling her cheeks heat in anger. "Lawrence, please. We're never getting back together. I'm sorry. I wasn't myself last night. I was drunk, upset…" Her voice was meant to be stern, but it shook with emotion instead.

"You used me?" he spat. "You get my hopes up and then you just discard me and continue with your happy life?"

"No, Lawrence. It's not like that."

"Why don't we see what your boyfriend makes of our kiss?"

She shook her head. How dare he try and threaten her. "You wouldn't know where to find him."

"I think The Black Door would be a good start."

Gabi's stomach flipped. She dropped back in her seat, all of a sudden feeling nauseous.

"Gabi, when we were together and you were dressing up like some tart pretending to meet Mallory, you think I didn't know there was someone else?"

Gabi swallowed.

"I knew you'd visited the club, and fallen for that wanker's charms. How can you be with someone who owns that kind of establishment?" She sensed the disgust in his voice.

"You knew all along?"

"I had my suspicions. Stupidly, I didn't think it'd last as long as it has. I thought you'd go through some wild rebellious phase, get it out of your system, let it run its course, and come back to me."

"Wait a minute," Gabi sat forward in her chair, her voice sharp. "How did you know he was the owner? How do you know what sort of *establishment* it is? I thought you never visited The Black Door." She tapped her foot against the floor, unable to keep still. "You told me those matches belonged to Tom." Gabi put a hand to her mouth. That time she had found personalised matches to The Black Door in Lawrence's pocket, and suspected him of cheating, she must have been right. Everything she had had with Lawrence had been a lie. Minus him mistreating her, the loyalty, predictability, and the love she'd thought she'd had with him, she'd been wrong. "So, when I questioned you that time, you lied to me?"

The line was silent.

"So, you did cheat on me?" she asked. "Answer me, Lawrence," she yelled.

"It was one time." She heard him sigh. "I stopped at the club for a quick beer on my way home, and ended up getting drunk."

"Who was she?"

"One of the dancers. It meant nothing."

"What did she look like?"

"What does it matter?"

"Tell me," she said through gritted teeth.

"Gabi, it was a while ago...I don't know...Good body, black hair..."

Probably Wendy. "You asshole." She clamped her lips together to stop the sobs that were threatening to escape. "You guilt tripped me on so many occasions about betraying you with Darion, and you'd already slept with someone else. There was a difference between me and you, Lawrence," she cried out. "You mistreated me. You neglected me, came home late, criticised me, controlled me and pushed me into the arms of another man." She wiped a stray tear away. "I was nothing but good to you." She blew out air again, utterly bewildered. "And that speech you gave me." She laughed mirthlessly. "You said no one could ever love me like you could. And I almost believed it. Shows how much you love me."

"I do love you. It was one mistake."

"I bet you cheated on me countless times, Lawrence. Loyalty was one of your good points, but now you don't even have that anymore."

"I was stressed with work, I was..."

"Don't even go there," she spat.

"Give me another chance, please."

"Never."

"I know you're unhappy. I can see it in you. He'll cheat on you too. Mark my words."

"How would you know how I feel?" She gasped. "Have you been following me?"

"Does it matter?"

"Yes, it does." She tried her hardest to keep her tone quiet.

"I miss you. I can't sit back and watch you get

hurt. Hypocritical, but I'm a changed man. We're good together. Believe me, please."

"Did you get a new car?"

"The Toyota? It's Tom's."

"If you come anywhere near me again, I will call the police." She tightened her grip on the phone. "And don't worry about mentioning the kiss to Darion. I was going to tell him everything myself."

She slammed the phone down and dropped back in her chair, taking deep breaths. She had felt guilty about the way she had treated Lawrence for months, and he'd cheated on her anyway. Would he have really married her, had children with her holding that secret? It didn't even bear thinking about. At least when she had got intimate with Darion, she had tried countless times to end the relationship with Lawrence. She had then ended it, with no intention of getting back with him.

She was outraged that he had been following her, watching her with Darion. Did he really think she would go running back to him? He was crazier than she'd thought.

She was about to stand up to make a coffee when her mobile rang. Taking it out of her bag, she noticed it was Darion. *Shit.* She bit her lip, wondering whether she should answer, whether she could act normal with him.

"Hello."

"Gabi," his low, sexy sounding voice met her ears. It sent a delicious chill through her body, which at that moment she hated.

"How are you?"

"I'm good. I'm just at home watching

television."

"Are you not going to work?"

"I'll pop in on the evening. I spend too much time there, Gabi. I need a break."

"Oh. Is everything okay there?"

"Yeah. We've made a fortune these past weeks. I've paid off my vehicles and everything." She detected the happiness in his tone and was pleased. "We need to go out and celebrate at some point."

"Sure."

"How was the rest of your weekend with Mallory?"

Gabi squeezed her lids shut. "It was good." She wondered whether to tell him about Lawrence stalking her. She decided against it. She hoped threatening to inform the police would cause him to back off.

"I'm glad to hear it. Am I seeing you later?"

"I've got a dance class. I could pop by the club after?"

"You do that." Silence. "I can't wait to see you." He groaned as if he was frustrated.

She opened her mouth, and then closed it, at a loss for words. She was relieved when he continued talking.

"Darlin'." She heard him take a deep breath. "I do love you…you know that, right?"

Gabi swallowed. Her heart raced. She felt a hot flush spread up her chest. "I love you too."

"I'm so grateful you're being patient with me." With what? When it came to him declaring his feelings, or when it came to swinging? She was about to ask but he cut her off. "Anyway, I'll let you get back to work."

"Okay."

"See ya, Gabi."

"Bye."

Gabi dissolved into a fit of tears. She buried her head in her hands. All she'd wanted was for Darion to open up to her, to trust her, and she had destroyed it. She needed to come clean about the kiss and soon, in case Lawrence got to him first. And if he didn't, it wasn't something she wanted hanging over her head. Honesty had to be the best policy, no matter what.

She clapped a hand over her mouth as if she were about to be sick. How would Darion react? What if she lost him?

Chapter Thirty-Six

It was 9:15 p.m. when Gabi entered The Black Door. Dance class had managed to occupy her mind for an hour. She'd then showered at The Royal Dance Academy and hurried home. She'd slipped into a navy, tight knee-length dress, and cream stilettos to match her clutch bag. She'd straightened her hair to perfection so it hung silkily down her back. She felt good on the outside, however inside, she was a quivering wreck.

As she meandered into the room, she scanned the place for Darion. No sign of him. Assuming he was busy in the office, she pulled out a stool and ordered a white wine. A woman she had never seen before served her. Darion hadn't mentioned he'd hired new staff. Gabi was disheartened to see she was gorgeous. As she handed her the wine, she introduced herself as Jasmine. She advised her that Darion was on the telephone and would be with her shortly. Gabi was about to make polite chit chat with her when Lexi strode over, grinning.

"Gabi. How's it going, pretty lady?"

She held back a sigh. "Good. How are things with you?"

"Great." Her mouth moved as she chewed gum. "I'm sorry if I've been a moody bitch lately. Work has been stressing me out."

"That's okay. Are things running smoothly here now?"

"For now, yeah." She flicked her hair back. "Eva must have waved a magic fucking wand, because the place is booming."

Gabi felt envy twist her heart. So Eva was a great asset to the place, and obviously sticking around for the foreseeable future. "Have you heard anything from Gina?"

"She sent me a text message saying that she was still in London. Johnny's with her, so I think she's okay."

"Any news on her mom?"

"Nah. She was very brief. I tried to call her, but her mobile was switched off."

"If you speak with her, send her my wishes."

"I will."

Gabi scratched her head for a second, deep in thought. "Lexi." She looked up. "Can I ask you something?"

"Of course."

"Does, um…Does Darion ever flirt with Eva, or anything?" she asked, linking her hands together. She was unsure whether she was asking out of distrust, or whether she was trying to make herself feel better about her kiss with Lawrence.

"Gabi." Lexi shot her a serious look. "Darion never flirts with Eva. He can't stand being in the same room as her."

Gabi chewed the inside of her cheek, unsure of what to respond with. She felt a pain in the back of her throat. Darion's loyalty made her feel guiltier. "Do you think he still has feelings for her, though?"

"I wouldn't know." She shrugged. "I'm sorry."

She nodded.

"I've gotta go speak with my favourite client, but we'll catch up properly soon, K?"

Gabi offered her a smile.

She focused on the stage where Wendy was occupying the stage. Gabi watched her intently as she hung upside down on the pole, opening her legs wide in the splits, her hair falling underneath her. She seemed to move with such ease, such confidence. The audience clapped and wolf whistled. Gabi wondered whether she should question Wendy about Lawrence, but then decided against it. What good would it bring? He had cheated and that was that. There was no point in dragging up the past.

She averted her gaze, and toyed with the stem of her glass. She hoped Darion wouldn't be too long. Just as she picked her drink up to take another sip, she felt a chill run through her body. *Oh no. Not now.* She gulped half of her wine back quickly, and turned her head to face Eva. She was taken aback when she sat down.

"Jasmine. I'll have a vodka and Coke."

"Sure."

"Hey, Gabi." Eva flashed her a saccharine smile

which didn't meet her eyes.

"Hi."

"Where's Daz?"

"On a call."

Jasmine handed Eva her drink, and then left them alone, whilst she served other customers.

"So…" Eva took a sip of her drink, before setting it down. "How were your antics in the playrooms?" She giggled. "Maybe you're not so prissy after all."

Gabi couldn't help but retaliate to Eva's bitchiness. "Wouldn't you like to know?"

"Sweetheart, I have been on every surface, worn every outfit, used every whip, and experienced more with Darion in those rooms than you ever will." She licked her lips. "You might want to remember that."

"Wow." Gabi shot her a look. "You almost sound proud of that."

"Your boyfriend was."

Gabi drew in a breath.

"I will get Darion back." Eva pushed herself to her feet. She swigged back the remains of her drink, and added, "It may be taking longer than expected, but he will see sense, and when he does, he will return to me."

"You're so sad that you have to use the club as a weapon."

"He loves the club, Gabi. So do I. You don't." She pointed a finger. "With me, Darion doesn't have to make sacrifices. He won't be restricted from enjoying the playrooms. He can have *everything* with me."

"Whatever," Gabi mumbled, not having the energy to fight.

"May the best woman win."

Gabi didn't even watch as Eva sashayed off. *Conniving bitch,* she thought, a sour taste appearing in her mouth. Maybe Eva would win once Darion found out the truth about Lawrence.

"Gabi."

She perked up at the sound of Darion's voice. He stood confidently, towering over her, his green eyes sparkling. A slow, wicked smile formed on his face. The muscles in her stomach clenched. He was wearing black jeans, a white top, and black blazer. She guessed he must have met a client earlier.

"Hi."

Sauntering toward her, he cupped her face in his hands and pressed his lips against her mouth. They were gentle, lingering kisses that caused her stomach to somersault, and tingles to shoot through her body.

"Look at these lovebirds."

Gabi pulled away with a soft giggle, to see Lexi approach the bar and help herself to a drink. She took a sip before saying, "So, when's the wedding?" she teased.

"Lexi," Darion's tone was stern.

"Any babies on the horizon?" She laughed. "Okay. At least tell me you've met each other's families?"

Gabi stared into her wine…anything but meet Darion's stare. Was she worthy of meeting his family? Did she even want him to meet her family when she wasn't sure if they'd even last when all was revealed?

"C'mon. I'm a woman, Darion." Lexi placed her glass down. "If I were Gabi and I'd been hooking up with a dude for a while, I'd be driving myself crazy, wondering where it was headed, or whether I was just some booty call, and—"

"Do you want me to meet your family, Gabi?" Darion asked her outright. His expression was devoid of emotion.

"Um…" she spluttered, at a loss for words. Did she? Before the Lawrence situation, she wouldn't have liked anything more than to introduce him to her parents. She was certain she saw a slight frown crease his forehead and so said, "Yes, I'd like that." But did he want to meet her family, as Lexi had put him on the spot, or because he wanted the relationship to reach the next stage?

She remained staring at him, waiting for her invitation to meet his family, but there was none. Her heart sank, as she wondered if he was ashamed of her for some particular reason.

"Follow me," he said, his voice low and husky.

Gabi finished her drink and followed him toward the office. He stroked her buttocks, causing her body to fill with heat.

"You look fuckin' amazing, Gabi." His predatory stare swept over her.

"Thank you." She tucked a strand behind her ear. "You look good too."

In the office, he placed a palm on her stomach and backed her against the counter. Gabi slid onto it. She felt a fluttering of nerves in her stomach, feeling the magnetic pull between them. She swallowed the lump in her throat and inhaled audibly.

Darion's gaze lingered on her lips for a moment. A slow, salacious grin surfaced on his face. He reached around and slowly unzipped her dress. In one swift movement, he lifted it over her head, tossing it to the floor. Gabi was about to playfully complain at the cost of that dress when he caught her mouth in a firm, demanding kiss. His tongue darted out, finding hers, massaging it with an overwhelming urgency. His hands cupped her face as he possessed her with his mouth.

Tearing away, breathless, she noticed his lips were red, swollen. He wet them with his tongue. Gabi swallowed. His hands fell to her chest, where he peeled her bra down, exposing her full breasts. His mouth captured a hardened nipple; his warm, wet mouth awakening every nerve ending. Gabi's head rolled backwards as she closed her eyes and moaned softly. Darion pulled back to kiss the pink peak gently. His breath was hot on her skin. His lips landed several more tender kisses on it.

Lifting her into his arms, he carried her to the other side of the room. Gabi felt herself being lowered onto the sofa. As he removed his blazer and t-shirt, she waited with bated breath for his next move, her tummy tightening in both excitement and anticipation. *Could he be any hotter?*

Spreading her legs, he tore her thong down her legs, the material tickling her, until they came off her ankles. His gaze took her in, glinting naughtily, as if he was wondering what to do first with his prize.

As he ran his hands up her legs, Gabi felt herself getting moist, aroused…throbbing for contact. She lay back, balancing herself on her elbows. As he placed firm kisses along her thighs, she felt her inner muscles clenching. She arched her back when he began to circle her clit with the tips of his fingers. Vibrations shot through her, making her tremble.

"Hmmmm…" she moaned softly.

Languidly inserting a finger, he slid in and out. The way his blazing eyes cast down, watching what he was doing intently, aiming to please her, aroused her further. As he continued to penetrate her with his fingers, he unzipped his jeans with his free hand and released his erection. Gabi could see he was hard, thick, and ready for her.

Climbing onto the sofa, he spread her legs further, and kneeled between them. He slapped his cock on her entrance a couple of times, causing her sex to throb. As he circled the moist tip of it against her, she clenched her teeth. With his hand around his penis, he stroked up and down the length a few times. Gabi could see the desperate hunger on his face. His body must have been pulsing with the same needy ache she felt.

"Get a condom," she said softly.

Darion's eyes darted around the room frantically. "I don't have one in here."

"We can't risk it…" she panted as he continued to stroke his tip against her, causing her to wriggle impatiently.

"Just this once," he murmured, his voice thick with longing.

Before she could deny him, Darion slowly guided himself, easing into her slowly. As he went in deeper, Gabi gasped, delirious with lust. The feel of him bare was sensational. He moved in and out of her at a slow pace, knowing by now that she needed her body to get familiar with his. When he was in all the way, the rhythm increased.

Gabi watched as Darion screwed up his face in what must have been in pleasure. A sigh left his lips as he closed his eyes and threw his head back. Pounding into her quickly, she cried out, overwhelmed with emotions.

She breathed in the scent of him, the smell of his intoxicating aftershave. She gripped his biceps, loving the way they felt, how muscular and firm they were. She then traced her palms along his smooth chest before reaching around for his buttocks, pulling him as close as possible. *Faster. Deeper. Harder,* she silently begged, needing more, wanting everything he had to offer. All of him.

Darion returned his fierce stare on her, his irises darkening as if he could read her thoughts.

"You want me to be rough?" he asked, challenging her with a lift of his brows.

Gabi looked down, feeling her heartbeat build. "Yes."

His dirty sounding laugh made her inner muscles tighten as the exquisite feelings increased. His left hand moved to cup her behind where he lifted her into his thrusts, which were now fast, deep, and hard. He captured her ear in his mouth and tongued it, slowly, swirling it around inside. His breath was hot, tickling, and exciting her. She'd never known it could be such a turn-on. Her abdomen tightened as pleasure engulfed her.

His mouth trailed down her cheek with firm kisses. When he got to her neck, he sunk his teeth in roughly. *Ow!* She tensed her legs, digging the heels of her feet into the sofa. He nibbled down her neck and bit her again roughly.

She was surprised when he clamped his right hand tightly around her throat. His wicked eyes bored into hers. He continued to jerk his hips into her, his cock hitting her sensitive areas, his balls slapping against her rear.

"Gabi…" He panted. "You're so fuckin'…sexy." His expression now looked dazed, drunken, his eyes half closed, as he allowed the sensations to take over.

Her breathing was shallow as his fingers squeezed even further around her neck. She liked the way he dominated her, took charge. His mouth curled back into a snarl. His hips bucked upwards relentlessly, driving her closer and closer to an orgasm. Tension coiled in her stomach as she felt herself building. When he released her neck, she sucked in air.

Without thinking of her actions first, she slapped him across the face. The sharp sound of the hit, and his eyes widening, told her that she may have lashed out too hard. She expected Darion to throw daggers in her direction, however he grinned slowly. Before she knew it, he tugged her nipple roughly with his teeth. She grabbed fistfuls of his hair, wondering how pain could bring pleasure at the same time.

"Darion," she moaned out as he repeated the

assault on her nipple.

Swivelling his hips teasingly, he let out a low, sinister laugh, knowing exactly the effect he was having on her, almost sending her over the edge. Her nails clawed at his buttocks. She felt him throbbing inside her. Gripping her shoulders, he pounded away endlessly. Gabi rocked upwards, mirroring his frantic movements. How she wished it would never stop, that they could go for hours and hours.

Her chest tightened, her pulse increasing, her breaths short and shallow. He dipped his thumb into her wet mouth, his pupils raw and glowing, intent on her. She flicked her tongue over it and sucked it softly. Satisfied grunts escaped from his lips.

"Oh, Gabi…" his voice was rough. "I'm close…" His face looked tired, but devilish with his darkening expression. She could see the perspiration glistening on his forehead.

"And me," she mumbled, clenching her teeth, craving release.

She felt her chest expanding, her breathing having become erratic. With one last breath, Gabi felt her inner muscles tensing, quivering, as an orgasm exploded through her. She shuddered, convulsing around him, gasping and crying out. She clung onto him tightly. Her heart slammed rapidly in her chest as she desperately sucked in air.

Darion began to tremble and writhe. With his lids squeezed shut, his groans filled the air, and he exploded inside her. He filled her completely, making her body sink further into the sofa. Then he stilled for a moment before his rigid body went limp and he dropped onto her. She could feel the rising and falling of his chest with his heavy panting.

Gabi wasn't sure how long they remained on the sofa, her stroking his hair, and him tracing his thumb gently along her arm. Her breathing had resumed to normal, and her muscles had gained strength again. Lifting his head, Darion pressed his lips against her temple tenderly, and climbed to his feet.

Gabi scanned the floor for her dress, desperate to get to the bathroom and clean herself up.

"So, it looks like I'll be getting to know a lot more about you, Gabriella Woods."

"Yep." It wasn't fair. Why should Darion learn about her upbringing, meet her family, hear about her past, and she learn nothing about him in return? She was sick of being kept in the dark when it came to his past. Maybe if she met his parents too, it would strengthen their bond, make her confession a little easier, and add hope to him perhaps forgiving her. She gathered the courage and asked, "Will I be meeting your parents?"

She noticed him straighten his posture, his hand buried in his hair. "I don't think you'll like them."

She eased herself off the sofa. "I'd still like to meet them. I want to know everything about you too."

With a little nod he said, "If that's what you want."

"What happened to your arm?" she asked, noticing the inch cut to his skin.

Darion looked down at it. "Some drunk was throwing glasses around. Scared Lexi." He yanked on his top. "He caught my arm."

"Darion, you need to be careful," she said firmly. "What if he caught your stomach, or…" She shrugged. "I don't know…your neck." It didn't even bear thinking about.

"I'll *never* let anything happen to those girls, Gabi." When he brought his face up to look at her, his eyes darkened, his stare menacing. "And god help anyone who ever tries to hurt you."

She felt a cold chill run up her spine, unsure of what Darion was capable of. But as he stepped toward her, claiming her mouth with his own, she knew he was just protective over them all. He was scared of losing people in his life. He was afraid of being alone. But then again, he was also afraid of *being* with someone.

Now she knew why. Her little secret flashed in her mind once more.

Chapter Thirty-Seven

"I like these gifts," Suzie squealed happily. She was sat cross-legged on the floor with presents before her: a cream fleece blanket, dressing gown, a tiny hat and gloves, picture albums, teddy bears, and toys. "Thank you, girls."

It was Thursday evening. The week had flown by. Work and dance class had been going well for Gabi. She was up to date on her workload at the office, and had managed to pick up on all of the new moves in her dance lesson. She was also reading a lot more at home, and practicing her cooking. She wasn't sure whether she was doing it out of enjoyment, or to occupy her mind.

"You really didn't have to get me all of this," Suzie's voice dragged her back to the present.

"We wanted to." Gabi smiled. "We got everything cream, as we still don't know the sex of the baby."

"I have a scan in a couple of weeks, so fingers

crossed I'll find out then."

"Have you thought of any names yet?" Mallory cradled her cup of coffee.

"I've been looking online, but nothing has jumped out at me."

"You'll get there," Mallory reassured her. "Anyway, where's Marcus?"

"He should be home soon. He's been working overtime lately. He wants everything to be perfect for the baby."

"Bless."

"So." Suzie looked from Gabi to Mallory. "Enough about me and the baby. What's going on in your lives?"

"Well." Mallory beamed. "As you know, I've booked a holiday. Me and Steve go to the Maldives soon." She clapped her hands in excitement.

"You lucky cow." Suzie laughed.

"It's all right for some," Gabi teased with a laugh.

"So, Gabi. How are things going with Darion?"

She clamped her hands together, and paused before saying, "Good. For now. We're meeting each other's families soon."

Mallory's eyes danced with merriment. She was clearly pleased for her. "I'm so glad the relationship is reaching another level, Gab." She nudged her with her elbow.

"Lexi put us both on the spot, so we couldn't back out, really."

"I'm sure everything will be okay."

"I guess time will tell."

She decided not to reveal her drunken mistake to

the girls. Although they were likely to give her advice rather than lecture her, she was ashamed.

"So." Suzie stood up. "Who wants more coffee?"

***

Darion

Darion smiled as he took in the bustling crowd surrounding him. He was standing near the door, holding a flute of champagne, speaking with Tiana. There was laughter and chatter all around, and he noticed everybody seemed to be at ease, enjoying themselves. Eva had managed to pull off a successful masked theme night. Everywhere he looked he saw eye-masks in almost every colour. Even the men had donned plain black ones. It added excitement. People could keep their identities hidden whilst doing whatever they pleased.

"She's really given the club a lift, Daz," Tiana said, nodding toward Eva.

Darion focused on Eva. She was standing amongst a group of men, talking, giggling, and flicking back her hair flirtatiously. They tapped their flutes together, obviously in a toast to something.

"I suppose. Although it wasn't in bad shape before." He wasn't about to let Eva take all of the credit.

"How's Gina?"

He shrugged a shoulder. "She messaged Lexi stating that she's fine, and that surgery went well for her mom." He sipped his drink. "I haven't heard from her."

"It's probably Johnny preventing her from calling. He knows you pair had quite a past."

He turned to face Tiana. "Is she happy with him?"

She nodded. "I think so."

"That's all that matters."

He missed Gina like crazy. If she was happy though, then no way would he intervene. It was about time she had a steady relationship. She'd dated losers most of her life.

He set his flute on the side and meandered through the dancing bodies. The smell of alcohol and perfume wafted through his nostrils. He noticed looks of admiration from women he passed, and felt his ego swell. Who didn't want to feel worthy, appreciated even?

"Where's Eva?" he asked the barmaid, noticing that Eva was no longer in the room. He wanted to be civil, do the right thing and congratulate her on the event. He knew they weren't easy to organise.

"As in your ex-wife?"

"Do you know any other Evas?" he asked.

"Actually, I don't." She giggled. "Not like her, anyway."

He remained tight-lipped.

"She's back there." She jerked her head in the direction of the playrooms.

Maybe she was checking on the girls that dressed up for role-play, or ensuring everything was running smoothly. He decided to inspect the rooms himself, see how busy they were. As soon as he strolled down the red carpet and passed the rope, he was in the corridor to the playrooms. He blinked, his eyes having to adjust to the change in lighting, as he was instantly bathed in a red glow.

He peered in each room he went by, getting a view of writhing, naked bodies, mostly fornicating, or pleasuring themselves solo. Moaning and groaning filled his ears, and the smell of sex and perspiration met his nostrils. As a stunning brunette shuddered and cried out, an orgasm tearing through her, her gaze locked with Darion's. He swallowed the lump that had appeared in his throat. The playrooms were as enticing as ever—the erotic nakedness making him stare in awe.

Turning himself away from the scene before him, he thought of Gabi and the rules. Never would he break them. As he neared toward the room with the four rotating beds, a familiar cry of agonised ecstasy sliced through him. He squeezed his eyes shut for a brief second. A part of him knew it was best to leave the playrooms; the other part was curious, needing clarification on how he really felt about Eva. He found her lying spread-eagled on a bed, wearing only a black lacy thong. Her false breasts were prominently displayed as she arched her back in obvious pleasure. He could see her wrists were bound together by a leather cord. He was unable to tear his eyes away from the scene. A man hovered over her, placing kisses down her stomach. Eva was no longer his. There was no familiar sexual thrill at seeing her in those circumstances. He turned on his heel.

"Darion?"

Stopping still, he looked back over his shoulder.

Eva was in a seated position, making no attempt to cover her naked body. "Were you after me?" Her lips curved upwards.

"I wanted a word, but it's not important."

"I'll be out soon." She held up her wrists. "As you can see, I'm a little tied up."

Back in the bar, he settled down on the sofa in his private booth. He left the curtain open so he could see everything that was going on. Usually he would have had girls fussing all over him, joining him in the booth, sharing champagne. He couldn't decide whether he missed that lifestyle or not.

One of his bartenders brought a glass of whisky over. As she handed it to him, the condensation from the ice cubes dripped from the glass.

"Helen, is this how you bring drinks to the customers?" He placed it on the table and rubbed his hands together. "Always on a napkin," he ordered her.

The pretty blonde, usually confident and flirtatious, cowered slightly, her cheeks turning pink. She apologised profusely.

Feeling guilt tighten his chest, he said in a tone as soft and soothing as he could muster, "It doesn't matter. Just remember for next time, darlin'."

"I will." She looked down, fiddling with her hair. Darion was amused. She had worked for him for years. How she could still be coy was beyond him.

He placed his hand on hers, giving it a gentle squeeze. "I know it's busy in here tonight. You're doing a good job."

"The shift seems to fly by the busier I am." She smiled tightly. "You fancy some company?"

He leant back on the sofa and draped his arm on the back of it casually. "I'm good."

"Well, if you need anything, give me a shout."

He noticed her take in his appearance. He was wearing black jeans, a matching shirt, and a smart blazer. His hair was slicked back, and his jaw line was free of stubble for once. He knew he reeked of aftershave. He always dressed well for the clients, especially for the private parties.

"Will do," he responded, which seemed to break her daze.

"Um…I…" she stuttered.

"Helen, a Martini wouldn't go amiss." Eva appeared, plopping herself down on the sofa beside him.

"Sure." Helen hurried off.

"So, Darion," she purred, her pupils gleaming under the spotlights. "What did you want me for?" He could see from her hazy eyes that she was drunk.

"I was coming to congratulate you. The turn out tonight is fantastic."

Her eyes widened, shock registering on her face. "Oh."

He picked up his whisky and took a sip before setting it back down on the table.

"Couldn't it wait? You came looking for me in the playrooms to tell me that?" Her brow rose.

Darion traced his finger along his bottom lip. "Why else would I come looking for you?"

She let out a low, mischievous laugh, leaning forward so he got a view of her cleavage. "For reasons I can only dream."

Darion pushed himself to his feet. Towering over her, he said, "Keep dreaming, Eva."

He didn't wait for her reaction. Instead, he left the room. He felt her glare burning holes into his back.

Chapter Thirty-Eight

Darion tightened his hold on Gabi's hand. How the hell had he been badgered into meeting Gabi's family? Lexi. He made a mental note in his head to remind her to keep out of his business, especially when it came to relationships. He couldn't help but worry that things were moving too fast. What was it that he even wanted? Before he could answer the questions swirling around in his mind, Gabi squeezed his hand.

He blinked and took in the surroundings. An immaculate grass lawn was complete with colourful flowers, under a cerulean sky. The sun was blaring for a change, heating his face. He slowly made his way toward the cream four storey building. Not too far from Hyde Park, they were in Mayfair, an expensive, luxurious part of London. His breath held tight in his throat. He tried to hide the surprise on his face. It appeared as if Gabi really had lived a sheltered life. He could bet she had never gone without anything whilst growing up. She had advised him that her parents were retired doctors. They went on several vacations throughout the year.

"So, your brother is home now?" he asked.

She nodded. A huge grin was plastered on her face as if she could barely contain her excitement. "For a short while, yes."

A tiny part of him was actually looking forward to meeting her parents. He wanted to know more about Gabi. He supposed he also wanted them to like him, to welcome him with open arms. He doubted he could handle rejection should it come. Eva's parents hadn't exactly been friendly. They reminded him of his own parents. He chewed his lower lip.

"Mom, it's me, Gabi," she called into the intercom.

Darion heard a buzzing sound followed by a click, which indicated that the door was open. As they proceeded along the shiny marble floor toward the elevator, Darion pushed down the sleeves of his navy shirt. When he was before the elevator mirror, he fastened two buttons at the collar. Gabi wrapped her arms around his waist tightly and planted a kiss on his cheek.

"Don't be nervous. They will love you."

Darion rubbed his forehead. "I'm not nervous."

Turning around to face her, he pulled her into him. Her big brown eyes were shimmering with happiness. Her beautiful, pure smile had a way of melting his heart. The emotions he was feeling were unfamiliar, slightly unnerving. He definitely must have loved Gabi, for she made him feel as weak as she did strong. He felt he could get through anything, and do anything having her by his side. Without her, he felt a little empty, lost—always wondering what she was doing.

He brought his hands up to cup her face. He pressed his lips against her mouth. After a few gentle pecks, he slipped his tongue inside, massaging hers with urgency. He couldn't help but groan as the kiss became deeper, and she rubbed her pelvis against him. His teeth clashed against hers as he kissed her ever harder, backing her against the wall. His hands slid underneath her pretty black dress.

"Darion…" She pulled away. "We can't."

He inhaled a breath, noticing that her lips were engorged. They looked tempting, even more kissable than usual. "I want you, Gabi." He reached out to grab her.

She swatted his hand away, a playful smile tilting her lips. "Behave."

The elevator doors pinged open. *Shit!* He massaged the back of his neck, feeling his muscles become unbearably tense. *Relax. They will like you.*

As soon as Gabi pressed the bell at a red door, it flew open, as if the person beyond it had been waiting eagerly near it. A woman who appeared to be in her sixties, with the same long, blonde hair as Gabi, and kind eyes, forcefully yanked her into a hug.

"Oh, sweetheart. It's been too long."

"I know it has, Mom. But I never know when you're home. The telephone always rings out."

"I'm sorry, dear. It is very rare that we're in

these days."

"I've told you to get a mobile."

She waved her hand in the air dismissively. "Gabi, the world is controlled by technology. I don't want people to be able to get hold of me every second of the day." She laughed. "You must be Darion."

Darion offered his hand for her to shake, however she embraced him tightly. He was slightly taken aback, but at the same time filled with warmth at the welcome.

"This is my mom, Joy, as you've probably guessed."

Joy. The name certainly suits her.

"Gabi." A man, appearing to be in his mid-sixties, approached. He was dressed smartly in a grey shirt and black trousers. His hair was also brown, however streaked with grey strands, obviously free of colour dye, unlike his wife. His skin had the same olive colour Gabi's had. He squeezed Gabi into a tight hug, and then turned to face him.

"Mr. Milano." He held out his hand. "Nice to meet you. I'm Nicholas, Gabi's dad."

Darion clasped his hand in a firm shake.

"Supper is almost ready. Samuel's just serving it up as we speak."

Darion followed them into a large dining room. The décor was a mixture of white and gold colouring, from the cushion of the chairs, to the painted walls. He noticed a glass cabinet stocked with family photographs. He felt his stomach flip, noticing how different it was from his parents' home. He didn't remember ever seeing photographs throughout the house.

"Please, sit."

He made himself comfortable on a chair. When he noticed Gabi's dad prop his elbows on the table, he did the same. He didn't know why but he all of a sudden felt like a choir boy wanting to make a good impression. He felt so out of his depth with these people, but also relaxed and welcome. *Fuck.* He held in a chuckle. What the hell would they think if they knew he lived the lifestyle of a swinger, that he had introduced their precious daughter into his world of dark desires? No wonder Gabi had been drawn to him. He bet she'd never experienced excitement like it in her life. The most excitement she'd probably ever seen growing up was being allowed to eat chocolate after eight.

"Samuel." Gabi jumped out of her seat and wrapped her arms around her brother when he entered.

Darion noticed he was an attractive looking lad, also with dark hair. When Gabi introduced him, he was surprised to find his arms were decorated with tattoos. Darion shot out of his seat and offered his hand.

"Hey, man." Samuel pulled him into a loose hug instead, patting him on the back.

Once he and Gabi were left alone at the table, her family in the kitchen, he muttered under his breath, "So you're a posh bird." He licked his lips, smiling at her playfully.

"I'm not posh," she exclaimed.

"Gabi, come on."

"Darion. My mom and dad were brought up in Hackney. They did well at school, secured good jobs and…"

"Went up in the world. I can see."

"They're not posh. You'll see." Her eyes gleamed as if there was more to her parents than met the eye.

"Darion, we didn't know which meat you liked, so we cooked a bit of everything. I hope you like chicken, lamb, or pork." Joy regarded him, setting down a tray of different meats.

"I like them all. Thank you."

They were soon digging into the buffet before them. There was meat, a variety of vegetables, potatoes, and other foods that Darion didn't recognise, complete with gravy, mint, and cranberry sauce. It smelt divine and was heaven to his taste buds.

"So, Darion." Nicholas looked up. "What is it that you do?"

He felt his spine stiffen. It was the question he had been dreading. He glanced at Gabi.

"I told you, Dad. He owns a gentlemen's club."

He tightened his grip on his fork, wishing Gabi could have just stated that it was a normal bar. Now they would probably assume he was a sleazy pervert. Not that they'd be wrong. However, that aspect of his life would have been better kept private in the circumstances.

"I hear they do well these days." Nicholas nodded in what appeared to be approval. "Good for you, son."

Darion turned his head quickly, wishing the

shock that definitely would have surfaced on his face wasn't so clear. He felt himself swell with pride. Nobody had ever congratulated him on his business before. Well, his aunt did, but the people he had most wanted to hear it from—his parents—hadn't.

"Maybe when the girls are out gallivanting along Bond Street one day, you and I could—"

"Nicholas." Joy slapped him on the arm, with a soft laugh.

"This is why I don't do girlfriends. Restrictions." Samuel shook his head, beaming. "I wouldn't mind checking the club out."

"Excuse me." Gabi shot him a look. "You don't do girlfriends because you hate long distant relationships, not because of the restrictions you believe they place upon you."

"Keep telling yourself that, Gabi." He laughed. "I like being a man of freewill."

Darion popped a potato in his mouth, liking Gabi's family even more. He had been wary at first, believing they would be slightly stuck-up; however they were far from it, having a great sense of humour.

"Gabi said you like bikes and cars," Samuel said, his mouth full. "Me too. I want to get a bike at some point."

"Yeah." He nodded. "I've got the R1."

"Nice."

"So, Gabi, how's work? How's Mallory and Suzie?" her mother asked, lifting her glass of wine to her lips.

"Everything's great, Mom."

Darion turned his head to see Nicholas opening a tin. Cigars. He felt himself perk up. Maybe they had something in common after all. He didn't hesitate at taking one when offered.

"After dinner, we can smoke these in the playroom."

Playroom. He couldn't refrain from smiling. He caught Gabi staring at him. She shook her head with a giggle, as if to say, *Not that sort of playroom.*

Joy groaned. "Nicholas and his games room. I tell you, the minute Gabi moved out, he was splurging on a pool table, dart board, computer consoles, and a mini bar."

"It's the best room in the house, to be fair," Samuel informed him.

"Sounds it," Darion agreed.

He tensed when he felt a hand massaging him through his jeans. He glanced at Gabi sitting beside him. At the dinner table, with her family present? The girl must have more guts than he'd thought. He felt himself hardening as she continued to caress him. He tried his hardest to keep a straight face, and concentrate on chewing his food. But it felt so good. He gripped his fork as her rubbing became firmer.

"Gabi," he whispered. "What are you doing?"

She stared at him, her eyes wide and full of mischief. She leant closer and said quietly, "I want you, now."

He almost choked on his food. The words he often used rolling from Gabi's tongue sounded sexy, and he was completely seduced.

"Let's go to the bathroom."

He shook his head.

289

"Am I seeing a shy side to Darion Milano?" Her brow rose as she stared at him questioningly.

"More like a respectable side."

"I thought there was never a wrong time or place when it came to sex."

"There is now."

She removed her hand. Darion felt his shoulders sag in disappointment, although he knew it was for the best. He'd ravage her once they stepped foot in the elevator.

The next few hours seemed to fly by. Darion had played pool with Samuel and Nicholas, whilst Gabi remained in the kitchen with her mom, helping wash up. He felt more at home there than he ever had in his own home. When it came to leaving, a small part of him actually wished they could have stayed even longer. Gabi made a promise to see them more often. Waving enthusiastically, he followed her into the elevator.

As soon as the doors closed, he slammed her against the wall, possessing her mouth with his own. He attacked her clothes, bunching her dress up around her waist, and tearing her underwear off.

"You want me, do you?" he asked.

"Yes, I do," she responded, tugging his hair and ramming her tongue down his throat.

Darion ran his hands up Gabi's smooth legs. He buried his face into the crook of her neck, inhaling the smell of her sweet perfume. Showering her with kisses, he then pulled down the neckline of her dress, freeing her pert breasts. He took one into his mouth, sucking on it hungrily, desperately. He then caressed her behind. He groaned in satisfaction at how nice her body felt under his palms. He couldn't get enough of her.

"Ah, Gabi…" He frantically fiddled with the zipper on his jeans. He released his throbbing erection, urgently needing sweet release.

Chapter Thirty-Nine

Gabi

Darion rubbed his cock against her a couple of times, causing her sex to throb. As he circled the tip between her legs, she clenched her teeth, pulling him closer. She wanted him so bad. She looked down to see his fingers were wrapped around his shaft as he guided it into her, the moist head sliding in. As his length went in deeper, she sucked in air. His hips collided against hers as he rocked back and forth, moving in and out slowly. When he was in all of the way, the rhythm became faster. She studied how he screwed up his features, grimacing in pleasure. A sigh left his lips as he closed his lids and threw his head back.

"Gabriella Woods..." he groaned. "You feel so fucking good."

He gripped her hair as he jerked into her so powerfully, she almost couldn't take it, the pleasure intense. She cried out incoherently.

"One of these days…" he breathed heavily into her ear, his fierce stare intent on her. "I'm going to claim every little part of you." He squeezed her rear, roughly. "And you're going to love it."

She felt vibrations between her legs, which rippled through her stomach, as he returned to her clit. He circled it with his thumb as he pounded into her. Her abdomen tightened as pleasure took over.

"Don't stop…" she pleaded, clawing at his shirt, pulling him against her.

What the hell? She glared at him when he withdrew, taking a step back. Oh no. She was so close. Her inner muscles throbbed and ached, needing to be satisfied.

"Darion. Don't you dare."

"I think we should practice tantric sex." His tongue darted out to wet his lips. "Let's bring each other close to orgasm and stop. We can go all day."

"Not now." She grabbed him by his upper arm, pulling him into her.

She cried out when he filled her again, hitting her sensitive spot. She thrust her hips back and forth, mirroring his actions, urgently needing the heavy, swirling ache in her stomach to go.

"You want me to fuck you hard?" he asked, his eyes dark, possessed, a sadistic look on his face. Oh, how she adored that sexy look.

"Yes."

Gabi didn't think it could feel any more pleasurable, but she was wrong. He slowly slid in and out. Her breathing hitched. In and out. The pace was torturous. He was teasing her, preparing her.

She gripped his buttocks, needing to be filled even more.

"Okay. Fast it is."

He slammed into her so hard her body crashed against the wall. He bucked his hips at a frenetic pace, his features strained. His cock filled her deliciously, increasing her breathing and moaning. She caught sight of them in the mirror, which further piqued her arousal. Watching him fucking her was better than observing other couples in the playrooms.

She could see his ass bobbing, the expressions on his face. She glanced down to examine his cock sliding in, and then out. It was moist with her arousal, so thick and hard. She was unable to tear away from watching their bodies connecting.

"You like that?" he asked, leaning back slightly to give her a clearer view. His head dropped as he also watched his cock entering and leaving her sex.

"One day, we'll set up a camera. Watch ourselves." He bit her ear. "Would you like that?"

She felt heat flood through her chest and into her cheeks. Would she? She decided that she might. She nodded.

"We're gonna do so much together sexually, Gabi." His tone was seductive, husky, promising. "Just you wait and see."

He sent her over the edge. She curled her fingers. As he continued to hit into her, she sucked in air. Her stomach and lungs tightened. She clutched him one final time and convulsed on a loud groan, exploding over and over. Darion followed closely, shuddering, his head thrown back, crying out.

Wow, Gabi thought with a soft laugh. She almost buckled on her weak knees, her vision blurry as she felt disoriented for a second. Balancing her weight on Darion, she cuddled him tightly.

***

The car journey to Darion's parents' house was quiet, except for music, which Gabi assumed Darion had played to avoid conversation. She remained staring out of the window, taking in the sights. The tidy streets of Mayfair were replaced with streets which were littered, and instead of seeing girls laden with designer shopping bags, and people in suits, she saw street gangs, and drunks stumbling around.

She twiddled with her nails, and tried to ignore the rolling of her stomach. She couldn't decide whether she was nervous because she was meeting his parents and didn't know what to expect, or whether it was because it seemed pointless, as she believed that soon enough, she and Darion would be over. How could he forgive her? She had done the one thing he despised—cheated, betrayed him outside of the playrooms.

When the car came to a halt forty minutes later, Gabi blinked rapidly. Sitting up in her seat, she rubbed her head. She must have fallen asleep. Glancing at Darion, she saw he was biting his lower lip, lost in a daze.

"Are you okay?" she asked, unbuckling her seatbelt.

He turned to face her. "I'm not sure this is a

good idea, Gabi."

Me either, she thought. *Let's save ourselves the hassle and go home.* "You don't have to introduce me to your parents," she said. "Maybe we are moving too fast."

"Gabi." He shot her a look. "You've wanted nothing more than for our relationship to be exclusive." His lips curled into a smile. "Everything Lexi said is true. If you need more stability, and this is the way to show you that I care, then so be it."

Gabi turned her head away. She would have liked it in the past, yes. But things had changed since then.

He nodded toward a red Seat Leon. "Dion is here too."

Gabi took out lip-gloss from her bag. She wiped the wand across her lips, coating them with a shimmery pink colour. After she quickly ran a brush through her hair, she pulled herself out of the car, the door of which Darion was holding open.

"I meant what I said about my parents. They're not nice people."

"What did they do to you, Darion?" she asked.

"It's more a case of what they didn't do." He stuffed his hands in his jean pockets.

"Milano, long time, no see," a man called out from across the street.

Darion acknowledged him with a nod of the head.

"Nice car."

"Thanks."

Gabi followed Darion toward a house. Judging from the size of it, and the windows at the front, she guessed it had four bedrooms. The garden was untidy, the grass needed a cut, and the wilting flowers desperately needed watering. When she was before the front door, she also couldn't help but notice it needed a good slick of paint, and the window needed a scrub.

"My mom works two jobs. She doesn't get around to getting everything done," Darion informed Gabi as he ducked his head. She wasn't sure whether it was in embarrassment or annoyance. "I've offered to help. They won't accept."

He curled his fingers into a fist and knocked on the glass.

"Who is it?" she heard a female yell from the other side.

"Darion."

The door creaked open. Gabi came face to face with a stunning woman, who she assumed was Dion. Her hair was brown with thin blonde streaks all over. She had Darion's green eyes and full lips. Her body was petite and concealed in a white vest top and ripped blue denim jeans. She had no shoes on her feet, only black socks.

"What do you want?" Her stare swept over Darion.

"To start with? A coffee."

She shook her head, and smiled. "You asshole." She flung her arms around his neck. "You never visit anymore."

"We both know why that is."

"Yeah, well, doesn't stop you popping by my house." She peered over his shoulder. "Nice car! I thought you only had the Jeep?"

"I have a bike too."

"It's all right for some." Her eyes lit up, as if she was proud of her big brother. "You look smart, Daz."

He rubbed the stubble on his chin, as if finding it difficult to accept a compliment. "This is Gabi." He stepped back. "Gabi, this is Dion."

"Hi, Gabi." Dion gave her the once over. "Nice to meet you. She's certainly an upgrade on Eva." She nudged Darion with a wink.

"Who's at the door, Dion?" a male voice boomed from inside.

"It's Darion." She moved aside for them to enter.

Gabi took in the hallway. She'd expected it to be adorned with family photographs like most houses were, however the walls were bare. When she entered the living room, closely behind Darion, she could see that a man, more than likely his dad, was watching boxing on television, a bottle of Corona in his hand.

"You remembered where we live then?" his dad huffed.

"Just about," Darion responded, pulling out a chair near a table. He dropped down onto it. He pointed at another chair, indicating for Gabi to sit.

Reluctantly, she sat down. His dad hadn't even looked up from the television. Only when the boxing had finished did he rise to his feet. He was an older version of Darion—tall, green eyes, dark hair, and the same slightly tanned complexion. His family had good genes. So far they were all above average in looks. His face broke into a smile as he studied Gabi.

"New girlfriend again?" he asked. "Can never keep up with them."

A laugh which sounded uncomfortable left Darion's mouth. "The apple doesn't fall far from the tree."

"Too right it doesn't."

"Gabi, this is my dad, Luca."

Gabi looked at Darion, knowing surprise must have surfaced on her face.

"What?" Darion asked. "Gabi, don't tell me you didn't know I have Italian in my blood."

She laughed, feeling her face flame. "I…"

"Didn't the surname give it away?"

"My parents were from Portofino," his dad informed her. "So, who are you?"

Darion, the Italian stallion. Yummy. "Um, Gabriella," she responded.

"Gabriella? Spanish ancestors?"

She shook her head. "No. My mom just liked the name. Nothing exotic about my family tree."

"I'd disagree," Luca said, a twinkle appearing in his eye.

Darion rolled his eyes.

"Anyway, why are you here, Darion?" He turned his attention back to Darion, a puzzled expression on his face.

"I was in the area."

"Darion, Gabi," Dion shouted from the kitchen. "We're outta coffee. You want tea? Squash?"

"Tea will be fine," Darion responded. "Gabi?"

"I'm okay."

"Where's Mom?"

"Working. Where else?"

Gabi chewed her nail, not knowing where to place herself. The tension in the room was so intense it almost seemed tangible. Darion's relationship with his parents was nothing like she had with hers. She could see he was uncomfortable as he tapped his foot on the floor and crossed his arms across his chest.

She was slightly relieved when Dion returned with a cup of tea. She placed it on the table.

"Where's Jane?"

Dion threw him a look. "She's upstairs." Standing in the doorway, she shouted, "Odelia. Uncle Darion is here."

Gabi could hear the sound of hurried footsteps booming down the stairs. A pretty girl who looked similar to Dion rushed into the room. She appeared to be about six in age. She flung her arms around Darion's neck.

"Daz, where have you been?"

"Working."

"Nanny said you work with prostitutes. What's a prostitute?"

Darion leant back in his chair with a sigh.

"Don't use that word again," Dion snapped.

"Use what word?"

Gabi turned her attention to the door. A woman who must have been his mom appeared, her arms full with bags, of which milk bottles, cereal boxes, and fruit was visible. Darion hurriedly approached her, taking bags from her arms. Gabi could tell by the circles under her eyes, and her drooped shoulders, that she was exhausted. Her hair was greyer than it was brown, and hung lifelessly flat down her back. It was clear she would have been beautiful when she was younger. She could even have been beautiful now, although it looked like she'd given up on her appearance a long time ago.

"Prostitutes," Odelia repeated. "You said Darion works with them."

"Well, they do sell their bodies for money," his mom said before leaving the room. "And turn that television down, Luca. Are you deaf or something?"

Darion followed his mom, leaving Gabi twiddling with her thumbs. She felt unwelcome, desperately wishing they could leave. Dion began making small talk, asking Gabi where she was from, and how she and Darion had met. She revealed she was a single mom, and only lived a street away. She apologised for her parents' behavior under her breath, and said she wished she could say it was just an off day, but it wasn't.

"The only reason I visit is because Odelia, for some crazy reason, adores them. I guess she knows no better."

"Mom, this is Gabi. Gabi, this is my mom, Whitney," Darion gave the introductions when he returned.

"Hi." Gabi flashed her a smile.

"Hi," she responded flatly, seeming disinterested. She dropped onto the sofa, next to Luca.

"Work okay?" Darion asked his mom, obviously trying to make polite conversation.

"What do you think?"

Silence descended upon the room.

"It's been years since I opened the club, and you

still haven't visited," Darion said firmly.

"I'm not interested in visiting that sort of place." Whitney screwed her face up. "Your dad might have a thing for cheap tittie bars, but I haven't."

Gabi noticed Darion's face fall. She doubted she had ever seen his eyes look so sad. She saw his Adam's apple dip as he swallowed. Drumming his fingers on the tabletop, he must have remembered his drink, and so reached over to grab it.

"Right, I'm going out," his dad said, standing up.

"See what I mean?" Whitney shook her head.

"There's nothing else to do around here."

"Dad, I can give you a ride if you wait. I'm not staying long."

"My car might not have cost over twenty grand like yours, but it gets me down the road."

Darion opened his mouth to speak, and then obviously thinking better of it, closed it.

"I think Darion's done great with the club," Dion said as she braided Odelia's hair. "And his car is amazing. Give him a break."

"Don't start." Whitney shot Dion a look.

"Would it kill you to congratulate him for once?"

"Dion, stop." Darion held his palm in the air. "It's okay."

"No," she huffed. "They never congratulated you when you passed your GSCE's, or when you opened the club, or when you could finally afford nice things. Oh, and when you got married. It's not right."

"Oh, here we go." His mother grabbed the television remote and turned the volume higher.

"This is why I'm always out." Luca pulled on his

jacket. "I've got a miserable wife."

"I wouldn't be miserable if you hadn't come into my life," she snapped.

"Oh yeah, because you'd be a fucking trolley dolly now, flying to exotic locations. Well, you're a mother instead. Deal with it. That ship sailed a long time ago."

"You can talk. If it wasn't for me, you'd still be in prison, not making up for lost time by sleeping around."

"My daughter is in the room," Dion yelled. "And we have company."

"I'm not gonna pretend everything is perfect just because we have company." Whitney folded her arms across her chest.

"It's called politeness," Dion said through clenched teeth.

"See you soon, Odelia." Luca bent down and pinched the girl's cheek.

"Are you going to see prostitutes? Nan says you do."

"Odelia! What did I say about using that word?"

"Unfortunately, your grandpa doesn't have that much money."

"Get a job then," Whitney shouted. "Oh, I forgot. You have a criminal record for theft."

"I was young and stupid." Luca sighed. "Gabi, good luck with my son." He gave her a brief wave and left the room.

"I'm sick of this shit," Dion muttered under her breath.

"I'm sick of this shit," Odelia repeated.

Dion gasped, but then seeing the funny side, she

started laughing. Darion followed suit.

"Gabi, can I get you a drink, some food?" Darion asked, standing up.

"No, thanks. I'm okay." The sooner they left the better.

As Odelia began telling Gabi about school and her friends, Gabi watched as Darion approached Whitney and sat down. She could see his mouth moving, his face etched with worry, but she couldn't make out what he was saying. He placed a hand on Whitney's arm, but she edged away. The hurt and rejection was apparent on Darion's face. He abruptly stood up again and shoved his hand into his pocket.

"You don't need to work two jobs, I tell you all of the time. I'll send you money."

Whitney threw him a look of disgust. "I'm not some charity case."

"Mom, I—"

"You come here, with your fancy car, your fancy clothes, throwing money around, thinking you're better than us."

Darion blew out an exasperated puff of air, as if not believing his ears.

"Mom, he's only trying to help."

"I'm leaving," Darion said. He crouched down and handed Odelia a wad of money. "You buy yourself something nice, okay?"

"Wow." Her face lit up. "Mom, look how much money is here."

"Darion, you don't have to do that."

"I want to. Here." He handed Dion money. "Take this."

"No, Daz."

"Take it," he said, his tone firm. "Come on, Gabi."

Gabi grabbed her handbag and clambered to her feet. "It was nice meeting you." She wasn't surprised when his mom didn't respond. "Dion, Odelia, nice meeting you both." She gave them a little wave.

"It was lovely meeting you, Gabi. Maybe one day the four of us can go out?" Dion smiled.

Odelia clapped her hands together with excitement. "Can we?"

"Yeah." Darion nodded. "Call me." He ruffled Odelia's head. "Be a good girl for mommy, Jane."

Dion slapped him on the arm playfully. "Don't be a stranger."

As they made their way back to the car, Gabi felt a heavy ache in her throat. She could have cried on the spot for Darion. It was clear that no matter what he did, or tried to do, his parents never showed they were proud of him. What a horrible way to grow up. She could see that Darion was trying to put on a brave face with a smile, but she knew he was hurting.

She climbed into the car, after he opened her door. Strapping her seatbelt on, she leant her head on the window. She felt a shooting pain in her heart, and emptiness in her stomach. She felt even worse for what she had done.

Chapter Forty

"I'm so sorry, Gabi," Lexi said, the sincerity apparent in her eyes. "I only suggested it because I really want you pair to get serious."

Gabi smiled tightly. She knew Lexi only had good intentions.

"I didn't realise his parents were like that." She shrugged. "Darion never talks about them. He may have to Gina, but not to me."

"It's okay. I just feel really bad for him. I can tell he's hurting. I wish I could help."

"Gabi, he's thirty-six now. If he doesn't have a close relationship with them now, it's likely he never will."

Gabi lifted her glass of wine to her lips and took a sip. "Do you think I should check he's okay?"

"He will be. He said he had to make an important phone call."

Ever since they had returned from his parents' house, Gabi had been sitting at the bar for half an hour—alone. Darion had fled to his office saying he needed to take care of something.

"Gabi, my favourite client is here. I'm gonna see if he wants a dance." She squeezed her hand. "It will all be okay."

When Lexi vanished into the crowd, Gabi stared into her wine. She didn't fancy making small talk with Jasmine. She wasn't in the mood. She felt her mobile vibrating through her bag, which was on her lap. Pulling it out, she pursed her lips, wondering who would be calling her on an unknown number. She pressed answer, and held it to her ear.

"Hello."

"Gabi."

"Lawrence," she hissed. "How did you get my number?"

"Suzie gave it to me. I told her I'd found some important stuff of yours which you'd left here."

"And is that true?"

"Well…" he began, "If I searched the attic, I'd probably find something."

"Why are you calling me?" She rubbed her temple, a part of her knowing full well the reason for his call.

"I can't stop thinking about you, Gabi, seeing you, the kiss, talking with you. I want you. The only thing keeping us apart is that man."

"That's not true," she snapped, "I don't want to get back with you because we're not compatible. I don't have any regrets about leaving you. I'm with someone else."

"I know if he wasn't in the picture, give or take a few weeks, you'd be back here with me, where you belong."

"Don't ever call me again. I swear, I will call the

police."

"Have you told him yet?"

Her breath caught in her throat.

"If you don't tell him, Gabi, I will."

"Why are you doing this?"

"I want you back," he spat. "I will do *anything* to get you back, Gabi. I need you. I want to make up for everything I did wrong. Give me a chance."

"No."

"You've still got your engagement ring," he said softly.

Shit! After all that time she had forgotten to return it to him. Had he seen it as a sign of hope? That she hadn't been able to part with it. "I'll ensure you get it back."

"Gabi, please…"

"Lawrence, you slept with a stripper, and would've married me hiding that secret. Fuck you."

She ended the call. She sat there for a moment, her body shaking with rage. Putting her mobile back into her bag, she rested her head on her arms, which were flat on the bar surface. She was exhausted. It really had been the day from hell. After a minute, she sat up and swigged back some of her wine as she studied the room. Lawrence threatening her made her muscles stiff and her stomach churn. Would he really visit the club and tell Darion everything? She guessed he probably would. Lawrence was bitter. He wouldn't go down without a fight. No way would he sit back and watch Gabi happily move on with her life, whilst he was alone and miserable. She wanted to reveal everything to Darion, but when the timing was right. Now, she didn't even have that option. What if Lawrence rang or visited the club to speak with Darion? She needed to get to Darion before Lawrence did. If he heard it from Lawrence, then there was no way in hell there was even a tiny chance of him forgiving her. Plus, it would hurt him so much more.

***

Gabi watched as Darion shakily poured another drink, not noticing that he was spilling some on the desk. She'd seen him tipsy lots of times, however never completely drunk. She came to the conclusion he wasn't a horrible, rowdy drunk—far from it. He wasn't deliriously happy either. He was the same, except his guard came down. Although a smile remained on his face, troubled lines creased his forehead. She wasn't sure whether it was the light reflecting in his black pupils, or whether it was tears teetering on his lids. No. It couldn't be tears. She knew Darion kept everything bottled up. He saw crying as a sign of weakness.

"Gabi," he murmured. He now had that lewd, mischievous expression as if he were thinking of sex. "Come here."

As she rose to her feet and slowly took steps toward him, she felt the full weight of his scrutiny. His gaze swept over her body, his lips upturned. He devoured and worshipped her with his stare. He patted his knee, indicating for her to sit. She did as commanded. The feeling of him rigid against her, and the sadness apparent in his eyes when up close, made her wrap her arms around his shoulders.

Burying her face in his chest, she inhaled his scent. It was a mixture of his cologne and a slight twang of cigarette smoke.

She sat up abruptly when she heard his gentle snores. He had fallen asleep. His expression wasn't the face of someone in a deep, peaceful sleep, a nice thought or dream swimming in their mind. His features were screwed up, his brows pinched together with worry. Gabi pressed her lips gently on his.

"Gabi." His eyes shot open.

She rested her hand on his knee. He didn't reject it, nor welcome it. It was only when she began caressing it, did he look up. His green eyes clouded with obvious desire and longing.

"Are you okay?"

He shifted in the chair, causing her to perch on the edge of the desk instead. Darion stood up and stretched, causing his shirt to ride up and reveal his tight abdomen.

Retrieving his cigarettes from his pocket, he stuffed one into his mouth, and lit it. Only when he'd taken a long, slow drag, did he speak. "I'm fine, Gabi." He blew smoke out. "Come on, let's have a drink."

Gabi reluctantly followed him out of the office. She had to pace to keep up with his long, hurried strides. Sliding onto a stool, she shook her head as Darion began pouring Absinthe into two shot glasses. The strong smell alone made her screw up her face.

"I'm not drinking that again."

"Gabi," he said, his tone silky smooth, "live a

little." He slid the glass toward her. He doused his cigarette in the ashtray, and picked up his glass. "Let's have a little fun." He was trying to block out his problems with alcohol, trying to have as much fun as possible so he could force himself to be happy, to be rid of the feelings of hurt and rejection. She knew how he worked now. A slow, dangerous smile slid across his face, his expression darkening. Bringing the glass to his lips, he downed the liquid in one. His tongue darted out and lapped up the remains on his lips.

Gabi felt desire pool between her legs. She groaned inwardly. She couldn't understand how almost everything he did and everything about him turned her on, from the sound of his husky, sexy voice, his smoldering stare, his intoxicating scent, to the way that he moved so gracefully with confidence. She craved his touch. As if reading her mind, Darion let out a dirty sounding laugh before biting his lip, undressing her with his stare.

"Drink up, darlin'."

"Are you trying to get me drunk, Mr. Milano?"

"Yes," he replied, his voice husky. "I am. Gabriella Woods."

"And why might that be?" She necked back the drink. She screwed up her face as it washed down her throat and chest and settled in her stomach making it churn. She coughed. *Damn.* It was harsh.

Darion jerked his head to the ceiling, his brows shooting up suggestively. "Time to get kinky."

Gabi remained still for a moment, feeling her legs weaken. Her mind was flooded with images and words like one blurry movie. Darion kissing

Leah's stomach, tracing his way down, getting lower and lower. His fingers yanking at her underwear, slowly tearing it down her legs, and discarding it to the floor. Darion's lips on hers, hungrily, possessively, his eyes boring into hers, then the colour changing from green to blue…Lawrence's eyes, Lawrence's face, Lawrence's lips, fast, firm, needy.

"Have you told him yet? If you don't tell him, Gabi, I will." The words rang loud in her ears.

"If you don't keep your man happy, sweetheart…someone else will," Eva's sultry tone replaced it. *"I have been on every surface, worn every outfit, used every whip, and experienced more with Darion in those rooms than you ever will. I will get Darion back."*

"If you don't tell him, Gabi, I will."

"I will get Darion back." The words whirled around in her mind repeatedly.

Oh my god. She inhaled a deep breath of air, feeling a throbbing pain in her temples, the forming of a headache. She squeezed her lids shut for a moment. When she heard a bleep on her mobile, she opened them, and quickly fished it out of her bag. She discreetly checked the text message, her swirling stomach giving her an idea of who it may be.

Lawrence: I wonder if a trip to The Black Door is in order.

"Ready?" Darion asked, holding out his palm.

No! "Yes," she responded, putting her mobile

away. She took hold of his hand and allowed him to lead her upstairs.

Chapter Forty-One

Present Day

Once they were upstairs, Darion didn't waste time ordering any more drinks, or sitting down. He led her straight to the back of the room, toward the black door. The lively crowd was all one big blur. The sound of chatter and laughter pounded in her ears. The room was spinning. She was a nervous wreck. When they crossed the rope, Gabi swallowed. Darion was eager, as always, pleasure on his mind. Little did he know that he'd soon be experiencing pain.

He checked with Gabi to ensure she was fine with going in the playrooms. Although the rooms weren't open to the members for at least ten minutes, she knew Darion wanted her to go all of the way, to swap partners, to get intimate in one of the open rooms and be watched. She also knew he never wanted her to feel uncomfortable, nor would he ever force something on her which she disliked.

She let go of his hand, worrying thoughts consuming her. All she could think of was Lawrence entering the club. The kiss couldn't be revealed that way. No way. Not after everything Darion had been through lately: Eva's shock return, Gina leaving, his parents rejecting him shamelessly.

Once they were eventually in the dungeon suite, Gabi knew there and then that even if she hadn't betrayed him, and all was normal, she couldn't have sex whilst people watched. Nor could she ever share him. The swinger's lifestyle wasn't for her.

Her identity had already been stripped when she'd experienced the rooms before. She had allowed Darion to pleasure her whilst other bodies writhed around them, surrounded by an orgy. She had kissed men and women, strangers. She had allowed Darion to restrain her with leather cuffs in the dungeon suite in the past, and whip her naked body. She had worn fantasy outfits that she never would have chosen herself. Her body had been touched by several hands that hadn't been Darion's. She had turned her back on normality the day she had met him. She was surrounded by voyeurs, exhibitionists, fetishists, and people with fantasies beyond her wildest imagination. Who was she?

She took a deep, steady breath and asked Darion if they could talk. He tried to reassure her that she would enjoy the experience. He then almost sent her tumbling when he seized her face and kissed her. When she pulled back, he asked her what was wrong.

"There's something I have to tell you."

It was confession time.

Gabi felt the atmosphere change in the room dramatically. Wrapping her arms around herself, the murderous expression on Darion's face made her sob. It wasn't because she was afraid of him, for she knew he'd never hurt her. It was because she was about to destroy their relationship.

She took a step backwards. She had never seen him so angry before. She knew she had deeply hurt him. She hated herself for being so stupid, for ruining the trust between them they were slowly building on. Now, instead of feeling close to him, she couldn't have felt more distant. But it certainly wasn't all her fault. Darion had played a big part too. He should never have introduced her to his world. He should never have tried to change her.

"What do you need to tell me?" he repeated, his tone cold.

She focused on the ground. She couldn't meet Darion's eyes, which were full of hate, disappointment, and pain. He wasn't stupid. Of course he knew what was coming. He had seen it many times before. She could hear his erratic breathing, his chest rapidly rising and falling with each breath. His hands were trembling, and his posture was slouched, as if he no longer had the energy to stand. All confidence he had a moment ago had diminished.

"I did something stupid."

Darion turned his back on her and paced the room, back and forth. He ran his hand through his hair and released a puff of exasperation. Eventually, he sat on the edge of the bed. Silence loomed over them like a dark cloud that was seconds away from pouring down with torrential rain.

Gabi hastily wiped a tear away that slid down her cheek.

"What did you do?" he asked, his voice shaky, obviously a mixture of emotions.

Gabi swallowed the lump in her throat. She took a deep breath, and looked at him. "I kissed my ex-fiancé." She squeezed her lids shut, afraid of what she would see. Would he be flushed with rage, or breaking down in pain?

"Why would you do that?" he asked, his voice barely above a whisper.

She opened her eyes. He rose to his feet, his features hardening.

"It was you who wanted the relationship to be exclusive," he reminded her. "And yet I allowed you to have anyone between these walls."

"I didn't do it for pleasure, Darion," she cried out. "I was feeling lost...confused...it was after that time with Jayce and Leah. I couldn't handle seeing you with her." She looked down and wrapped her arms around herself. "I couldn't handle Eva being back, also. It all got too much for me."

Darion rubbed his palms up and down his face. "This is why I found it difficult to tell you I loved you, even when every part of me did. Because I knew shit like this would happen. I knew that if I fucking loved you, it would be too good to be true." She could see the rage on his face, the cords in his neck taut; his fists clenched either side of him.

Her heart thudded in anticipation, waiting in fear for his next move.

"I'm so sorry, Darion," she whispered. "I regretted it instantly."

"You know, I've been unsure about my feelings for Eva, but I *never* would have dreamt of acting upon it, Gabi. Ever."

Gabi wiped at her soaked cheeks.

Darion stood before her, so close she could feel the warmth radiating from him. She could see the devastation in his eyes. "It's over."

Her stomach dropped. She sucked in air. It was what she had expected. Knowing she had nothing to lose anymore, she decided she wasn't going down without a fight, without having her say.

"I made one drunken mistake when I was doubting our relationship, unsure of where it was headed, *hating* what it involved. You don't mind me kissing other men when it suits you." She stared up at him.

"That's something we agreed on," he said. "Something for *our* sexual gratification. Something we shared in these playrooms. Together. You kissed another man behind my back for your own reasons. You're no better than Eva."

With all of the force she had, Gabi lifted her hand, and slapped it hard across Darion's face. His head jerked sideways from the impact. She felt the sting of it, and the blood rush through her palm. Darion slowly turned his head, and she noticed she had cut his lower lip. His tongue appeared and licked the blood away. His dark, devilish eyes bored into hers.

Gabi waited with bated breath, wondering how he was going to react. A part of her desperately wanted that familiar wicked smile to show, that glint to appear in his green irises, for him to slam her against the wall, and possess her with his mouth, claim her with his hands, whisper obscenities in her ear, and fuck her harder than he ever had before. She deserved punishment and she wanted it so bad.

"After all this time, I worried that I'd be the one to hurt you. But it was you that caused the hurt. Maybe it was me that needed the warning."

"Do you think I wasn't hurt when you wanted to sleep with other women?" she spat, feeling her cheeks burn.

"You knew what I was about."

"Yeah. Well, I'm an insecure wreck when I feel unloved, when I'm not told I'm loved, so now you know what I'm about."

He remained silent.

"Do you know what I once read?" She glared at him. "If you have to prove your worth to a man, then he isn't the one."

Darion shook his head. "We weren't meant to last anyway," he said, the sadness apparent in his trembling tone. "Happiness is always within my reach, but never to have."

Gabi felt her heart skip a beat.

"Goodbye, Gabi," he said, his voice so soft she barely heard it, yet the impact of it was as strong and effective as if he had screamed it in her face. She recognised the hurt, pain, and rejection in his eyes one final time before he turned his back on her. He left the room.

Gabi stilled for a moment, in complete and utter

shock, not knowing what to do. He had been right. She had wanted the relationship to be serious. Not only had Darion changed her, but she had also changed him. Although she hadn't directly expressed it to him, she wanted him to give up swinging, leave the club, and commit to her and only her. She had wanted nothing more than to get him to open up, to let her in, to allow himself to be loved, and to love back. She had wanted to show him he could trust her. He obviously couldn't.

She slid to her knees, and the tears fell freely as she cried hysterically. *Asshole!* He hadn't been a saint. She remained sitting there in the red glow of the room for what felt like an eternity. When she felt ready to go home, she wiped her eyes, and slowly dragged herself to her feet. She almost jumped out of her skin when she saw a figure leant against the door. Moving closer, her stomach flipped. It was Eva.

"I heard what happened," she said, crossing her arms across her chest. "Looks like we're not so different after all."

"We're very different, Eva. I kissed someone. I didn't fuck them."

"The sin is still the same—betrayal, lies, deceit. You've lost him, Gabi."

"What? And you think he'll get back with you?" She snorted. "With the betrayal, lies, and deceit?"

"There's hope."

"Fuck you," she spat. "You don't love Darion. You're happy to share him." She shook her head. "I never wanted to share him. *Ever.*"

"Because you're boring, sweetheart. Vanilla."

"I'd rather be vanilla than a whore."

"Oh, Gabi." Eva laughed loudly. "Don't you know that men like a lady in the street, and a freak in the sheets?"

"Men have fun with women like you," Gabi said. "They don't settle down with them, have babies, and live the good life. You're only as useful as those sex toys over there." Gabi smirked. "But even those get 'same old.' Chemistry and passion dies. Then what do you have left, Eva? From where I'm standing, it doesn't seem like much."

Eva's mouth fell open.

"If Darion still loves you, and he wants you back, I promise I won't stand in your way. I want him to be happy."

Eva's eyes widened in surprise. Her features then softened, as if she suddenly had a newfound respect for her. Gabi wished her luck, and fled out of the playrooms as quickly as she could. She didn't bother glancing back at the glowing red window as she climbed into a taxi ten minutes later. As far as she was concerned, it was the window to hell.

Chapter Forty-Two

Gabi kicked off her black Louboutin heels, and tucked her legs underneath her. It was Monday morning, and she couldn't concentrate on anything. Being without Darion was like missing a limb. She didn't have him messaging and calling her throughout the day. She didn't have him to cuddle up to at night. She didn't have his big, protective arms around her making her feel safe. She missed everything about him—his captivating eyes, his sexy smile, his gorgeous body, his sultry voice. Life was also boring not having a man puzzle to try to figure out, the excitement of spontaneous plans, the dramas he always shared. Everything was back to being *dull.* Ordinary.

She had a piercing pain in her heart that wouldn't go away. She yawned for what was probably the fifth time that day. She had been unable to sleep last night. She kept replaying the confession in her head, how broken Darion had looked.

She clicked the keyboard of her computer, causing the screen to light up. Maybe if she knew why Darion was the way he was, why he had the desires and fantasies he did, then she could understand him a bit better, and the way his complex mind worked. Or maybe she was trying to figure him out to convince herself they weren't suited, that she was better off without him.

She typed in *exhibitionism* in the Internet browser. Several websites displayed before her. She clicked on one, and read the psychological reasons for *some* exhibitionists.

Exhibitionism can be a desire to be observed whilst having sex with other people. The behaviour can be linked to the person having poor social and interpersonal skills.

This was probably true in Darion's case, she decided. His parents barely made conversation with him. She continued to read.

Some individuals are unable to establish a conventional sexual relationship.

Again, she thought of Darion's past relationships, which he'd said had been brief, except for Eva, who he married, who was also an exhibitionist, and whatever else.

Some want attention; and need people to think highly of them.

Next, Gabi typed in voyeurism.

Voyeurism, the risk of getting caught appeals to adrenaline junkies. It's the thrill of it. These types of people may have low self-esteem, and unresolved family conflicts.

It sounded fitting. Although Darion displayed an air of confidence, Gabi knew he was unsure of his abilities deep down, lacked confidence, and was damaged. His upbringing hadn't been normal. He didn't have a good example of what a normal relationship should be like, nor did he know how it felt to have loving parents.

Although Eva had suggested swinging to Darion, he had continued it when they had separated, obviously becoming addicted to it. Maybe he always would have desired it, but just hadn't known it then.

She took hold of her cup and swigged back some of her coffee. A tap came on the door, followed by Mallory entering.

"Hey, Gab." She beamed, sitting on the chair opposite.

"Hi, Mal," she responded, hoping her tone didn't come out as glum as she felt. She quickly closed the Internet page.

"Shit. What happened to you?"

"What do you mean?"

"Gabi, you look as pretty as a dog's arse."

"Thanks, Mal."

"I'm sorry, but your hair looks a right mess, you look like you haven't slept a wink, your nail varnish is chipped all over, *so* unlike you…and you've a coffee stain on your shirt." She shook her head.

Gabi glanced down. She noticed a coffee splodge on her shirt. *Damn.* She hadn't even realised. It must have happened when she'd hastily picked it up whilst daydreaming.

"If this is because of a sexy all-nighter with Darion, I might just forgive you." She laughed.

"I wish," she mumbled.

"Well, how did it go with meeting each other's family?"

"My family liked him a lot. And his family were…not nice, at all."

"Oh. Why not?"

"It's obvious they're not affectionate, loving, positive, or uplifting in any way, which explains why Darion, deep down, is insecure, scared of commitment, and basically…fucked up."

"What a shame."

"And I messed up bad, Mal." Gabi's head dropped into her hands.

"What did you do, Gab?"

She looked up to see Mallory's worried expression. "Remember when Lawrence took me home that night?"

"Oh, no." She shook her head. "That bastard. I knew he would take advantage."

"I'm as much to blame, and it was just a kiss. But a kiss, sex—it's all the same to Darion. I cheated."

"Cheated? Gabi, he wants to share you in the playrooms. Why would a poxy kiss bother him?"

"It's not necessarily the act itself, but the

betrayal of it. Because all he's ever wanted is a loving, doting girlfriend, who is loyal when he's *not* around. And I failed. What happens in the playrooms is an agreement between us. There are rules."

"Well, is it over between you both?"

Gabi nodded. She felt tears blur her vision. She wiped them away hastily. "The kiss with Lawrence meant nothing. I was upset, feeling insecure, lost."

Mallory rested her elbows on the table with a long sigh. "Why did you tell Darion? Gabi, for the sake of your relationship, you could have kept one tiny secret."

"I couldn't do that. I felt I owed it him to tell the truth." She fiddled with her fingernails, her heart drumming in her chest. "Lawrence threatened to tell him too."

"I could seriously wring Lawrence's neck."

"He wants me back. For some stupid reason, he thinks that if Darion isn't in the picture, that I'll give him a chance." She rubbed her aching temples. "Do you remember that time when I thought Lawrence had cheated on me, and I first visited The Black Door?"

Mallory nodded.

"He did cheat on me. With one of the dancers."

"What?" Mallory exclaimed. "I knew he was fucking fake." She walked toward the window and sat on the ledge.

"And that's not all. He's been following me for ages, watching me."

"I knew Lawrence was a little strange, but that takes the biscuit." She shook her head. "I wonder if he knew we'd be at Sasha's that night."

Gabi shrugged. It was a possibility.

"Have you called the police?"

"No. I told him I would. It appears he's backed off with stalking me."

"I hope so. What will you do about Darion?"

"What can I do?"

"Ring him."

"He won't want to speak with me, Mal. I know it. You should have seen the way he looked at me." She burst into uncontrollable sobs.

Mallory stood beside her, rubbing her back soothingly. "It will be okay. Darion will come around. He has to. He loves you."

"What if he doesn't?"

"I don't know."

"I've never felt this way about someone before. I can't stop thinking about him. How can I go from Darion to a normal relationship? I'll always be comparing it, knowing I'm missing out, settling for second best." She chewed her nail. "I sound pathetic." She sighed heavily. "I hate the hold he has over me. Why can't I forget about him, Mal?"

"Because you're in love, and you can't control it. It takes over like some fucking disease."

"I loved Lawrence, but it was never this strong." She kicked the leg of the table. "How could I have kissed him?"

"Who the hell hasn't confided in, or sought comfort from an ex before? It's common. It happens, Gab. If Darion can't forgive you for something so trivial, then he doesn't deserve you. No one is perfect."

"How are things with you, anyway?" she asked, eager for a change of subject.

"I'm just counting down the days until we go on holiday."

"Is Steve excited?"

"He can't wait."

"Have you heard from Suzie? I've got a bone to pick with her." Gabi laughed softly. "She gave Lawrence my new number."

"Oh shit."

"It doesn't matter. He lied to get it out of her. I'll need to change it again."

"Suzie's fine, anyway. And pre-warn her next time, so Lawrence doesn't get it out of her again."

"I will."

Mallory made her way to the door. "As much as I'd like to stay and chat, I've got a load of manuscripts to read."

"Same," she said. "Thanks for listening as always, Mal."

"Anytime."

When the door closed after Mallory, Gabi picked up her iPhone. She scrolled to Darion's number, and pressed the call button. Holding it to her ear, she sat further back in her chair. An automated message stated that the mobile was switched off. She contemplated ringing Lexi, and then decided against it. Lexi would be on Darion's side—she had to be. Drumming her fingers on the table, she called Darion's office number before she lost her courage.

"Hello," a smooth voice purred through the line.

Gabi ended the call quickly. Eva was answering his telephone. Were they back together? Had she persuaded Darion into giving her another chance? She clamped her lips together to suppress a choking sob that threatened to escape. Before she was able to stand up and head for the kitchen, her mobile rang. She snatched it up.

"Hello."

"Gabi."

"I told Darion everything. Leave me alone, Lawrence."

"If you need time to think about things, Gabi—"

"I'm not getting back with you," she yelled. She slouched in her chair, praying her colleagues on the other side of the door didn't hear. "I'll post the engagement ring back to you." Her tone was now low.

"I love you, Gabi."

"No, Lawrence, you didn't. You loved the idea of me, of what you wanted me to be. You didn't love the person I was, for you wanted to change everything about me, from my clothes, to my friends, to my passion for dancing. You wanted me to be a miserable little housewife, raising your children. Our relationship was not only boring, but lonely. We weren't matched."

"We can work on that."

"Goodbye, Lawrence."

She ended the call. She made a mental note to purchase a new sim-card again as soon as she left the office. She knew it was probably best if she also left Darion to it. If he wanted her back, he knew where she was. Glancing at the clock, she saw that she had five hours until dance class. She hoped it would help her relax, and make her forget about her problems for a short while.

Chapter Forty-Three

Darion

Darion pulled on his helmet, climbed on his bike, and started the engine. Gripping the handlebars tightly, he sped off. He didn't care where he was going. The sky was black, the roads deserted, and the only sound was the howling wind. He predicted it'd rain. He probably should have taken the Jeep, or his Audi, but he wanted the adrenaline rush he got from his motorbike.

As he made his way down country roads, he felt specks of rain land on his hands. He drove faster. The wind was sharp against his face, coldly filling his lungs. The green fields passed in a blur. He drove even faster until he could no longer focus on his surroundings. The rain was lashing down now, dripping from his jacket, soaking through his jeans. He glanced up at the grey sky, which reflected his dismal mood.

He felt a little light-headed, dizzy for some reason. Maybe it was due to the fact he hadn't eaten a decent meal in days. His stomach churned, and he swallowed the tangy taste that burnt his throat, feeling as if he would vomit.

He missed Gabi. He loved her, and yet he hated her. Was it his fault she had kissed her ex-fiancé? Had he pushed her too far? His mind was a hurricane of thoughts and emotions. He kept slipping from anger, to hurt, to guilt.

A flashing light blared in his eyes, and the sound of a loud horn filled his ears. He blinked repeatedly, his vision blinded. *Shit!* He swerved to the right quickly, and braked. He must have drifted into the wrong lane, lost in his thoughts. His heart slammed against his chest as he caught his breath.

When his pulse returned to normal and the shock had subsided, he dug into his pocket. He pulled out his mobile. He needed to talk to someone desperately. He couldn't be left alone with his thoughts. He couldn't go back to drinking until he passed out, gambling his hard-earned money away. He attempted to call Gina. Pressing the speaker icon, the ringing tones echoed in his ears. His shoulders sagged in disappointment when she didn't answer. Johnny must have forbid her from talking to him.

Stuffing the mobile back in his pocket, he decided he'd go to the club. Perhaps work would take his mind off Gina, Eva, and Gabi. He just realised that he'd lost them all.

***

It had been a couple of weeks and Darion hadn't heard a word from Gabi. He was slightly surprised. Maybe he hadn't meant anything to her at all. Perhaps she had gotten back with her ex-fiancé. He slouched in his chair, and reached for a cigar. Placing it between his lips, he picked up his lighter and lit it.

Only when he'd smoked it, did he lean forward, and switch on his computer. He checked his bank account online. The club was doing amazing. Profit had tripled. Even still, it didn't lift his mood. What was the point in having money if he had no one to share it with, no one to spoil?

He closed the Internet browser, and spent the next half an hour checking that membership applications matched identification cards. He then put in an order for fifty black plastic membership cards, emblazoned in gold swirly writing. When in receipt, he would then post them to the new clients, along with a welcome letter and an invitation to the club.

"Daz?"

He straightened his posture when he heard a knock at the door. Lexi walked in, closing it gently behind her.

"Hey, boss."

"Hi, Lex."

"How's it going?" She threw him a sympathetic look.

"Not good," he admitted. There was no point in lying about it. He knew his appearance gave him away. He had a few days' old stubble covering his jaw, his eyelids felt heavy, and he knew his face was paler than usual. No matter how long he slept, he still felt exhausted, and he lacked motivation. Lexi had bought him some vitamin pills, and offered to cook for him each day, but he'd declined. He'd well and truly lost his appetite.

Pulling out a chair, Lexi sat opposite him. "Is there anything I can do to help?"

"I don't know what sort of help I need, Lex. It seems like history repeats itself over and over in my life." He sighed heavily and rose to his feet. "Fancy a drink?"

"No, thanks."

Darion poured himself a generous glass of whisky. Taking a large swig, he resumed sitting at his desk.

"What am I doing wrong, Lex?" He tapped his fingers on the surface. "It seems I either love too much, or not enough."

When it'd come to Eva he had declared his feelings endlessly. Having been without love growing up, he'd sure taken advantage of her showering him with affection, the way she had been unable to keep her hands off him, wanting to bed him all of the time. He liked the way that love had made him feel. Being able to look after someone else, care for them, and put them before himself felt rewarding. It made him happy. Eva, on the other hand had hated it. She had told him he was needy, made her feel suffocated. With Gabi, he had tried to tone his feelings down a bit, hide how much he really adored her, by not saying the four letter word too often, and it had got him nowhere. He couldn't win.

334

"Don't hold back on love, ever," Lexi's stern tone surprised him. "Love freely. Be who you are."

"It's over, Lex. It has to be."

"You can't avoid moving on in life because you're afraid of history repeating itself. You'll forever be a prisoner of your past."

He shrugged a shoulder, at a loss for words.

"Darion." Lexi grabbed his hand. "There's a difference between Eva and Gabi. Eva's a whore. Gabi's a lost soul. When Eva cheated on you, she lied about it. Gabi made one tiny mistake. She came clean. Doesn't her honesty mean anything?" She looked at him questioningly. "We're human. We make mistakes. It's what we do afterwards that counts. I truly believe that Gabi is sorry. I *know* she wouldn't hurt you again."

He chewed his bottom lip whilst in thought.

"Give the girl a break. Your lifestyle is hardly the norm. You wanted her to participate in the playrooms. She probably didn't know what the hell was going on. Then you rarely ever told her you loved her, or made her feel secure. I'm sorry, but you're partly to blame."

Darion rubbed his stubble. Everything she was saying was true, he wasn't about to dispute it. "What do I do?"

"It all depends on what you want. Do you want to be loved, or adored?"

He was silent.

"Gabi and the playrooms offer you totally different things. Are you willing to give up the life you love for the love of your life?"

Darion blew out an exasperated puff of air. He

had two choices: to continue being adored and lusted after in the playrooms, a life of fun, without the hurt. Or trust one woman with his heart, who could break it into a million pieces or love him right back. Forever.

"Sometimes it takes a bad thing to bring two people together, to make them stronger."

"What if it goes wrong?" he asked, hating that his tone was shaky with emotion.

"What if it goes right?" she challenged him. "Sometimes we have to take a risk in life." She shrugged. "And if anyone's a risk-taker, it's you, Daz." She stood up and walked to his side of the desk. "If she hurts you again, then she didn't deserve you. You will know then. But if you don't give it a go, you could live a life of what ifs and regrets."

"I hate this relationship shit."

Lexi grabbed hold of his hand and yanked him to his feet. He allowed her to pull him into a tight hug. It was just what he needed. He felt an ache in his throat. His heart tightened. Ashamed for being emotional, Darion drew in a sharp breath, and looked up at the ceiling. It wasn't just Gabi that had him hurting. It was his parents. Thirty-six years had passed, and not once could they praise him, compliment him, or support him. If only they showed him they cared. Maybe then he wouldn't be so messed up, scared of commitment, doubting himself constantly, and living ruthlessly.

"Call Gabi. Give it one last try. I know you love her, even if you don't like to say it much. I've seen the change in you. She's what you need."

"Hmmm," he mumbled.

"And get the answers you need from Eva too. You can't move on until you've got closure. What she did eats away at you. You need to let it go." She stroked his back with soft, circular movements of her palm.

"Did anyone ever tell you you're good at this stuff?" He half smiled, pulling away. "Why did I ever go to Gina when you were here all along?"

"Because Gina had other spectacular talents, I believe."

Darion chuckled. "That she did. Although you weren't bad, Lexi." He winked.

Her mouth dropped as she slapped him on the arm playfully. "I could never let loose with you sexually. I always felt shy at how fucking beautiful you were naked, and how skilled you were in the bedroom."

"You serious?"

"Piss off, you arrogant arse." She giggled.

Darion grinned as he followed Lexi out into the corridor. He was pleased he had the girls to turn to. Gina may have been away, but Lexi and Marnie were there for him, just as he was for them.

"Good luck with Eva." Lexi winked.

"Thanks." He rubbed the back of his neck. "I have a feeling I need all the luck I can get."

Chapter Forty-Four

Gabi

Gabi was in the kitchen cooking pasta. She stood there stirring the sauce in absentmindedly. She wasn't particularly looking forward to eating the plain tomato and basil pasta; however it was all she found in the cupboard that was quick and easy to make. She remembered Darion in the kitchen, taking out tons of different ingredients, saying he liked to rustle up fancy dishes. If only he was with her, to advise her on how to give it extra flavour. She had already added pepper, but it didn't do much. She sighed heavily, feeling herself deflate. How was it possible to miss someone so much?

How she wished he would creep up behind her, wrap her into a tight hug, kiss her neck, and stare at her with those smouldering green eyes, and offer her that lewd, mischievous smile of his. Would anyone ever look at her like that again, so intently, so full of desire and longing? The passion he had for her was raw, animalistic, and so very real. She craved his hands and tongue on her body, wanted to feel him buried deep inside her. She needed his intoxicating smell. Her fingers ached to touch his hair, wishing she could grab it roughly. Her lips missed his full mouth, the way he possessed her, claimed her, invading inside with his tongue. She felt a ball of fire in her stomach as she became wildly aroused.

Darion was addictive. He was like a drug she couldn't go a day without. The high was thrilling, but the come-down was depressing. He'd opened up all sorts of emotions in her. There were so many times when she'd desperately wanted to tell him how she felt about him, state the four letter word…however, nine times out of ten, she'd held back. She hadn't wanted to scare him away. She had waited mostly for him to say the words first, so she knew he hadn't just been mirroring her words. Groaning inwardly, she squeezed her lids shut. *Forget about him. What's done is done.*

"Gabi, I want you now," his smooth, sexy, persuasive voice played in her mind. Darion Milano. She had a feeling that recovering from the break-up certainly wouldn't be easy.

"Shit," she mumbled when a burning smell filled her nostrils. She stirred the pasta, which was now sticking to the pan.

She switched off the hob and emptied the gross looking pasta into a dish. She couldn't be bothered to cook something else. Exhaustion had taken over her. Her muscles ached, her eyelids were heavy, and she'd been unable to stop yawning.

She settled in front of the television, and wolfed the food down hungrily. Twenty minutes later, she retired to her bedroom. Taking out her mobile from her pocket, she checked the screen, force of habit. Who was she expecting? It wasn't like Darion had a way of contacting her, since she had changed her number again. She had wondered whether she should visit the club, try and apologise for a final time, but then the other part of her knew she couldn't face the rejection if he turned her away. She collapsed on the bed. She couldn't even begin to imagine how Darion must be feeling.

As her attention met the bedside table, she sat up abruptly. She opened the drawer and took out a black velvet box. It creaked as she opened it. The diamond of the white gold band sparkled in the light. She ran her finger over it. Life seemed to appear simpler with a wedding band on the finger, made a person feel wanted, accepted, more secure, like they had their life all mapped out. She wondered if she would ever be engaged again, whether she would ever get married, and to the right person. She envied those people who had found their soul mate, that one person they knew they wanted to be with forever. Closing the lid, she placed the box back in the drawer, and made a mental note to have it returned to Lawrence.

Dropping back on the bed, she took hold of the remote and flicked the television on. She settled on an episode of *Sex And The City*. Perhaps Carrie, Miranda, Charlotte, or Samantha would have some advice for her, or a motto which would uplift her spirits, especially when it came to Darion. The title of the episode appeared—*Three's a crowd*. Gabi shook her head with an incredulous laugh. How ironic.

***

Darion

Darion's hands were shaking ever so slightly as he mounted the stairs to find Eva. He was almost certain he could hear the slamming of his heart against his chest. He licked his dry lips to moisten them, and cleared his throat. Was he really ready for answers? Could he handle hearing why she cheated on him?

He pushed open the door and took a few tentative steps inside. It wasn't due to open for another couple of hours. Rock n' roll music was playing at a low volume. The room was immaculate, every single surface gleaming under the glow of the chandeliers.

He noticed Eva sitting at the bar with a pen in her hand and a piece of paper before her. Her forehead was creased in concentration. She only looked up when he pulled out a stool and sat beside her.

"Darion." Her eyes widened as pleasant surprise crossed her face. "What brings you here?"

"I need to ask you something, Eva," he began, averting his gaze for a moment. "I've wanted to ask you this for a long time, but I couldn't find you. And then I didn't know if I could even get the words out."

"What is it?" She shifted on the stool, as if suddenly in discomfort.

"Why did you cheat on me with Vinnie?"

Eva sighed heavily and flicked back her glossy black mane. "Is that all you wanted, to drag up the past?"

"I need to know," he said sternly, linking his hands together.

"And there was me thinking we'd have a nice, polite conversation for once," she scoffed, and picked up her drink.

Darion watched as her full, red glossed lips met the glass. He could see her delicate throat moving as the liquid went down. When she placed the glass on the side, her tongue licked the drink droplets away. She stared up at him under her thick, dark lashes, her green eyes holding his stare.

"This conversation can never go down polite," he said, unable to hide the resentment in his tone.

"Why don't we talk about you?" She laughed mercilessly. "Where's your frigid, prissy little lady?"

"Watch your mouth, Eva."

She stood up abruptly, placing her hand on her hip. "Look at you defending her." She shook her head. "You really have got it fucking bad."

Darion remained silent.

"I don't know why." Eva took another long swig of her drink. Darion could see her nostrils flaring with anger, as jealousy had obviously consumed her. "You're going to forgive her, aren't you? Yet you couldn't forgive me."

"You slept with someone else. Gabi briefly kissed her ex."

"You're pussy whipped." She laughed again, a loud, cruel laugh that made Darion slouch slightly, feeling foolish, feeling ashamed for being in love.

Was he pussy whipped? He smoothed his hair back with his palms. No. He was in love. He couldn't control it, couldn't deny it, couldn't live without it. Gabi made him want to be a better person. She brought out the good in him, the playful side, whilst he brought out the devil in her, the naughtiness. They were a perfect combination. They both complimented each other, experienced new things together, trying to adapt to one another's lifestyle.

With Eva, they had shared great sex. With Gabi, he had that and more. They shared the same interests. They both loved music. They liked watching movies. They enjoyed eating out at restaurants. They had fun at the bar, getting merry. They were even content when just lying on the sofa or in bed together, with nothing else going on around them. *Shit.* He realised he really had been playing the boyfriend role. Except for getting kinky in the playrooms, it suddenly dawned on him that he had been enjoying a *normal* relationship. He had been doing what normal couples did. Gabi thought he hadn't let her in, but he had. She had his heart. She had his mind, his soul. She had everything he had to offer. All that was missing was that four letter word, which he found difficult to say. L-O-V-E.

Then it hit him like a sharp slap in the face that

felt so real he could have tumbled from his seat. He snagged his lip between his teeth, feeling fear tighten his stomach. He also felt warmth flooding his chest at the same time. He knew exactly what he had to do. More importantly, he *wanted* to do it.

"Fuck me sideways," Eva spat, bringing him out of his daze. "You've got smitten written all over your face. What the hell has happened to Darion Milano?"

He took out a cigarette, stuffed it into his mouth, and flicked the lighter. "He's seen the light," he said. Eyeing the flame, he chuckled lightly at the scenario.

Eva stepped closer. "Do you want a boring life? Is that what you really want?"

"Define boring," he said flatly, blowing smoke from the side of his mouth. "You mean bedding the same woman for the rest of my life, having children with that woman, probably even marrying that woman, growing old with that woman, sharing stories and memories of more than just a sexual nature?" He took the cigarette between two fingers and nodded. "Then yeah, I do want a boring life."

Eva's eyes widened, her mouth falling open as if in shock. Darion now realised that boring was better than chasing excitement constantly. With boring, he'd know where he stood. Chemistry and passion faded over time, along with the excitement. Then what? You were either left disappointed with someone whereby beyond the chemistry, you had nothing in common with at all, someone who valued excitement more than they did friendship, loyalty, support and love.

Darion had always believed that as you only lived once, you had to make the most of it. Yes, he had been making the most of it the wrong way. His broken heart and damaged, lonely soul had made him a selfish man that cared only about the pleasures in life, whether it was spending money on fancy items, sleeping around, using women as if they were toys, seeking enjoyment in things that were bad for him. But really, the only real pleasure in life that made you feel good was how you made someone else feel. How you contributed to their life. How you picked them up when they were feeling down, supported them when they didn't believe in their dreams, complimented them when they felt insecure.

He thought of when he most felt happy. It was when Gabi was smiling, when her eyes were lit up, when her sweet sounding laugh filled his ears. He wanted to care for and protect her.

Stubbing his cigarette in the ashtray, he slowly rose to his feet. Towering over Eva, he asked again, "Tell me why you did it."

"What?" Her brow furrowed in confusion as she feigned stupidity.

"We had rules. We slept with other people to satisfy one another. When you were in that room with Vinnie, I wasn't there. You weren't doing it for me, Eva."

She looked at the floor for a moment. Eventually she focused on him again, her eyes watery. "I was seeing how far I could push you."

He felt his spine stiffen as he became dumbstruck. He wasn't sure he'd heard her right.

"What?"

"We always used to play games, test one another, argue and then make up. I wanted to see how you'd react...whether you'd come into that room so mad, and jealous, and sexy..."

"You cheated on me to see how I'd react?" He shook his head in bewilderment. "The door was locked, Eva," his said through clenched teeth. "I sat outside that door for fucking half an hour, whilst you fucked someone else behind my back."

"I took it too far. I'm sorry." He noticed a tear roll down her cheek. She held out her arms, as if to embrace him.

Darion took a step back as if she was a hot flame which would burn him. "You told me Vinnie was giving you a massage, that you needed somewhere to relax. Your story has changed again, Eva." He glared at her. "You had a relationship with Vinnie afterwards."

She shrugged a shoulder. "I lost you," she replied, her voice shaking with emotion. Her lips were trembling. "What else could I do?"

"If you loved me, you wouldn't have given up so easily."

He noticed the quick familiar scowl flash on Eva's face, the way she used to roll her eyes whenever he discussed feelings. How she used to make him feel worthless, like it was weak to need reassurance all of the time, to be told he was loved. All of a sudden the confused emotions he felt for her crystallised into hate. Eva and his parents were the reason he was scared of saying, "I love you," to anyone. How could he be that brainwashed, that hurt, to believe that declaring love could ever be a bad thing, when realistically, it was the *best* thing?

"It was all just a blessing in disguise," he muttered, blinking rapidly, coming to his senses. "You were never the one for me, Eva."

As he took in the black leather corset she wearing, her silicone breasts spilling over the top, her black ripped jeans, her hair splayed over her shoulders, her face covered with an inch of make-up, he noticed something he never had before.

"And do you know something?" He leant into her so his nose was a millimeter away from hers. He heard her swallow, saw the fear and anxiety in her eyes. "Everything about you is *cheap*."

As he turned his back on her, he couldn't believe what he ever saw in her.

"Oh, and Eva, there's one more thing I have to tell you," he said over his shoulder. "You aren't gonna like it."

Chapter Forty-Five

Gabi

"Gabi. Just go," Mallory said sternly.

Gabi clutched her mobile to her ear. "What if he sends me away?" She bit her lip.

"It's better to find out than to always wonder."

"Maybe." She sighed heavily.

Gabi had been unable to sleep, tossing and turning in bed. It wasn't even yet midnight. She had tried to concentrate on the television, but it hadn't kept her occupied. She'd then had a long soak in the bath, thinking it'd relax her and make her sleepy. No such luck. Darion was invading her mind like some sort of disease. She knew she needed to speak with him, to see if he was willing to give her a second chance. She couldn't bear it any longer, having no contact, driving herself insane, replaying every bit of their last conversation in her mind.

"I've never done anything like this in my life,

Mal. I almost feel a bit stalker-ish."

"It takes guts and courage to own up to what you've done, to take responsibility, and face it head on. If Darion's a decent man, then he will, at least, respect you for it."

She couldn't believe she was about to show up at The Black Door unannounced, but Mallory was right. It was better to know than to always wonder.

She didn't know whether Darion despised her and never wanted to see her again, or whether he still cared, but was too stubborn to do anything about it.

"Ring me back later. I want to know how it goes."

"Okay."

"Good luck, Gabi. You can do this."

"Thanks, Mal."

"If it doesn't go down well, then you're welcome to come here. I don't want you to be alone and upset."

Her stomach churned. *What if it all goes horribly wrong?* she worried.

"Speak soon, sweetie."

"Bye, Mal. I don't know what I ever would have done without you."

Ending the call, she placed it into her tote bag. She removed a towel from her head and sat before the dressing table. *I can do this,* she told herself over and over.

She spent the next thirty minutes blow drying her hair, and applying make-up. She then dressed in grey jeans, a white shirt, and matching white heels. Flinging her bag over her shoulder, she hurried out of the apartment to her car. The quicker she got there, the better. She needed to face her demons and get her speech over and done with.

Just under an hour of driving, Gabi was at the club. It was busy as usual. She spotted Marnie dancing on the stage, Lexi sitting beside a client, and Wendy occupying one of the poles. Jasmine was leant against the bar, tapping away on her mobile. She looked up when Gabi was before her.

"Hey."

"Hi. Is Darion around?"

"Yeah. He's in his office." She placed her mobile in her pocket. "Do you want me to get him?"

"Please." Gabi slid onto a stool. "Jasmine," she called out, before she left the room. "Could I have a drink first?"

"Sure. What do you want?"

"Um…Make it a shot of Absinthe."

Jasmine threw her head back with a laugh. "Gabi, if you're on the hard stuff, then something isn't right."

"We'll soon see."

Lexi was now leading the client into a private booth. She hadn't noticed that Gabi was there. She felt a little relieved, not wanting to stay at the club for any longer than was necessary. When Jasmine handed her the shot glass full of green liquid, Gabi held it to her lips. The strong smell caused her stomach to somersault. She downed it in one quickly. *Urgh!* She placed her palm to her chest, which felt on fire.

"That sure is the devil's drink," she said, spotting

the devil logo on the front of the bottle.

"You know you can get Absinthe in red and black too?"

"Are they even stronger?" she gasped.

"I'm not sure." Jasmine pursed her lips. "Maybe we'll get some in stock."

"Keep them well away from me," Gabi told her.

"Anyway." Jasmine smiled brightly. "I'll go and get Darion.

"Okay…I'll be on that sofa in the corner." She pointed to a sofa in a quiet corner, where she knew they'd have privacy, without people around them being able to hear their conversation.

Gabi crossed the room slowly, glancing at people briefly as she passed them. Her hands were damp with sweat. Her heart was pounding at a frenetic pace. Inhaling a deep breath, she tried to ignore the rush of paranoid thoughts in her head…that Darion wouldn't want to see her, that he'd get Lennie or Travis to escort her out of the club.

***

Darion

Darion switched his computer off and stood up, yawning. He couldn't focus on work. He decided he'd go home early and watch a movie, or something. Tomorrow would be a long day for him, and a special one at that. He couldn't wait to put his plan into action. Although he was absolutely terrified, and unsure of what the future held, he was definitely ready to take a risk. As he crouched down to grab his jacket, he heard a knock at the door. He stilled. If it was Eva, then she had some nerve. He wasn't in the mood for a full-blown argument, which he knew would follow, since he had told her one of his plans.

"Yeah?" he called out.

His muscles softened when Jasmine poked her head around the door. "Hi, Daz. I wasn't sure if you were sleeping."

"Everything okay?"

"Um…Gabi's here. She wants to see you."

Darion looked down as he rubbed his forehead. What did she want? He supposed that she'd saved him the journey of travelling to her apartment in the morning.

"I'll be out in a minute."

"Sure."

With quick strides across the room, Darion poured himself a glass of rum from the mini-bar. He gulped it down in seconds. Dutch courage. He knew if ever there was a time he needed it, it was then.

Looking down at himself, he scrutinised his appearance. The long sleeved black top he was wearing clung to his biceps. The black jeans were a good fit. He decided he looked decent. As he leant closer to the mirror, he noticed the sparkle had returned in his irises. That was happiness right there. There was no denying that his eyes always displayed his emotions.

Leaving his office, he sauntered toward the bar area. *"We're human. We make mistakes. It's what we do afterwards that counts. I truly believe that Gabi is sorry. I know she wouldn't hurt you again."*

Lexi's words rang loud and clear in his mind. She had been right. Gabi was nothing like Eva. Now he knew why Eva had cheated on him, it was clear as day that Eva had cheated by choice, with the intention of doing so. Gabi had cheated because she was probably caught off guard, upset, and confused at the time. A part of him needed to have faith that she wouldn't betray him again. *"You can't avoid moving on in life because you're afraid of history repeating itself. You'll forever be a prisoner of your past."*

He spotted Gabi sitting on a sofa at the far end of the room. She was twiddling her fingers, like she always did when she was nervous. As he approached her, it felt as if he was moving in slow motion. He saw the way her eyes flitted around the room, and when she brought her hand up to her mouth to chew a nail. Then her hands dropped to her lap, and she focused on the ground. Gabi. Beautiful, sweet Gabi. Her stunning legs were concealed in tight jeans, which would make her ass look amazing. Her tempting and delicious cleavage was visible because she had four buttons undone on her blouse. She was tapping her heel-clad foot, whether in impatience or nervousness, he didn't know.

He wanted nothing more than to slip off those heels, drag the jeans down her legs, and rip open her shirt. He wanted his mouth and tongue all over her. He felt his jeans becoming uncomfortably tight across the zipper, and knew he needed release desperately. He had never wanted Gabi so urgently before.

"Don't speak," he commanded, once he was towering over her.

She looked up with wide, wary eyes and swallowed.

"I'm gonna fuck you so good, you'll never wanna leave me."

He laughed softly as her cheeks flushed red, confusion showing itself on her face. Grabbing hold of her hand tightly, he yanked her to her feet. Leading her into the nearby bathroom, he locked the door to ensure they wouldn't be interrupted. Unlike the other bathroom near his office which was for the staff, this public bathroom was a room, with one toilet and sink, rather than separate cubicles.

"Darion." Gabi stared at him questioningly. "We need to talk."

"Not yet." He lifted her into his arms. "If you say one more word, Gabi, I'm gonna gag, restrain, and blindfold you." He wet his lips with his tongue before flicking it over hers. "The only noise you'll be making is screaming, darlin'."

Chapter Forty-Six

Gabi

Gabi felt herself being lifted onto a counter top, where a round bowl sink was at the other end of. She hadn't been in that bathroom before, hadn't even noticed the door at the corner of the club. She took in her surroundings, and admired how fancy it was. The counter matched the black tiled floor, which the reflection of the spotlights twinkled in. There were large oval, silver framed mirrors on every wall. A huge black vase took up one corner, black twigs spiralling out of it. Another corner held a shelf under a mirror, where a hairdryer, hair straightener, and tongs were attached to the wall. She noticed bottles near the sink: hand sanitiser, soap, perfume and spray. Darion really had ensured that there was absolutely everything available for the public, should they need anything. Comfort was of utmost importance when it came to the club.

"Darion, we should talk first," she said, her mind overruling her body. Although she didn't want to ruin the moment, she knew talking was far more important.

"Gabi." He yanked his top over his head and placed it onto the counter. "No talking."

She sighed heavily. She had no idea what was going to happen between them, and their relationship, but in that second, she knew she wanted him. Her mind had now gone fuzzy, and her greedy body was in full control...and it could *never* resist Darion Milano.

She leant back against the mirror and took in his washboard stomach and bulging biceps. His physique was so perfect; she was surprised he wasn't a professional stripper himself. Women would shower him with money, and Darion would definitely earn a fortune. Failing which, he could be a porn star, with the impressive size he was packing in his pants and expert skills in the bedroom.

Taking a step forward, he took hold of either side of her shirt with both hands and whipped it open forcefully. She was thankful her shirt buttons were press-on for they would have surely been scattering across the floor. She glanced down at her breasts, which were encased in a red, lacy bra. Her nipples were already hard peaks, yearning to be touched. She knew Darion noticed as his teeth snagged his bottom lip, as if impatient and craving them in his mouth, like he was a starved man. Darion removed her shirt and tossed it to the side. She was silent. Her breath caught in her throat, anticipation coursing through her veins, when he slipped off each of her shoes. He then fingered the button on her jeans. His stare remained on hers the whole time. Unfastening the button and pulling down the zip, he slowly tore her jeans down her legs.

"Fuck…" He growled in frustration. "I've missed this body."

Gabi squeezed her thighs together, feeling a delightful spasm shoot between them. Her head fell back slightly, and she parted her lips wider to inhale air.

With a slow shake of his head, his gaze clouding with desire, Darion said, "Don't you dare close those legs."

He took hold of her knees and pushed them apart. Gabi's skin prickled with awareness, every nerve end awakening, her body straining toward his. Darion gracefully slid to his knees. His mouth met her stomach, to which he placed tender kisses across her skin. Gabi arched her back. His mouth moved lower. She gripped the edge of the counter, urgently needing to feel his tongue and mouth on her now pulsing clit. To say she was sexually frustrated would be an understatement. She had missed Darion claiming her body, pleasuring her in a way that only he could.

When his lips pressed against her clit, on top of the thin material of her underwear, she moaned softly. His tongue flicked over it, once. Twice. Three times. She lifted her buttocks off the counter slightly, moving closer to his face. His mouth sucking her teasingly was torturous. She desperately wanted to feel him on her bare skin, to remove her underwear. But Darion began stroking her, with circular movements of his fingertips. A wicked smirk surfaced on his face, and she knew he was purposely tantalising her, getting her worked up until she was unable to take it, and begging for him.

Her clit throbbed, the muscles in her belly clenched hard with desire. A needy ache lingered in her body, urgently requiring more of what Darion was giving.

"Darion," she whimpered, as he continued to tongue her.

With a dirty sounding laugh, and knowing full well what she wanted, Darion slid her underwear down her legs and discarded them. Gabi felt a slight chill, but when Darion's wet, wide tongue met her clit, she felt pleasurable heat spread through her loins. Darion propped her legs up on his shoulders, giving him more access. Gabi bucked her hips, grinding onto his mouth, feeling the sharp graze of his stubble.

His stare was fixed on hers, and she could see the opening and widening of his mouth as his tongue flickered over her. Gripping her thighs roughly with his fingers, he pushed his face further into her, his tongue now darting inside. His satisfied grunts made it that more pleasurable, knowing he became aroused by the act.

Oh my god. Gabi cried out, unsure if she could take the fast, satisfying lashes of his tongue. As he prodded in and out, in and out, and then circling his tongue on her entrance, she squeezed her lids shut. He continued to change the rhythm, making her excitement build, and then drop. He kept bringing her to the brink of an orgasm, and then pulling away, prolonging her pleasure.

How did he know what to do so well? How did he know her body better than she knew it, to the extent that he knew exactly what she wanted, what motions of his tongue worked, and when to switch it up? It was like he was wired up to her brain, knowing when she was thinking, *lower, faster, slower, rougher, deeper,* for he seemed to do exactly as she desired.

"Oh, Darion…" She felt her lips trembling as she moaned.

When two fingers entered her, she cried out. With deep plunges, he filled her nicely, the tips of his fingers massaging her G spot. The slapping sound against her wetness filled her ears. Inserting a third finger, Darion's thrusts got deeper and faster. Gabi spread her legs wider to accommodate his thrusting hand.

"I want you, Darion…please," she pleaded.

With one final push of his fingers, he withdrew. Gabi's inner muscles clenched and throbbed, the emptiness torturous. Pushing himself to his feet, Darion towered over her, his close proximity both intimidating and thrilling. Her heartbeat increased and her mouth became dry.

Before she knew it, Darion's lips crashed against hers, hungrily, desperately. As his tongue invaded and explored her mouth, her groans mingled with his. She grabbed hold of his hair, yanking his face closer to hers. She kissed him savagely, greedily, having missed him so much. The tip of his tongue swirled around hers, then licked, and sucked it into his mouth, roughly, so it swelled instantly. She didn't care. She enjoyed every bit of it. Even when her jaw began to ache from kissing so much, she was unable to tear herself away. She could kiss him for hours. He was such a good kisser; she believed that she could probably come from it alone, if she wanted.

"Fuck..." Darion pulled back, his green irises wild with need, his expression dark and wicked.

Unbuttoning his jeans, he yanked them down, along with his boxers, to his knees. His erection sprang free, and Gabi could see he was rock-hard, in need of her. Slapping the wet tip of his cock on her entrance, Gabi drew in air. He circled it around her clit slowly, sending delightful vibrations through her body. When he slid in partway, she gasped. It was exactly what she wanted, what she needed. *More!* she silently screamed.

Darion pushed in even deeper. Her inner muscles clenched around him as he fit her snugly. It was as if their bodies were made for one another. They connected perfectly. Rocking her hips back and forth, Gabi bucked upwards, meeting him thrust for thrust. She looked over his shoulder and almost melted with desire. She could see his firm, sexy ass in the mirror behind him, which met his strong, muscular thighs. Watching him fuck her in the mirror was so erotic.

Pounding into her, she reached around him and grabbed his ass. She grabbed at the flesh tightly with her nails, yanking him into her, needing to feel every single inch he had to offer. When he slid in further, his balls slapped against her buttocks as he drove himself back and forth. His head was tilted upwards, as guttural cries left his throat.

"Did you miss me?" he asked, his teeth grazing her ear. His husky, sexy voice sent tingles on her neck.

"Yes," she groaned.

"How much?"

"Too much."

"Did you miss this?" As if to indicate his tongue, he licked inside her earlobe, which made her sigh softly.

"Yes."

"Did you miss these?" He pushed two fingers into her mouth, to which she swirled her tongue around slowly.

"Yes," she mumbled, her mouth still full.

"Did you miss this?" He slammed into her full force with his cock, causing her to yelp.

Bowing her head, she giggled, and nodded.

"Good," he said. His serious gaze was on her now, studying her intently. "I missed every little thing about you, Gabi."

Hearing him say that spread a warm, giddy feeling through her body.

Resuming what they were doing, Darion plunged into her relentlessly. She pursed her lips. It felt so good. He seized her face with his hands, and his expression suddenly turned fierce, as if he hated, but loved her at the same time. He was confused, and it was understandable. She just hoped he still cared for her the way that he used to. His focus flittered from her eyes to her mouth, and then he bit her lip, roughly. *Ah!* She licked her lip, trying to be rid of the stinging sensation.

He slammed into her more forcefully, heightening her excitement, making her heartbeat increase. She curled her legs around his back, grinding herself against him. Her abdomen tightened again, and she knew she was close. Darion's plunging became even faster, deeper, harder.

Gabi felt the tension coiling in her stomach. Her legs stiffened, and she sucked in air. Grabbing his ass again, she pulled him closer. She felt the spasms shoot through her, as her sex clenched around his cock. She was pulsing and throbbing when an intense orgasm caused her whole body to shudder violently, making her cry out continuously.

"Ah…Darion…" She gasped and inhaled deeply.

"Gabi," he groaned, slamming into her. His features screwed up as he emptied himself into her, pushing deeper, filling her, grunts leaving his mouth. He stilled for a moment, and then dropped his weight onto her, taking deep breaths.

Gabi felt her body relax. She willed her heartbeat to decrease, as it was pounding so fast it was almost painful. Her tense muscles had now softened, and she felt overcome with exhaustion.

Darion eventually tore himself away from her and rose to his feet.

"I forgot to give these some attention."

He pulled down her bra and released her breast. His mouth wrapped around her nipple. As his tongue swirled around it, making it rise to attention, Gabi found herself sinking lower onto the counter. She closed her eyes as he continued to lick and suck her breast greedily. He tweaked her other nipple with his thumb and forefinger, pulling on it.

"Ah…" Gabi sighed, feeling a hot ball of fire in the pit of her belly. She wanted him again. With Darion, no matter how many times they had sex, it never seemed enough. She was always left wanting more. Tugging the nipple with his teeth, he finally pulled back.

"Let's get dressed."

Chapter Forty-Seven

Gabi tugged her jeans and shirt on. As she was fastening the buttons, she caught the devilish, triumphant smile on Darion's face. *Smug bastard.* That was some session. The best sex she had had. Ever. Or maybe she thought that because she hadn't had him in so long. But where did it leave them? Had he forgiven her? Even if he was willing to give it another try, they still had the same obstacles threatening to come between them—Eva and The Black Door. Tucking a strand of hair behind her ear, Gabi blocked out the worrying thoughts, trying desperately not to let it affect the moment. She had to speak with Darion, and she had to be honest. He needed to know that swinging wasn't for her, that she never wanted to enter the playrooms again, that she couldn't bear the thought of sharing him.

She felt flushed and lightheaded, knowing that shortly, she would be telling him she couldn't be the woman he craved, the woman he wanted. She couldn't succumb to his desires and adapt to his dark world.

She brought her eyes up to meet his. His features were hardened, focused on the floor, as if he were worrying about something. He yanked his top over his head, and pushed up the sleeves. When his gaze locked with hers, she felt that magnetic pull between them which never seemed to go away, no matter what problems they faced.

He snagged his bottom lip with his teeth, devouring her greedily with his darkened irises, taking in every inch of her body slowly. Her breath held tight inside, and she felt the heat build in her cheeks. She was about to interlace her fingers, when he took a step forward and grabbed both of her hands. Silence overcame them for a moment. She wished she could wipe the frown lines from his forehead, magically rectify his past, take away the hurt and pain in his life which prevented him from being able to offer his heart freely. She wished he could be head over heels, crazy in love, to the point it was impossible to think of anything else. The love she had for him, where she wanted to shout it from the rooftops, the love that had her smiling to herself all day long—strong, uncontrollable, consuming every fibre of your being, love.

When his features softened, and a small smile tilted his lips, it was as if he could read her thoughts. He was telling her he desperately wanted to feel what she did, with the same intensity. He found it hard. She knew that. She squeezed her lids shut for a moment. She wanted to tell him she loved him. She wanted to tell him how much, how strong she felt it, how she never wanted to be without him, that if he forgave her, she would love him forever. But most of all, she wanted to hear it all back.

Tell me! her insides screamed, *tell me you love me, please!* She needed to hear it so bad, more than ever.

But when she saw him swallow, avert his eyes, and withdraw his hands, she didn't dare utter the words. As he turned his back on her, she felt the blood drain out of her veins, leaving her insides empty. She swallowed the emotions that were building in her throat, willing herself not to cry. She wrapped her arms around herself for comfort, to push away the rejection—it was no use. He was destroying her, just like Lawrence had done, making her feel unloved, unwanted, not good enough. Maybe she had been blind to it, so wrapped up in lust. Maybe Darion wasn't the man for her.

"Gabi." He broke her thoughts. "Come." He held out his hand. "We need to talk."

She felt her heart twist inside her chest. Reluctantly, she placed her hand in his. When they were back in the bar, she did a quick scan of the place. The dancers were at the bar, sitting, drinking, and talking. She noticed there was now a band on the stage, entertaining the audience. In that moment, it felt just like a normal bar. When they began playing "Believe" by Mumford & Sons, she couldn't help but feel the lyrics had been written especially to apply for Darion.

She felt a sharp current pierce through her when she noticed Eva. She was slouched on a stool at the bar, several drinks before her. As she shakily picked up her glass and took a sip, she failed to notice it spilling down her chin. Her usually silky hair hung in messy waves around her, and her seductive eyes were hazy. She was drunk. Gabi almost felt sorry for her, but then she remembered her words, *"You're boring, sweetheart. Vanilla."*

"Sit." Darion towered over her, and indicated with his hand for her to take up residence on the sofa.

She did as commanded. Darion slowly lowered himself onto the sofa opposite. She waited, gripping the edge of the cushion, wondering what was about to leave his lips. Perhaps she should speak first, so he knew the only person she could be was herself, and to see whether that was enough for him.

"Gabi…" he began.

"Let me speak," she said, wishing her voice wasn't so shaky and weak. Clearing her throat, she said, "I can't be the woman you want me to be, Darion."

He leant back and stroked his bottom lip slowly with his finger. Gabi felt desire flood through her pelvis, wishing he wasn't so distracting.

She continued, "The lifestyle you lead isn't for me. I really tried, so hard…"

"I know you tried," he soothed, his green eyes burning into hers. "I don't want this to be over." His fists were now clenched, as if he was trying his hardest to remain strong. "I *hate* you for what you did," he said, his tone calm. "But I can live with it. I pulled you in every direction, wanting you to fulfil my needs, my desires. It must have been overwhelming for you. I get that now. I can see why you did what you did."

She remained silent.

"I know there was nothing malicious about it. I know you didn't do it to hurt me, or because you no longer wanted me."

She nodded vehemently, agreeing with him.

"When I almost lost you, I realised that I *really* do need you, Gabi."

"But we're too different, Darion." She hesitated. How would the relationship last? "We want different things."

"You're wrong, Gabi." He inhaled and exhaled. "You're *wrong*," his voice broke with emotion. He lifted his head and stared up at the ceiling, clamping his jaw shut. Once he'd regained his composure, his eyes were back on her, the mask of strength on his face, the only emotion he felt comfortable with.

"I thought I wanted those things. I thought I needed swinging to feel good, desired, wanted, fulfilled." He sat up straight. "But I was wrong." His fingers were drumming on his leg. He appeared vulnerable and more handsome than she had ever seen him.

She silently willed him to continue, to finally open up to her.

"I enjoyed swinging. I liked other men lusting after my girls; it turned me on watching them. But now it all makes sense." He paused, and she saw his throat dip as he swallowed. "They were all nothing but trophy girlfriends, women that I liked to show off, liked to have fun with. Gina, Lexi, Marnie, Charlie, Eva…all of them. That can't have been love." His features twisted into disgust.

"That night in the playroom when Jayce was kissing you, and Leah was all over me, I wasn't myself. My heart wasn't in it for the first time. My dick wasn't in it for the first time." He let out a soft laugh. "And when I saw him touching and kissing you…" His cheeks flushed red as he ground his teeth, his nostrils flaring. "I wasn't turned on; I wanted to rip his fucking head off."

Gabi swallowed the lump that had appeared in her throat, listening, concentrating, and allowing him to talk—the most she had heard him speak since they had met.

"I only invited you to the dungeon suite for that final time to see if I could go through with it, to see if I could share you, to still enjoy that lifestyle. The lifestyle I have enjoyed for years." He shot her a serious look. "And I realised I couldn't do it."

What? Disbelief came out in a choked gasp. Was she hearing him right? Gabi was momentarily paralysed.

"One thing about you that I liked, Gabi—you never tried to change me, never told me to stop seeing Gina, or whoever in the beginning, even though I know you wanted me to. But I stopped anyway, for me, and you never ever pressured me to give up anything. I know swinging put you off, but you never gave me an ultimatum. Lately, I've realised on my own accord that I don't want to live that lifestyle anymore."

Their eyes locked, a strong intensity in his. There was that chemistry again, and so much more. That connection from when they had first met…it was still there…probably stronger than ever.

"And I just thought to myself, it couldn't have been love with any of them," he continued. "I've been beating myself up this whole time about Eva, but now I know I didn't love her, not compared to how I feel for you. It took time for me to realise, but Gabi, I had one thing going through my head that night in the playrooms." He leant forward and took hold of her hand, stroking it gently.

She felt a shiver run up her spine, her stomach in nervous knots. He always had an effect on her. He licked his lips and his dark vulnerable eyes continued to stare right at her. "I thought to myself, *no one*," he said, his tone stern, his expression menacing, "*no one* fucking touches *my* girl."

They were the words she'd always longed to hear. Gabi dissolved into tears with what little energy she had left, her lips quivering, her heart slamming against her chest. Their relationship had been a rollercoaster ride from day one. For a moment, she sat still…all of the suspense, worry, panic, and sorrow trickling away.

A man who had enjoyed a life of swinging, who never thought he would give it up, a man who had been cut up over his ex-wife for years, and had been empty and hollow from all of the one-night stands, a man who didn't care and got off on watching his partners being pleasured by others, was before her telling her how swinging wasn't what he wanted anymore.

"With those women, I must've lacked something, which is why I had agreed and done most of the things I did." He shrugged a shoulder. "Well, plus the fantasy and curiosity aspect. I pushed the excitement and passion further. Swinging kept it alive. But I *shouldn't* have done it with you, Gabi." His grip tightened around her hand.

"You were fucking perfect as you were. I made love to you." He let out an incredulous laugh, with a shake of his head. "I never made love to Eva. It's only just dawned on me." He brought his hands up to seize her face, to which his fingers tenderly stroked her wet cheeks, wiping away the tears. "I will never ever let someone so much as look at you, Gabi."

He pulled her to her feet and settled her onto his lap. Squeezing her into a tight, desperate embrace, he buried his face in the crook of her neck. "You're *mine*."

Gabi breathed in his smell, his sweet cologne. She closed her lids as he gently stroked her hair and then down to her back. She felt like she could burst with happiness. She wrapped her arms tightly around him, never wanting to let go.

Darion pulled back and his gaze lingered on her eyes, then her mouth, and he kissed her softly, a kiss that sent shivers through her whole body and made her heart melt. She responded, kissing him back urgently.

"I've told Eva I wanna sell the club."

Gabi studied his face for any signs he was being insincere. He wasn't. Her breathing suspended as she thought of what to say. It was like music to her ears.

"I love you, Gabriella Woods."

Her heart skipped a beat. "I love you too."

She saw his shoulders droop as he sighed, as if finally able to relax.

"Darion," she said softly. "I'm not Eva. You can tell me you love me every second of the day, and I'd want you to. I'd *never* get tired of hearing it."

He closed his eyes for a moment. When he opened them, she saw love, admiration, and longing. "Come and spend one last time in the playrooms with me." He ran his hand slowly up her leg, leaving tingles in its wake, making her stomach clench hard with desire. "Just you and me. You choose which room."

He grabbed hold of her face, his hands burying in her hair, and kissed her desperately, passionately. Their teeth smashed together, their lips swelling from the pressure, their moans colliding. Gabi kissed him like she'd never see him again, and yet she'd be seeing him every day for the rest of her life. She hoped, anyway.

Finally pulling away for air, she smiled and nodded. She knew exactly which room to choose— the one with the king-size bed, candles, roses, and soft lighting. Nothing could beat a bit of good old fashioned romance.

Chapter Forty-Eight

Darion

Darion tore away from Gabi when he felt his mobile vibrating in his pocket. He retrieved it and glanced at the screen. His brow furrowed in confusion. It was a number he didn't recognise.

"Gabi, go and order champagne. We'll celebrate new beginnings." He smiled. "I'm gonna take this call." He pressed his lips against her temple. "I'll meet you in the playrooms."

"Okay." She nodded.

He took hold of her hand and squeezed it. It took all of his willpower to pull away. He felt warmth spread through his body, feeling completely positive about their relationship, about a new start. As he wove his way through the crowd, circling past sofas, he caught sight of a teary Lexi, Marnie, and Wendy. Lexi gave him a little wave, and by the smile on her face, she looked like she'd burst with pride. All the girls had ever wanted was to see him happy, to see him settled. He'd previously informed them of his plans. He'd thought they would have been upset with his plans to sell the business, but they weren't. Darion had been in talks with an old friend about buying The Black Door. He'd promised that he'd keep the same employees.

Turning his head, he noticed Eva for the first time. He inhaled deeply. Now, rather than feeling unsure about her, he actually felt pity for her. He flashed her a tight smile. She wasn't a bad woman. She just wasn't the woman for him. He was taken aback when she smiled, as if genuinely pleased for him, for the change he was making in his life.

"Hello," he said when he'd finally answered the mobile, which hadn't stopped its persistent ringing.

He left the club and stepped into the dark night. As he listened to what the caller had to say, he felt the blood drain from his face. The mobile fell from his hand, and he watched as it dropped to the ground before hitting the concrete. The screen instantly smashed to pieces, the glass scattering everywhere—pieces that could never be fixed.

A sharp pain stabbed through his heart. He dropped onto the step, fearing his shaky legs would buckle beneath him. Tears threatened to spill down his face in uncontrollable sobs, years of built-up anger, sadness, pain, and fear. Ignoring his heaving chest, he clamped his lips together to prevent from breaking down. All of the hope he previously had rapidly diminished.

Lifting his head, he noticed there wasn't one single star to light up the black, lonely sky. He buried his head in his hands, and squeezed his eyes shut, wishing and praying to God that when he reopened them, it wasn't real. He wanted to go back into the bar, to the woman he loved, drink champagne, and celebrate a new start. Now, it felt like a new end, a different end.

He opened his eyes. His vision was blurred with stray tears, making him grit his teeth and silently scold himself for being weak. It *was* real. The mobile at his feet was damaged. The news echoed in his mind loud and clear, like a time bomb ticking in his aching brain.

Hastily wiping his face, he dragged himself to his feet. He rolled his shoulders back and took a deep breath. When he eventually made it upstairs in The Black Door, he mirrored Gabi's smile. He no longer felt like celebrating, but he took the champagne glass from her outstretched hand. He drained the contents as quickly as he could and poured himself another glass. He knew he was in for a long night of worrying thoughts.

Just when he thought he and Gabi could finally be happy, it now seemed impossible. As Darion always believed, happiness was always within his reach, but never to have. The news could shatter their world and destroy their relationship forever.

Book Playlist

Guns N' Roses–Knockin' On Heaven's Door
Queen–The Show Must Go On
Breaking Benjamin–The Diary Of Jane
Def Leppard–Pour Some Sugar On Me
EMF–You're Unbelievable
Alice In Chains–Again
My Darkest Days–Porn Star Dancing
Ghost–Cirice
Radiohead–Creep
Soundgarden–Live To Rise
Mumford & Sons–Believe
Ms Mr-Hurricane Ms Mr
Muse–Madness
Muse–Undisclosed Desires
Depeche Mode–I want It All
Depeche Mode–I Feel You
Paper Route–You Kill Me
Linkin Park–New Divide
Linkin Park–Breaking The Habit
Soho Dolls–Bang Bang Bang Bang
Halestorm–I Get Off
Garbage–#1 Crush
In This Moment–Sick Like Me
Kosheen–Recovery
Brandi Carlile–The Story
Indiana–Solo Dancing
Yeah Yeah Yeahs–Heads Will Roll